NO MAN'S LAND

NO MAN'S LAND

Davis Bunn

SEVERN
HOUSE

First world edition published in Great Britain and the USA in 2024
by Severn House, an imprint of Canongate Books Ltd,
14 High Street, Edinburgh EH1 1TE.

severnhouse.com

British Library Cataloguing-in-Publication Data
A CIP catalogue record for this title is available from the British Library.

ISBN-13: 978-1-4483-1252-8 (cased)
ISBN-13: 978-1-4483-1253-5 (e-book)

All Severn House titles are printed on acid-free paper.

Typeset by Palimpsest Book Production Ltd.,
Falkirk, Stirlingshire, Scotland.
Printed and bound in Great Britain by
TJ Books, Padstow, Cornwall.

Praise for Davis Bunn

"Impressive . . . Bunn keeps the suspense high"
Publishers Weekly on *The Rowan*

"A wild ride"
Kirkus Reviews on *Island of Time*

"A fast-paced, retro-feeling sci-fi mystery. Bunn offers readers
a sure guide through his far-future setting . . .
A pleasure. This is good fun"
Publishers Weekly on *Prime Directive*

"I absolutely loved this story! *The Rowan* is a powerful political
thriller that delves both into sci-fi and fantasy.
The result is a mesmerizing page turner"
David Lipman, producer of the *Iron Man* and *Shrek* films

"Bunn's imaginative thriller combines propulsive plotting with
sharp observations"
Publishers Weekly on *Burden of Proof*

"A stylistically complex work that lends
itself to a variety of audiences"
Library Journal Starred Review of *The Domino Effect*

About the author

Davis Bunn's novels have sold in excess of eight million copies in twenty-six languages. He has appeared on numerous national best-seller lists, and his novels have been Main or Featured Selections with every major US bookclub. Recent titles have been named Best Book of the Year by both *Library Journal* and *Suspense Magazine*, as well as earning Top Pick and starred reviews from *RT Reviews*, *Kirkus*, *Publishers Weekly*, and *Booklist*. Currently Davis serves as Writer-In-Residence at Regent's Park College, Oxford University. He speaks around the world on aspects of creative writing. Davis also publishes under the pseudonym of Thomas Locke.

This book is dedicated to
BOYD TONKIN
For The Many Sumptuous Intellectual Feasts

ONE

Five days earlier

Homeland field agent Kelly Kaiser knelt on the ridgeline's narrow lip, first in a line of six, including three Border Patrol officers and a pale bucktooth CI they had immediately named Rabbit. The kid was supposedly twenty-seven and looked fifteen, rail thin with heavy eyeglasses that kept sliding down his nose. She asked him, 'How long?'

The nearest Border Patrol officer was a grizzled veteran named Haig, who replied, 'Haven't met a coyote yet who can be bothered to tell time. Might be another two hours. Could be next week.'

But Kelly wasn't speaking to the officer. Rabbit answered, 'They're five minutes out.'

Haig grunted and looked the kid over more carefully. 'Know that for certain, do you?'

Kelly kept her gaze on the river's far side. She had inspected the kid several times, head to toe. Rabbit carried no comm link, no sidearm. Just the same, he had directed them to this point. And they were ordered to obey Rabbit's every word. And ask no questions. Not even request his real name.

Kelly touched her own comm link and said, 'Five minutes.' Down and to her left, Kelly's number two offered a thumbs up. Until yesterday, she and Barry Riggs and Darren Cotton were all junior agents yearning for the big time. Then the spook lady had waltzed in, pulled Kelly from the line of newbies and named her mission chief. Anyone other than Riggs and Cotton, she would have worried about blowback, resentment, maybe some subtle sabotage. But she was tight with these two. Her best friends since training.

Not to mention the secret they shared. The three of them. The reason why they put up with the spook lady's strange orders. And Rabbit. Their CI who apparently could see beyond the edge of night.

Their shared secret was important enough to have them accepting the conditions before the spook lady finished laying them out. As in, agree or go back to your Washington cubicle.

They didn't actually leap forward. But close.

One look at the spook's photos was enough. They showed the face of a man controlling the new Ojinaga route for both drugs and refugees.

This was the same drug lord who had murdered Kelly's fiancé. Their primary target, at least as far as Kelly was concerned. There was no way on earth she would turn down this chance for revenge.

The spook lady had not introduced herself when she arrived accompanied by a tall stone-faced staffer. The guy had merely stood there and frowned as the spook laid out her instructions. Which were almost as baffling as the mission itself. Infiltrate the Chihuahua state of northern Mexico, which was currently being invaded by a drug gang so new they were not even named. Follow any and all directives issued by Rabbit. Assault the final gathering point for refugees heading north and the drug lord's new compound. Both of which were heavily manned. Gather up all the refugees that Rabbit identified. Consider them such high-value targets that their safety was more important than the lives of Kelly's own team. And herself.

Bring them back.

Mission over.

They were positioned six miles outside the nowhere Texas town of Presidio. Kelly's teams lined the narrow ridge and formed two arms at river level. They faced the slow-moving Rio Grande, whose summertime level glowed muddy and sullen in the moonlight. Across from them shone the meager lights of Ojinaga, which until recently had remained relatively unscathed by the gang-related violence dominating Juarez eighty miles further west. This region was too dry, too removed from roads and safe passages north. Presidio was positioned between hundreds of square miles of national parks. The town itself was populated by gun-packing locals who hated drug-runners and the people-smugglers known as coyotes worse than summer heat.

Four minutes passed, five, then the patrol officer muttered, 'Well, stitch me up in a sack with ten horny toads.'

Which made no sense yet fit the moment perfectly.

Directly in front of their bivouac, four coyotes and three dozen or so illegals clambered up the river's muddy bank.

'Riggs. Cotton.'

'Riggs. Go.'

'Cotton here.'

'Green light. Tranqs only.'

Most of her agents were positioned in two narrow arroyos, shielded by mesquite and creosote bushes, flanking the entry point. Kelly flipped down her night-vision goggles and watched as all the two-legged green blobs jerked, spasmed and fell. She thought she heard a few quiet *pffts* but couldn't be sure.

The Border Patrol officer muttered, 'Spooks get all the best toys.'

It was easy enough to identify the coyotes – two men and two women, tougher and better dressed and well fed. All minus the wasting fatigue that stained the others over the long and harrowing weeks spent trekking to this place. The muddy northern bank of the Rio Grande. Gateway to a better life.

When Kelly descended the ridge, she pointed to the coyotes and said, 'Give them the antidote.' Then, 'Hold a second.'

Rabbit padded over and touched the shoulder of a woman. 'Not her. She culls young ones for the gangs.'

Haig, the patrol officer, frowned at the words. But he did not speak. Kelly assumed he was operating under orders as strange as her own. 'We only need one,' she told Rabbit. 'Since you're here, choose.'

'I can take us forward.'

'It's better to bring one with us,' Kelly replied. 'In case we need to signal.'

The kid did not argue. He studied the three supine figures, then pointed to the younger male. 'This one.'

Kelly motioned to Riggs, who injected the antidote. Little metal tubes, small as the cartridges, minus the tiny carbon-fiber wings. Offered to them without any outward concern over the cost, which must have been huge. Next-gen weaponry, ammunition, comm links, the works. Everything handed around by the spook lady and her number two, their casual gestures saying clear as shouts that they were focused on something far more important than the money involved.

They left the refugees and the three other guides with the Border Patrol officers and headed out. Crossing the sullen summertime river, scaling the southern bank, heading into Indian country.

The coyote's wrists were zipped in front, his mouth taped. He walked with Cotton's knife touching just below his right ear. Cotton served as watcher because his Spanish was almost perfect. The coyote was awake but disoriented and terrified. Occasionally, he stumbled over the rough ground, but Cotton's grip on his collar kept him upright.

Cotton hissed softly, gestured with his chin to the coyote, who had raised his hands and pointed.

Kelly could see nothing ahead. The night was silent. Just the same, the coyote knew his life hung by a thread. She gestured for Riggs and his team to join her. Together they moved forward.

Thirty yards further on, Kelly heard a quiet voice, a soft laugh. She gestured for the team to spread out.

Riggs and six agents kept on their night goggles. Kelly stripped hers off and stowed them in her thigh pouch. A soft *pfft*, a single shot, and their coyote-guide dropped. Cotton crawled up beside her. Ten meters, twelve, and six battered Kia Sedona minivans finally came into view.

A light flared as one of the drivers lit a cigarette. Nothing to Kelly but blinding for her agents. Someone, probably one of her team seeing their first live action, cursed softly. Scarcely more than a whisper. But the night was so quiet that one of the guards heard and barked to the others.

Kelly hit her comm link. 'Fire, fire.'

She had never handled the rifle before. Never fired a single round. The lack of recoil was far more disconcerting than the silence. A soft whispering cough, nothing more.

The six drivers went down while still searching the night for a target.

Kelly's final conversation with the spook lady, Agnes Pendalon, had taken place in the rear hold of a Boeing C717 military transport. Which was when Agnes had finally offered her name. Agnes Pendalon had not actually said she was CIA. But the way she moved, the severe attitude, the demand for immediate and unquestioned obedience, Kelly assumed the lady and her silent number two were both either military or Langley spooks.

Kelly stood over an open case of the strangest rifles she had ever seen. 'Is this a joke?'

'Do I strike you as a funny person, Kaiser?'

'Ma'am, you can't expect me and my teams to enter Mexico and rely on untested weaponry.'

'They are thoroughly tested and ready for any live-fire operation you might encounter.' When Kelly looked ready to argue, the woman snapped, 'This is all you will carry. Say the word and I'll strip you of this command.'

Kelly was beyond stoked. Her first assignment as lead agent. Standing in the midnight-clad aircraft, orders still ringing in her ears, heart at redline. No way she was giving this up. She remained silent. Worried. But still.

Pendalon lifted one rifle and one clip. 'Next-gen weapons. Handgun accurate to fifty meters, rifles to three hundred. Laser sight as well as standard Zeiss telescopic. Clip holds nine rounds as well as a fresh gas canister. Same clip fits both weapons.'

Despite herself, Kelly was beyond impressed. 'Can we at least take our sidearms as backup?'

'That's a sharp negative. You and your team are not to fire a single hot round. Clear?'

Barry Riggs had sidled up beside her, a collegiate all-star fullback who had passed on the pro game for this. A chance to stand by open hard cases of rifles and handguns and ammo, barrels and grips and firing pins and clips all of carbon fiber. Taking orders from a professional ghost. 'What's in the ammo?'

'Whatever we elect to feed into those canisters. In this case, a fast-acting nerve agent combined with a powerful sedative. Paralyzes in half a second; the opposition is out before they hit the ground.' She indicated slender cases stacked beside the clips. 'Neutralizing agent. Brings them back in twenty seconds.' Agnes Pendalon revealed a genuinely nasty smile. 'Other ammo you won't be using on this particular mission holds combinations of agents that are a good deal less pleasant.'

When neither Kelly nor Riggs spoke, Pendalon gestured to her number two, who began sealing the cases. 'These weapons have never been known to fail. I expect the same from you.'

Darren Cotton was a tall African American who would be handsome in anyone's books, male and female alike. He treated his looks and the attention like some throwaway items he'd been handed by a mall troll. Kelly had liked him from their first day in training. She and Cotton both dealt with people who wanted to slot them into the beautiful-people socket. Round pegs in square holes, the two of them. Kelly's father was pure Romanian, probably gypsy; he used to laugh over tales his own father and grandfather told of Roma wagons, the horses decorated with silk ribbons, the road open and beckoning. Locals who were anchored to poverty-stricken villages despised them as thieves, while envying their wandering ways. Kelly's mother was a blond beauty. Kelly had inherited the best of both,

her mother's looks and her father's adventurous nature. She and Cotton detested people who saw nothing more than what they wanted, who classed her as a possible romantic target. Including the three men who had done their best to lash her down, then wreck her life when she refused to meet their expectations. They formed her finest targets on the firing range and in close-quarter combat. That and the man waiting in their current destination. She hoped.

Kelly watched Cotton's team strip the six drivers of hats and kerchiefs and phones. Riggs stepped up beside her, offering a Colt sidearm. 'The drivers don't need them anymore.'

'No extra weapons,' Kelly replied. 'You heard Pendalon same as me.'

'You sure about that?' Riggs waggled the gun. 'Feels mighty good, holding a piece I understand.'

She could almost feel the serrated grip, how it would nestle inside her hand. She knew the balance, the trigger action, the recoil, the smell of cordite after firing hundreds of rounds. She *trusted* that sidearm.

Still . . .

She forced herself to turn away. 'We're on the clock, Riggs.'

Riggs looked ready to argue. In the end, though, he dropped the Colt into the dust and headed for the second vehicle.

They all wore communication units as high-tech as the guns. A padded wire hooked around Kelly's right ear held a tiny listening device and mike in place, the wire also serving as link to the unseen drone hovering on the border's other side. All comms were encrypted, never out of range, no distortion, voices sounding like they were seated in the minivan with her. She had to assume this included Agnes Pendalon and her number two, the spooks monitoring her every breath. The controls were on a pliable armband encircling her left wrist. Kelly keyed the controls now, as deft as if she'd been using this for years. 'Bus depot a half-klick and closing. Teams two and three proceed straight to the main compound. Wait for my signal. Stop any combatants who try to join the dance. Cotton, confirm.'

'Roger that.'

'Team one, on my six.' The expression came from pilots of the First World War, who described the nose of their aircraft as twelve o'clock. Watching their six formed a constant refrain during Kelly's training. Keeping an eye on what was behind them meant the difference between survival and going down in flames. 'All teams, make yourselves small.'

Kelly crouched with the others, until only the drivers in their borrowed shirts and hats were visible. She knelt in the front passenger seat's footwell, her head just far up so as to view out the front windscreen. This was no time for questioning orders or doubting their arms or wondering about the blade-faced woman who pulled all their strings. Now it all came down to the battle waiting fifty meters up ahead. And surviving the night.

The lights surrounding the village bus station burned an acrid yellow. The air through her open window was dry and scented by creosote and desert pine and dust and smoke and roasting meat. Music drifted from the cantina attached to the station's eastern side. A trio of tricked-out 4x4s were parked in front, lined up like horses at the hitching post. Every table in the dusty forecourt was full. All the patrons were heavily armed.

Kelly keyed her link. 'Team one, be advised. Multiple hostiles.'

A woman seated at the corner table called and waved as they passed.

Kelly told the agent driving her vehicle, 'Wave back.'

He did so, laconic and slow, just another guy tired from a long hot night. The woman laughed and rose from her chair, accompanied by two men. They started to follow the SUVs.

Cotton said in her ear, 'Three hostiles on the move.'

'Roger that.'

They rounded the building and pulled up next to two more SUVs and three busses standing silent for the night. They faced an empty garage with one bay door open, one interior light burning. No one in sight.

Beyond that, two narrow lanes branched off and ran dark into the gloom. Leading to their primary targets.

'All teams hold.' She told her driver, 'Go for the woman on my signal.'

He nodded, his gaze straight ahead, his face bland. Just another night at the office.

The woman called again, and her two companions spoke together.

Kelly's Spanish was adequate, but their slang was so heavy she did not understand a word. Not that it mattered. Adrenaline parsed the seconds. Kelly felt able to pull wings from insects hovering just beyond her window. 'Now.'

She gave her driver the two seconds required for him to open his door and rise and aim over the vehicle's roof. Then she straightened and shot the two men through her open window. Quick puffs of sound, a trio of astonished looks, and they were down. She told her team, 'Secure the hostiles.' She touched her wristband, 'Riggs.'

'Riggs. Go.'

'Move out. Stay safe. Hold position until we arrive.'

'Roger. Teams two and three, on me.'

Impossible that Kelly was expected to assault two heavily armed compounds and an outlier station with Riggs, Cotton and nine more agents. Impossible they were sent into combat by a knife-edged ghost woman, who ordered Kelly to proceed on intel provided by a bespectacled kid hovering in the SUV's rear seat. A man whose real name Kelly was ordered not to ask.

She told Rabbit, 'Stay here. Do not move.'

They rounded the buildings from both sides. Kelly's trio took the cantina, Cotton the depot. Straight in, five agents against three times the number of combatants. More.

Kelly fired off her nine rounds, reloaded, fired. No sound, no recoil. Five ghosts in black holding rifles and sidearms that seemed carved from the night itself. No flashes. No sign they were even firing, except for how every single gang member went down.

Sixty seconds, less, and it was over.

Kelly watched as her team zip-tied wrists and ankles, then gathered weapons and cellphones in a garbage can taken from the kitchen. 'How many?'

Cotton's grin and copper-adrenaline gaze were the only bright spots to the man. 'Thirty-four, counting the kitchen staff.'

'Good work.' She keyed her comm link. 'Riggs.'

'Riggs here.'

'Station secure. Heading out.'

'Roger. We're in position and holding. Main gates secure.'

She signaled her team. 'On the move.'

They returned to the minivans long enough for Kelly to gather up Rabbit. She positioned him in the middle of her team, protected on either side by experienced agents. They had heard the spook lady's orders same as Kelly. Rabbit's safety was paramount. Lose team members if required. Rabbit was to return unharmed. Failure was not an option.

They took the right-hand lane, a rubble-strewn road lined by refuse and weeds. Past the mechanic's yard and half a dozen broken-down vehicles, hulking shadows in the night. No illumination except for the trio of stark yellow lights up ahead – two above the guards' chairs, positioned to either side of a warehouse's open door. The third spilled from dusty and cracked office windows, all open to the mild desert breeze. The warehouse door was guarded by four *polleros*, gang members responsible for herding refugees.

Kelly whispered, 'My team, guards. Cotton, take the office. Fire when ready.'

Thirty seconds later, the eleven gang members were unconscious. Cotton confirmed, 'All secure.'

Kelly walked to where she could look through the office windows and inspected the prone and zip-tied combatants. She asked Cotton, 'Any sign of our primary target?'

'He's not here.'

Kelly turned away. 'Hit the lights.' She walked back to where Rabbit stood with his lone guard. 'Showtime.'

The warehouse was lined with seven rows of bunkbeds. The front section held a dozen or so trestle tables and benches. The rear contained a pair of shower rooms and toilets. The air was fetid with industrial cleaner and too many unwashed bodies and fear. Overhead lights dangled from rusting steel beams, the same harsh yellow as outside. It painted the faces peering worriedly from beneath blankets in hard, bleak lines.

Two agents served as close-quarter guards to their gangly CI. Kelly and Cotton moved more slowly, pulling down blankets where necessary, checking each face in turn, guns at the ready. Making sure no further *polleros* were hiding among the refugees. Hunting for their secret target. Coming up blank. The four of them tracked Rabbit down one aisle after the other. Every now and then, they repeated the same words in Spanish. Stay calm. Remain where you are.

Rabbit pointed out a mother and daughter in the first row; from the second, three women in their thirties. In the last two rows, there was just a husband and wife, both in their fifties or older. All of those he pointed to rose silently from their bunks, utterly awake and fully dressed, their packs at the ready. Unlike everyone else, this group observed Kelly's team without fear.

They followed Rabbit from the warehouse. Not Kelly or her team. The slender young man played the silent Pied Piper as they entered the darkness. As they exited, Rabbit told her, 'The others are in the main house.'

Kelly said to one of her team, 'Take these back to the vans. Stay on guard.'

Another interesting thing happened then. The guard gestured with his weapon, spoke to them in passable Spanish. These people, who should have been terror-stricken at the sight of armed strangers, simply stood and watched Rabbit. Waiting for orders. At least, that was how it seemed to Kelly.

All he did was nod.

They turned and followed the agent into the night.

Kelly watched until the last of them became mere shadows. Then she keyed her comm link. 'Riggs.'

'Riggs. Go.'

'Targets secure. We're heading your way. Your advance teams have the green light.'

'Roger that.'

They powered back down the narrow lane and took the second road at a full sprint. Then, 'We're fifty yards from the compound gates and closing.'

'Ah, Kelly . . .'

She lifted a fist, halting her team's forward momentum.

'Riggs. Talk to me.'

'I'm at the top of the main steps. Front door is wide open.'

'You were ordered to survey and hold.'

'Ah, yeah. Sure. But . . .' A cough. Muttered exchange with someone else. Then, 'They're all asleep.'

She stared at Cotton. They slowed and looked back to where Rabbit ran between two agents. 'Say again.'

'My advance crew tracked across the forecourt. Waved us forward. The exterior guards were all zonked. Including the four on the front patio. We're holding in the foyer. I can see six more – no, seven. We're shooting tranqs and zip-tying bodies that were already laid out like Christmas presents. Request permission to proceed.'

Kelly saw no reason to refuse. 'Go ahead. Stay alert.'

'Roger. Riggs out.'

She walked back to where Rabbit stood at the tail end of her crew. 'Is this your doing?'

The way he looked at her, bright eyes glimmering in the dim light, was a clear response. She had stepped over the line. No questions. He asked, 'Can I proceed?'

Kelly positioned Rabbit beside and behind her as she led her teams through the main gates. The front yard was wide as a football field, strewn with construction equipment and brand-new supercars. Kelly spotted a McLaren, several Ferraris and a pair of matching Porsche track cars. Beyond the graveled drive were stacks of unplanted trees and flowers. The night was rich with the odors of blossoms and tilled earth.

Bodies were laid out everywhere. Prone, unconscious, trussed ankles and wrists. Kelly counted fourteen and probably missed some.

They climbed the broad front steps and entered the domed foyer. The house smelled of sawdust and fresh paint and polish. To her right, six supine guards were laid out end to end.

Riggs stood by the main corridor, gun slack in his right hand. 'Ain't this just some weird voodoo.'

He led her down a hallway twenty feet wide, the ceiling domed and illuminated by a string of crystal chandeliers. The manor held an eerie silence, unbroken save for the soft chatter of Riggs's team. Kelly felt like a bashful visitor to some carnival house of mirrors. 'How many combatants?'

'Counting those in the front yard, thirty-nine so far.' Riggs glanced at Rabbit, who remained attached to Kelly's side. 'Maybe some fast-acting gas, but who set it off?'

Rabbit seemed immune to Riggs and his questions. Kelly felt the need for answers build like an electric current in her gut. Mysteries in the field meant risk. Risk led to death.

But in the end, the only question she posed was to Riggs. 'What about our target?'

'Still searching.' They reached a broad curving stairway midway down the main corridor. He pointed to their left. 'Main bedroom is that way.' He indicated the opposite direction. 'Down there are three steel doors with mock wood covers. We were waiting for you before blowing them open.'

Rabbit spoke for the first time since entering. 'There's no need. Those rooms are our target.' He started up, hurrying now. 'I can take it from here.'

Kelly held back, allowing Rabbit to proceed on his own. Three of Riggs's team stood sentry outside the doors. She signaled them to back off. As Rabbit approached the first door, Kelly's comm link came to life. 'Team Leader, come in.'

'Go ahead, Cotton.'

'We've identified our primary target.'

'What's your location?'

'Behind you, end of the corridor.'

Kelly swung about and spotted him grinning between massive double doors. Cotton offered a thumbs up.

An adrenaline-rich fury drenched her veins. Kelly was pleased to hear nothing showed in her voice when she spoke. 'Hold him.'

'Roger that.'

She turned back to where Rabbit stood by the first steel door. The keypad above the knob glowed red. Rabbit touched the pad.

The agent standing to Rabbit's left said, 'All three are locked.'

Rabbit did not seem to hear him. Ten seconds passed. Twenty. Then the keypad chimed once and the light went green.

Kelly lifted her weapon with her team. Ready.

The door opened from within. And . . .

A young woman, dark eyes above the pronounced cheekbones of a pure-blood indigenous South American, stepped forward. She was, in a word, beautiful. She was also weeping. No sound. Her tears fell and dripped down her front; her hands trembled as she reached out and touched Rabbit's face. Which was when Kelly realized her CI was weeping as well.

The young woman whispered words that were certainly not Spanish. Some regional dialect, or perhaps a different language entirely. Rabbit whispered back in English, 'I'm here. The worst is over. Everything is good now. We'll take you somewhere safe.'

She flowed forward, swift as water, her words a constant musical chant. The two of them embraced with what Kelly could only describe as hunger.

While they watched the couple, locks on the other two doors chimed.

The doors opened. People emerged. Kelly counted twenty-seven in all. She and her team stepped back, granting them room to approach Rabbit and the woman he held. Touching his head and shoulders and arms. Many of them weeping as well.

Finally, Kelly said, 'All right, enough.' She gestured to five of her team. 'Take them back to our rides. Rabbit, go with them and help get them loaded up.'

She waited until they had straggled out, then said, 'Let's get this done.'

She had twice been into homes formerly owned by drug lords. Even so, the master bedroom's opulence was blinding. All the furniture, including the massive four-poster bed, even the pediments on which lewd statues rested – everything was gold plated. She ignored the four women trussed on the bed and knelt by the naked man bound and sprawled unconscious on the silk carpet. 'Is it him?'

Riggs squatted on the man's other side. 'No question.' He offered his phone showing a mug shot of the same man.

He had gone by many names. *Filero* was the most recent, slang for Blade. Until recently, he had served as primary killer for the Juarez cartel. Suddenly, without warning, he had branched out on his own, taken over this formerly quiet little border town and established himself as a kingpin. Somehow managing to fend off attacks from the Juarez cartel, the Sinaloans, Zetas, everyone.

Until now.

Kelly said, 'Wake him up.'

Riggs himself injected the antidote. Thirty seconds later, the man's eyes opened. One brief instant, a single glance at Kelly and Riggs and the agents lining the far wall.

He smiled.

Kelly's orders with regard to him were as explicit as all the others that defined this impossible night. Radio in the Mexican military. And then depart the same way they had entered, bringing with them all those identified by Rabbit. Leave this man and his gang to the local authorities.

She had anticipated this moment ever since being sent on mission. Imagined the things she wanted to say. About the four agents this man had personally murdered. Two in particular. Her fiancé. And her favorite instructor from Quantico. A man revered by everyone in the room. The instructor who inspired every recruit under his care to do their best, rise to the challenge, endure the insanely difficult training, become federal agents. He and Kelly's fiancé and two more agents had traveled to Juarez on just another brief cross-border visit. Which happened to be the day this man killed his own boss and went rogue. Four federal agents in the wrong place at the wrong time. Dead at the hand of this man and his knife.

Now that she was here, Kelly found there was nothing that needed saying. The action was as simple as punctuating a thought.

She took her knife and cut the man's throat.

Thirty seconds later, she rose and met the gaze of every agent in the room. Granting them all a chance to object, condemn. 'Any blowback goes straight to me. I acted against your strenuous objections.' When they remained silent, she started for the door. 'We're all done here.'

TWO

Today

'I'm so sorry, Mr Hayes,' the CEO's secretary said for the third time. 'I'm sure they won't keep you waiting much longer.'

'No problem.' Denton Hayes had never before entered NovaCorp's executive suite. The insurance company's headquarters was a highrise in downtown LA, and the top-floor view was stupendous – along the Sunset Strip's asphalt river, through Hollywood and Beverly Hills, all the way to the sparkling Pacific.

Rachel Adams was rotund, intelligent and motherly. Denton guessed her age to be late fifties. He also suspected the PA could reveal a steely bark when required. She asked, 'Are you sure I can't get you something?'

'I'm fine, thanks.' Denton had been parked in the CEO's outer office for forty minutes. This after being woken at five by a frantic call from his boss, flown back from his current gig by private jet, and rushed here by limo from the John Wayne Airport.

There were worse ways to while away the hours.

Ten minutes later, the PA's phone chimed, and she ushered Denton into the conference room. Just three people were present. Richard Crandon, NovaCorp's head of claims and Denton's boss. A beautiful woman in her mid-thirties, Connor Breach, head of legal. Denton had never met the woman. But he knew the office rumors. How she had been promoted over other executives because of her not-so-secret relationship with the company's CEO.

Byron Sykes sat at the head of a table capable of seating eighteen. He was sleek in the manner of a well-groomed tiger. No amount of polish or money could fully disguise the man's predatory nature. The practiced smile, the firm handshake, the sincere words thanking Denton for making the time to meet with them. All just so much varnish.

'Are you sure we can't get you something? How about a sandwich?' Sykes gestured to the drinks cabinet adorning the inside wall. 'It's a little early in the day for me, but help yourself.'

'Thank you, Mr Sykes. I'm good.'

'Call me Byron, will you?' He slipped on reading glasses and opened a buff manila folder. 'You'll have to excuse me, Denton. I'm still being brought up to steam here. Do you mind if I ask a few questions?'

'Not at all.'

'You studied business and finance at USC. Masters in forensic accounting, turned down the invitation to enter their doctoral program and instead joined the LA police force.' Another smile in Denton's direction. 'There's a story here. I can feel it.'

'My father was a cop. A forensic accountant is a detective hunting the trail of numbers. The new chief was beefing up their white-collar division. I applied, and they accepted.'

'And you stayed on the force . . .'

'A little over four years.'

'And afterwards you became an independent consultant – is that correct?'

Denton accepted the chief's polite probing. 'For another two and a half years.'

'At which point you entered NovaCorp's orbit.'

'Right.' Denton pointed to his boss. 'Richard's predecessor hired me to look into two questionable claims.'

'Why didn't he use our in-house team?'

'You'll have to ask him. My impression was he had and didn't like their answers.'

Byron turned a page. 'As a result, you saved our company a considerable sum. Twice.'

Denton did not hear a question and remained silent.

'Which was when Richard's predecessor recruited you. That was . . .'

'Three and a half years ago.' He glanced at his boss, wondered why the man was sweating.

'From which point you have successfully resolved . . .'

His boss spoke for the first time that morning. 'Seven fraudulent claims.'

'Saving us thirty-seven million and change. A most impressive record.' Byron closed the file. Slipped off his reading specs. 'All right, I've seen enough. Connor?'

The attorney slipped a trio of forms across the table. 'We have a very sensitive case that requires your immediate attention.'

'Sensitive how?'

'That will be clarified once this paperwork is completed.' She glanced at the CEO, watched him rise from the chair and walk to the side windows. 'As of this moment, all your current cases have been reassigned.'

Denton glanced at his boss, who was equally surprised by this move. Richard protested, 'The Phoenix investigation has reached a crucial—'

'That is no longer Mr Hayes's concern.' She pointed to the documents. 'You need to sign the nondisclosure agreement before we can proceed.'

Which made no sense. 'My contract with NovaCorp includes nondisclosure.'

'Just the same, you need to sign. Those documents specifically cover anything and everything revealed by this new investigation.'

Byron Sykes addressed the window. 'You are to report to me and Ms Breach. No one else. Not one word.'

Denton's boss shifted in his seat. 'Byron, I really must—'

'That's how it has to be, Richard. Sorry.' One finger drifted in Denton's direction. 'The clock is ticking. Sign, please.'

Denton signed.

The chief turned, said, 'Leave us, please. Denton, stay where you are.'

The attorney started, 'Byron, perhaps it would be—'

'That will be all, Connor.' At sixty-four, Byron Sykes was a striking figure. Steel-grey hair matching his glacier gaze. Tall, craven features, and something else. A magnetic force. When the door clicked shut, Byron Sykes turned back to the window and said, 'I have a very bad feeling about this particular case.'

Denton had little experience with people holding this level of power, corporate or otherwise. He had no idea if the man had always been this way, or if the mantle came with the job. He rose, walked over and stood facing the chief's right side. 'Bad how?'

'I'm catching rumors. Added to this is a conversation yesterday evening with someone I would trust with my life. The end result is a series of issues that simply don't add up. If it's true . . .'

Denton waited, then, 'If what is true, sir?'

The chief shook his head. 'I'm not going to start this investigation by sharing my nightmare scenarios.' He turned and gripped Denton with his gaze. 'Richard has the file. That is the last contact you are to have with him regarding what you discover.'

'I don't understand.'

'And if I'm wrong, you never will. My concerns will fade and eventually disappear. But if I'm right . . .' He waved that aside. 'If you manage to resolve this within a week, you will receive an additional bonus of fifty thousand dollars.'

'Sir . . . Byron, I don't know—'

'Whatever you need in terms of resources, it is yours. Speak with Connor; she will make it happen. You have a blank check. Use my jet whenever necessary. Speed is everything.' New shadows carved hollows in the man's face. Cheeks, eye sockets, temples. 'I very much want to hear there's nothing to worry about. I'll be delighted to pay you that bonus and have you assure me it's just another bizarre claim.'

'But you don't think that's the situation?'

'What I think . . .' He shook his head. 'A man I trust – a member of our board, a doctor who saved my life seven years ago, he's afraid. He thinks this represents a series of events that could well destroy our company. I'm paying you to prove him wrong. Or tell me otherwise. And fast. You understand? Speed is everything here. If he's right, we may already be too late.'

'Sir, I'm sorry, but you're not making sense.'

The CEO ignored his protest. 'Read the file. Update Connor at least once each day. If you find anything that suggests a nightmare scenario, you are to contact me immediately. The file contains my and Connor's private numbers. Now get to work.'

THREE

Kelly Kaiser sat in the fourth-floor corridor of Homeland's headquarters, across the Potomac from Reagan National. The building was only a few years old, part of the new Homeland campus still under construction. But the wooden bench where she sat was something from an earlier era, stained and warped and hard as granite. As if generations of agents who had sweated out their final hours in federal employment had permanently damaged the surface.

She and her team had returned from Texas by way of the same military transport. Once they landed, Kelly had been separated from the others and driven straight to secure accommodations in Foggy Bottom. The building was used by all the agencies: a fortified housing block replete with wire-mesh windows, a forest of security cameras, electronic keypads that could be overridden from the front desk, armed security. As far as prisons went, it wasn't at all bad – gym, pool, private room, cable and a cafeteria serving excellent food.

Riggs and Cotton had been permitted one visit. Seated in the lounge, supervised by uniformed security. They related how the Mexican authorities had come unglued when they had discovered the drug lord's body, naked and trussed, blood from the neck wound staining the priceless Persian carpet. Her two lieutenants had smiled with genuine pleasure as they related several brief but scalding interviews with various officials, including the ambassador and Mexico's very own Minister of Interior.

Once back in her room, Kelly had wondered why such high-ranking individuals were personally involved. It made no sense. It wasn't like their anger was going to bring the guy back. The mystery lingered still, as she sat in the Homeland corridor and waited while the brass inside the conference room decided her fate. She knew part of it had to do with how the Mexican government wanted her arrested and returned to stand trial for murder. She probably should have cared more than she did. But just then, watching people studiously avoid glancing her way as they walked past, Kelly mostly missed her fiancé.

Senior Field Agent Nathan Bragg had been Virginia born and raised. He joined Homeland after law school. He had been a quiet, gentle man and die-hard patriot, who had wanted little more than to serve his country with distinction. Nathan had deserved a better and far longer career than he had achieved. He would have despised what she did in Mexico, shouted at her for days. Not that it mattered. Nathan had always been a better man, and carried higher standards, than Kelly.

She had lived without her man for ninety-seven hard days. Some hours she managed to go without feeling like his absence was a hollow ache so strong it would swallow her whole. Now, seated and waiting to hear how they would frame her dismissal, Kelly viewed her time in Mexico with a total lack of remorse. That Mexican drug lord had wounded her terribly. He had paid the price. End of story.

Her only concern was the careers of her team.

Darren Cotton had left half an hour ago, right after a faceless admin type had pointed her on to the bench. Cotton had grimaced in her direction before two agents had firmly escorted him away.

Now Barry Riggs emerged, the same two agents serving as guard dogs. He tried to speak, but the instant he opened his mouth, the female agent snapped, 'Eyes front!'

Barry offered Kelly a mock salute and departed. Kelly held on to Barry's simple act of friendship as the pair returned and said, 'OK, Kaiser. You're up.'

Kelly entered the room well aware that her life as she knew it, the only job she had ever really wanted, was drawing to a close. She was ten days from her thirtieth birthday and felt a hundred and ten.

Agnes Pendalon, the spook lady who had sent them on the mission, was seated between two men. She introduced them as Grey Mathers, her number two, and Colonel Reuben Langdon, Pentagon liaison. Kelly was both confused and disconcerted even before she took her seat. She glanced behind her. The room was empty, the escorts gone. Disappeared.

Pendalon said, 'As far as you and your team are concerned, the most important purpose of your ops was to grant you first-hand knowledge of our new enemy. One we can't see, or identify, or take aim at through any so-called normal means.'

Kelly said, 'I thought this was a formal review.'

'Leading to your dismissal.' Pendalon nodded. 'From the viewpoint of everyone else, that is precisely what just happened. From this moment, your remit is off the books. Do you have any trouble with that?'

Her heart seemed incapable of maintaining a steady rhythm. Kelly started to ask if Pendalon had expected all along that the drug lord would not survive. Then decided it was best to offer a simple, 'No, ma'am.'

'I need you to select a second-in-command and six more from those who traveled with you to Mexico. They will be the initial members of your new frontline team. We can discuss adding more if or when the work requires. But for the moment, we need your ops footprint to remain both small and unseen.'

'Where will we be serving?'

'Your first field assignment is Los Angeles. Starting this afternoon.'

'And the other agents who accompanied me to Mexico?'

'They will serve as your intel backup. They will be based at our new dedicated HQ in Reston.'

Before Pendalon had finished speaking, Kelly was ready. 'I'd like Barry Riggs as my number two. Darren Cotton should serve as point on the in-house team.' She named the others to accompany her. And waited.

Pendalon watched as her number two typed into his laptop, studied the contents, then offer her a nod. Agnes turned back to Kelly and demanded, 'Why Riggs and not Cotton as your backup?'

'If our remit includes adapting to unexpected threats . . .'

'You have just defined the primary risk of your new assignment,' Pendalon confirmed.

'When it comes to facing new threats, Barry Riggs has the fastest reflexes I've ever encountered.' Kelly hesitated, then added, 'Darren's wife is expecting their third. Until we know what we're facing, all those with me on the frontline should be single.'

Pendalon glanced at her silent aide, received another nod in response. 'Very well. You and your lieutenants are hereby granted TS/SCI status. Your first duty is to decide how much the rest of your team should know.'

Top Secret, Sensitive Compartmentalized Intel was the highest level of DOD clearance. Something normally reserved for senior officers and ranking members of the White House and Congressional intelligence communities. Just the same, Kelly replied, 'With your permission, ma'am, I think they should know everything. They trust me; I trust them.'

Pendalon thought a moment, then told her silent aides, 'Get them ready.' She then waited until it was just the two of them in the room. 'I think you should know. Nathan Bragg was killed while investigating the enemy you will now be hunting.'

Kelly felt the words slam her from all sides. 'He said—'

'That they were down for a routine inspection with their counter-parts in Mexican intelligence. True and not true. We – my team – have been concerned that our new enemy has infiltrated the drug gangs and those trying to cross the border. Or perhaps the gangs became alerted to the potential of harnessing the enemy. We don't know yet, but we will soon.' Pendalon waved that aside. 'Your former fiancé was part of our first attempt to get a handle on what is happening south of the border. I thought you should know.'

It took her several breaths to manage, 'I don't understand.'

'You will soon enough.' Pendalon rose to her feet. 'This will most likely be your last visit to Homeland. You have ten minutes to clear your desk and say your farewells. Make it sound like an involuntary dismissal. A ride is waiting out front.'

FOUR

D enton took the elevator down to the eighth floor and entered his cubicle. Central aisle cubicles were generally despised and assigned to the newest paper-pushers, interns, and employees on the way out. The other investigators assumed Denton was barely holding on to his job, a guy who was no threat to their own advancement. Which was exactly what Denton wanted.

Denton's space was right up against the windowless rear wall and granted him a view over the entire floor. No one could approach him unseen. A ceiling a/c unit blasted a constant frigid note. The lighting was artificial and fairly awful. Denton was not there often enough to care.

He knew his boss and NovaCorp's head of legal waited for him in Richard's office. Denton couldn't start on the investigation until he obtained the relevant file. Just the same, he seated himself, leaned against the concrete wall and mentally ran through what had just happened. Motionless. When he was a child, several teachers had thought him slow, the way he sat cocooned in silence, scarcely seeming to breathe. Sometimes for hours. In reality, this was when Denton was busiest. And in some respects also when he was happiest. Sifting. Sorting. Analyzing. Preparing himself for whatever came next.

When he was ready, he left the cubicle and walked back down the central aisle. Over to where Richard's glass wall was smokey, opaque. The inward-facing windows to Richard's office and the floor's three conference rooms were equipped with electrochromic glass. Switch it on and the window not just turned milky but jammed most listening devices. This was Richard's way of hanging up a *Do Not Disturb* sign.

Denton knocked, waited until the electronic lock clicked opened, then entered.

Richard greeted him with his customary, 'Is there anything you wish to report?'

Now that his boss was free from the CEO's presence, his standard irritation was back in control. Richard Crandon was a man bound by rules. He liked full reports. He demanded detailed written overviews of all investigations, every day spent outside the office, every cent listed on expense accounts. Denton knew Richard would never have hired him. Denton's methods did not fit inside Richard's tight little box. But by the time Richard had become VP of claims, Denton's success record had granted him lifetime job security. If he wanted it.

Denton had no problem with Richard's rulebook. It gave him a formal method for sorting through the mysteries attached to most of his cases. A number of the other investigators thought Richard Crandon was a constant and perpetual pain. Denton neither liked nor disliked the man.

Denton replied, 'I'm not sure I should answer that.'

'No. Definitely not,' Connor said. To Richard, 'You were wrong to even ask.'

'This is my division. My team. My investigation.'

'Not this time.' When Richard looked ready to argue, she added, 'Let me know if the chief needs to spell that out more clearly.'

Richard subsided. Fumed.

Connor rose, slipped the lone file off Richard's desk. 'Let's relocate to your office.'

'Investigators have cubicles,' Richard snapped.

'Not this investigator and not this case. Is there a spare office?'

Richard reluctantly allowed, 'We use the small conference room for laying out evidence on major cases.'

Connor asked, 'Does the door lock?'

Richard said, 'This is getting ridiculous.'

Denton thought his boss had a point but merely replied, 'Numerical keypad.'

'I'll have Security come up. No one but the chief, you and I can have access. Understand?'

Richard protested, 'This is a missing house. Not the launch codes to World War Three.'

Denton asked, 'Sorry. Missing house?'

'A private home in Beverly Flats,' Richard said.

'I strictly work major corporate,' Denton said.

'You do what the chief tells you. Clear?'

'Yes and no.'

Connor started for the door. 'Let's move this conversation to your new office.'

The smaller conference room was down the side aisle, back near Denton's cubicle. Every eye in the bullpen watched their progress. As they entered, Denton glanced back. Richard stood in his doorway. Arms crossed. Fuming.

The conference room was mid-level corporate, bland and functional and spartan. Connor entered first, said, 'Lock us in. Opaque the glass.' When he had done so, she asked, 'Is this place swept for bugs?'

'Richard was right. This is overkill.'

'I'll have Security do a sweep when they change the locks.'

'Will you tell me what's going on?'

Connor surprised him then. She walked to the windows. Clenched her arms together at gut level. 'You've heard the rumors about me and Byron.'

Denton took his time. Stepped to the table's far end. Drew out the top chair. Settled. Waited.

'It's bogus. A complete and utter lie, fabricated by people who are jealous of my rise.' She tilted her head, and auburn-rich hair fell over one shoulder. She inspected him in the window's reflection. 'Do you have a problem with that?'

She wore a navy jacket over a grey shift of raw silk. Her arms and legs were tanned and strong. Denton knew she had played tennis for her university team. He knew a lot about her because he had checked her out. 'Should I?'

'Do you have a problem with me?'

He liked how she asked that. Getting the issue out in the open. 'If you mean, how the chairman has ordered you to usurp my boss's position, the answer is no. Not at all.'

She walked over, selected a chair three down from his. 'I'm good at my job. Excellent, in fact.'

Denton saw no need to respond.

'Byron and I are friends. The opposition has that much right. He's come to trust me with a number of issues that are . . .'

'Highly sensitive.'

She nodded. 'Something about this case has him running scared.'

'Because of a missing house?'

'I have no idea. But I've never seen him like this. He won't talk to me. All I know for certain . . . Night before last, Byron had dinner with his closest friend on the board. He hasn't been the same since.'

'Who is the board member?'

'Why is that important?'

'I won't know until you tell me.'

'Sanjib Gupta.'

'Ah.'

'You know about him?'

'Doctor Gupta is head of UCLA Medical School. Former oncologist, now one of the world's foremost experts in the epidemiology of human longevity.'

She went quiet. Then, 'You've researched the entire board?'

'The board, the company directors. Yes.'

'Including me?'

'Connor Biggins Breach. Thirty-one, Stanford Law Review, clerk to Supreme Court Justice Alito, junior partner with Hill and Cleat, recruited six years ago to take on the NovaCorp's contracts division, promoted four times since.'

Another pause, then, 'That is both spooky and impressive.'

'Call Gupta. Tell him we need to meet.'

'I'm not sure—'

'Soon as possible.' He indicated the file. 'I'll spend the rest of today bringing myself up to speed on this house. Ask if we can meet him tonight.'

'Is this a test?'

He liked how she asked. No heat. Simply enquiring. Setting out the ground rules. 'I need to know how far this goes. With you and me. Are you willing to do whatever it takes? At which point do I go straight—'

'I'll set it up. Can I come?'

'That's not for me to say. Ask your boss. Gupta's private residence would probably be best. If not, somewhere off the books.'

'You know where he lives?'

'Different question. Same response.'

She rose, walked to the door, turned off the electronic field. 'Again. Spooky.'

FIVE

Three days earlier

G rey Mathers, Pendalon's number two, was a tall fellow in his mid-thirties. Suit to match his name, regulation haircut, massive build, gunner's eyes. Flat and hard. The man looked exactly what he was: a watchful, savvy agent, ready to spring into action. He addressed them with a crisp no-nonsense air, utterly without humor. He reminded Kelly of her favorite instructors at Quantico, the type who wanted their students to understand, who urged them to rise up, to succeed. Kelly hoped this same spirit was reflected in Mathers. If Pendalon's warnings with regard to unnamed threats were valid, Kelly's life and those of the frontline team depended on it.

They were seated in the first two rows, office chairs pulled up to lines of linoleum-topped rectangular tables with folding metal legs. Grey stood behind an identical table at the front of the room. On his left, a display screen had been rolled down from the ceiling. A small AV projector hung in a ceiling cradle. The room was well lit and windowless.

Behind them, in the rear left corner, sat Rabbit. Silent, watchful.

Kelly was still coming to terms with Pendalon's news that their assignment was somehow tied to her fiancé's murder. She found herself waiting for the rage to set in. Or maybe bone-deep sorrow. Something. Instead, all she felt was a crystalizing of forces. A clarity of purpose. A readiness for whatever came next.

Or so she thought.

The classroom occupied one corner of a faceless Reston office building's ground floor. From beyond their chamber came the constant muted sound of construction chaos. Grey's words were punctuated by thuds and hammering and the distant whine of electric saws. He gave no sign he even heard. Upon her arrival, Kelly had caught glimpses of a full army of workers moving at double speed, stripping out walls, laying cables, unpacking a vast array of electronic gear.

Grey opened a leather carry-case, extracted an armload of stapled pages and began passing them out. One to each agent. 'You are to study these, memorize what you can, then pass them back. Anyone attempting to retain pages or take screenshots of what you read will be imprisoned. No notes. No discussing what you read with anyone outside this room. You have thirty minutes. Begin.'

Kelly had always been a fast study. Not page-at-a-glance. But close. Her hand shot up.

'Yes.'

'Sir, is this confirmed, definite, concrete intel?'

'Affirmative.'

'Excuse me, but why haven't we heard about this before now?'

'A valid question. I will answer once you have completed reading.' He pointed. 'Twenty-eight minutes. Go.'

The pages were beyond astonishing. Nothing could have prepared Kelly for what she read. When she was done, she returned to the beginning and started over. Not because she might have missed something. Buying time. Trying to digest the impossible.

The document's last page included a brief bio of the author, Valentina Garnier. Kelly had read one of the woman's books, a first-hand account of family life under the Taliban. For which Garnier had won a Pulitzer. Hers was a recognizable face after appearing on any number of national talk shows. The fact that she had authored these incredible pages added credence to what Kelly read.

Finally, Mathers said, 'OK, time's up. Pass your documents to the front.'

It was Cotton who demanded, 'Is this some sort of test?'

'Yes, but not in the sense that you mean.' Grey Mathers counted the documents before slipping the pages into his carry-all. Then he opened his laptop. 'We are setting up a new squad. Your first assignment begins today. But first we need to make certain you can handle the truth.'

Riggs muttered, 'The *truth*.'

'This, ladies and gentlemen, is as real as it gets.' Mathers typed swiftly. 'An alien race has invaded humanity. It is now us versus them. We have one slim chance to maintain control of our future. It requires swift, calculated action. At times, it will require a certain ruthlessness.'

One of her agents asked, 'Standard rules of engagement? Geneva Convention?'

Mathers checked something on the screen, then straightened.

'This is part of your test. For the period of your engagement, however long it takes, you are operating under the Prevention of Terrorism Act. From this point on, you are fighting a secret war.'

'But—'

'Hold your questions.' The overhead projector came to life, shining a *Top Secret* symbol on the front screen. Double red lines made diagonal slashes. Mathers said, 'You in the back. Kill the lights.'

The video images, shot from multiple mobile phones and professionally spliced together, proved even more disconcerting than the documents. First was a rowan tree surrounded by crystal guardians, offering leaves that turned to golden threads before being ingested by all who approached. Then the crystals shattered before the tree itself was consumed by a heatless fire.

Next, a two-story wooden craft flew to the edge of space and back. Without sound or power. Just as the article had described.

And finally, a second rowan tree, massive in size, impossibly situated in the mountainous deserts of southern Morocco. This time, the tree's crystal guardians were shaped like palms. They watched as a crowd of people, every race and age, ingested the shimmering golden threads. Then the view switched to a spot high on a ridgeline. From there they watched an incoming Tomahawk missile. Which destroyed the entire valley. Numerous participants escaped beneath a protective dust shield thirty miles across.

The video ended. The room remained silent. Professional agents rendered utterly speechless.

'Lights.'

When the room was illuminated, Kelly discovered that Agnes Pendalon had entered and was now seated beside Grey Mathers. The blade-faced woman said, 'We face an enemy we cannot see, much less name. All we know for certain is that the number of infected is growing. But for this one brief moment, we have a slim chance of winning this fight.'

Mathers pointed to Kelly. 'Ask your question.'

Kelly thought she knew. But asked in case it had not yet occurred to the others. 'How have we not heard about this before now?'

Pendalon answered. 'The answer, Agent Kaiser, is that a coalition of intelligence agencies and heads of state now encircle the globe. What was unthinkable last month is now our only hope of survival. All governments, all cultures and societies face the same urgency.'

Mathers broke in, 'Doesn't mean everybody is holding hands and singing in harmony.'

'If only.' Pendalon gestured to the blank wall behind her, as if stabbing a map. 'There's an Indian reservation in northern Canada that we suspect is harboring a community of the infected. Two of the smaller and poorer Greek islands. Another off Croatia. We are classing these as dark zones.'

'Three more islands in the Pacific, maybe four.' Mathers pointed to the silent Rabbit. 'Thanks to our secret allies within their ranks, we managed to halt an invasion of a small town in Texas and another outside Chicago before they could take hold.'

Pendalon went on, 'We and our allies in this battle are using algorithmic weapons developed by the Chinese to censor and suppress internet services and social media sites.'

Mathers pointed to his leather case. 'These articles were sent to publications around the globe. When the alternative was put to them, most voluntarily stifled the news. Regarding the others, the senior staff are now guests of their respective governments. They are classed as enemies of the state.'

Kelly felt the frigid tension grip everyone on her team. Trained Homeland agents knew being classed as an enemy of the state carried huge significance. An individual or group had willfully threatened a nation's safety and sovereignty, usually by an act of treason. In such instances, the gloves came off.

'Questions?' Agnes Pendalon clearly expected none. She pointed to Kelly. 'A crew bus is out front. You and your frontline team are wheels up in one hour.'

SIX

Denton waited until he was parked by the house to phone Connor.

Correction. Where the house *used* to be.

When Connor answered, he slid the file into his lap. 'I know this family.'

'Know them how, and how well?'

'The man, Professor Sean Stiles, we've met. Twice. His wife . . .'

'Yes?'

Denton knew it was only a question of time before they discovered this. Still, it was hard to acknowledge, 'She and I have had a relationship.'

'This is getting repetitious. Still, you've got to admit, it's spooky.' A pause, then, 'The chairman needs to know.'

'Understood.'

'Hold one.'

Denton watched an old guy walk past, a West Highland terrier on a leash. The dog walked with an arthritic limp. The old man paused and studied Denton for a long moment, then walked on.

Connor came back on. 'Byron says it has no bearing on the case, and you are to proceed.'

Denton liked how the promised access was proving to be genuine. 'From this point on, all work-related calls between us need to be via new burner phones. You need to buy one first chance you get. Ditto for the chairman. Make a note of this number.'

When he had read it off, she asked, 'Is that necessary?'

'No idea. Don't share it with anyone but the chairman. And don't call me again on my standard line.'

He heard a chime from her phone, then Connor said, 'I have to go. Byron wants to see me.'

'Can you tell him you'll be five minutes? I want you to hear a conversation.'

'Hang on.' A briefer pause, then, 'Five minutes.'

'Maybe less.' He used his new burner to make the call, then put the new phone on his car's speaker system.

'Robbery Homicide, this is Detective Burns.'

'It's Denton.'

The voice brightened. 'Hey, man. Long time. Didn't recognize the number. How's it going, working on the other side of the aisle?'

'The pay's definitely better.'

'I hear you. What's up?'

'The Stiles case.'

'Sorry. Doesn't ring a bell.'

'The missing house.'

'Oh, man. Don't tell me that's one of yours.'

'Afraid so. What can you tell me?'

'Other than it's got the UFO conspiracy nuts swarming, not a lot. Have you seen the place?'

'I'm there now.'

'An entire house, including the cellar and garage and foundations. Poof. Far as I'm concerned, space invaders works as good as anything.'

'Who's handling the investigation?'

'Such as it is. You remember Celeste Jones?'

'Sorry. No.'

'She's OK. On the level. She and the lieutenant are scratching their heads on this one. Probably be glad to hear somebody else is on the hunt for answers. You want me to see if she's in?'

'That would be great, thanks.'

'Hold on. Tell your pop I said we need him back on the force.'

When the phone went quiet, Denton lifted the other phone and asked, 'Connor?'

'Still here.'

'That was my dad's former partner.'

The other phone clicked, then a woman's voice came over the car speakers. 'Jones.'

'Detective, this is Denton Hayes, investigator with NovaCorp.'

'You're at the scene?'

'Parked across the street. Staring at the spot where a house we insure should be standing.'

'Any UFO nut-jobs inside the tape?'

'The place is empty. Literally. Has forensics been out?'

'They report a big nada. No prints, fire, explosion, the works. The neighbors report nothing out of the ordinary. They're as baffled as us.' A pause, then, 'You need to check out the pipes. And the wiring.'

'What about them?'

'Everything is capped. Sealed. Craziest thing I've ever seen.'

'The woman who reported the . . .'

'We're calling it a theft. For the moment.'

'What can you tell me about Ryan Stiles?'

'Other than she's missing, not a lot.'

Denton studied the empty space. 'Missing?'

'Ryan Stiles called at seventeen minutes past midnight. Reported her house had been stolen and her husband was missing. Patrol officers responded. House was definitely not there. Detectives brought her into Ramparts, took a statement. Apparently, Ms Stiles gave a false contact number and address where she'd be staying.'

'I don't understand.'

'I got to tell you, we're not searching very hard. Without the wife, there's really not a lot we need to be investigating. She never signed the complaint, which means we can officially let this one slide. It also gives us an out with the news teams, who have been swarming almost as bad as the alien hunters. I'm surprised you haven't already heard about this.'

'NovaCorp just pulled me off a case in Arizona. Can I stop by, take a look at your report?'

'Long as this is a quid pro quo, sure.'

'Anything I discover regarding the . . .'

'Theft. Aliens. Whatever.'

'I'll stop by soon.' He cut the connection, then, 'Connor?'

NovaCorp's attorney said, 'So the official police line is aliens.'

SEVEN

Two days earlier

A silent Homeland agent drove Kelly to her Adams Morgan apartment and waited while she packed. Kelly was hungry, so she made a salad and ate while she prepared for departure. She washed up, then stood in her kitchen nook, staring at the lonely plate and glass and utensils. There had been two of everything for twenty-two wonderful months.

She swallowed the slow-burning rage and went through the apartment's three rooms, turning off the lights, saying farewell to a life that was already over. As she locked the front door and started out, she was fairly certain a different person would next walk through that door.

When the agent dropped her off, Darren Cotton was standing on the sidewalk outside Reagan National's private air terminal. Kelly expected a rant, an argument, a plea. But all he said was, 'Promise me one thing.'

She wanted to respond, *Anything*. But she couldn't. So she dropped her case and waited.

'First chance you get, you bring me out. Me and all the others wishing we were on the front line. Now. Today. Watching your back.'

Kelly shouldn't have felt the burn behind her eyes. Her need for friends and comforts and a man she would never hold again left her wanting to keel over and lie there on the concrete and weep until all the tears were gone. But she had tried that. And it didn't work. There were always more tears. Always another empty dawn.

So she said, 'I can't. You know I can't. And you shouldn't have asked. But it's OK. I would have asked the same thing in your position.'

Cotton crossed his arms, bunched his shoulders, scowled at the concrete sidewalk between them.

'I need someone Barry and I know and trust to be lead back here in the home office. Part of this is being the strong voice on the other end. Linking us to HQ. Being the only person talking when we're going into action.'

He jerked a nod. 'I can do that.'

'Next. My guess is, you're going to be flooded with raw intel. We need a clearer grasp on exactly what's happening. Somebody who can lift the rocks and take a good hard look inside the shadows. And keep all our team on the right compass heading. Despite everything.'

Cotton looked at her. 'I wish I could disagree. I really do.'

'Third and last. We're trusting people we don't know. They claim we're entering a high-risk environment, but we don't have a handle on them, their motives or who's pulling their strings. This has to change. And fast.'

He looked beyond bitter. Still, 'You know what I'm going to say.'

She almost smiled. 'Your wife will thank me.'

'Not strong enough,' Cotton replied. 'She'll put you up for sainthood.'

'Do this, Darren. Take charge here. Build an in-house team we can rely on. For all of us. Please.'

'You owe me.'

'I owe you a lot now.' She hefted her case. 'When you save our lives, I'll owe you everything.'

They flew west on a Gulfstream 800, the ride of choice for senior officials not traveling on the government's top-of-the-line BBJs. Rabbit sat slightly removed from Riggs and the rest of Kelly's team, a nylon backpack and leather carry-all by his feet. After they boarded, Kelly made a point of shaking his hand along with all the others, showing by deed rather than words that the guy was now part of their team.

Their orders were clear enough. Agents from Homeland's LA office were to meet them at the airport. They were to spend the afternoon getting squared away, setting up an office completely isolated from Homeland's other ops. That evening – tomorrow morning at the latest – Grey Mathers would be in touch with specifics.

Half an hour into the flight, the co-pilot drifted back, said they'd be landing in four and a half hours, asked if anyone was up for a snack. The jet became filled with the fragrances of fresh-baked bread and coffee. They gathered by the kitchen, made sandwiches, filtered back to a pair of stations by the wings. Kelly took an aisle seat, Riggs across from her. The other four agents were seated to either side of the aisle. Nine in all, seven men and two women counting herself and Rabbit, who remained seated back by the kitchenette, alone. Kelly knew she needed to do something about that, but not just yet. She finished her sandwich, accepted another mug of coffee, then decided it was time.

Barry Riggs was silent, watchful, ready when she launched in. She talked like it was just the two of them, but pitching her voice loud enough to carry. 'The AIC, or whatever we're supposed to call her.'

'Agnes Pendalon,' Barry said. 'AIC works for me.'

'She said our targets in Ojinaga were behind Nathan's murder.'

Bodies shifted as all her team drew in closer. 'When did she drop that bombshell?'

'End of my private review. Just tossed it out, like your basic oh-by-the-way.'

Barry's features hardened to onyx. Nathan had been one of his closest friends since the academy. But all he said was, 'You believe her?'

'You know, it fits with something Nathan said before he shipped out. I asked him why he was going. He had no connection to Mexico, wasn't working the drug gangs.' Kelly lifted her mug, decided she couldn't take another swallow just then. She set it back down. 'He made a joke of it. Laughed and said he'd been assigned to chase ghosts. But I could tell he was worried. Or scared. Something.'

Barry tracked movement behind her. Rabbit started to slip into a chair one station back and across the aisle. But Kelly motioned to Barry, who rose from his seat and gestured for Rabbit to take his place. Rabbit hesitated, then complied, placing himself directly across from Kelly. Barry stood in the aisle, resting his hip on the back of Rabbit's chair. Intent.

Barry said, 'I can't imagine Nathan Bragg being frightened by much of anything.'

'Going in dark and uncertain of the target,' Kelly replied. She'd thought of little else. 'Following orders that made no sense.'

'Just like us,' Barry suggested. 'I suppose that would do it.'

'My guess is, Homeland tried to handle this through normal chains of command,' Kelly said. 'A new, unknown threat to be treated like everything else. Send in an experienced team, ask questions, make some useful contacts, try to determine if the danger really exists.'

'Made perfect sense,' Barry said. 'Until a senior agent and a young rising star, and two other agents, all got themselves killed in Juarez.'

'Suddenly, a routine investigation went horribly wrong,' Kelly said, liking how they were moving in mental tandem. 'Then the top brass probably fell all over themselves, passing it off before the blowback cost careers.'

'Which brings us to Pendalon and Mathers and our own set of mystery orders,' Barry said.

'Head down to Ojinaga,' Kelly said. 'Take instructions from a guy whose name we're not allowed to ask.'

'Rescue a clutch of refugees, can't tell them from all the others we leave behind,' Barry said.

'Take out an entire drug gang with weapons we didn't even know existed until we're out in the field,' Kelly said.

'Enter a drug lord's fortified compound,' Barry said. 'Try not to fall over bodies snoring in the dust.'

'Rescue another set of refugees,' Kelly said. 'Only these are being kept behind fortified steel doors.'

'Not to mention electronic locks that bang open when we ask.'

'They didn't bang.' Rabbit spoke for the first time. 'No bangs.'

Kelly took that as the signal she had been hoping for, ever since Rabbit appeared planeside. 'So are you officially part of our team, moving forward?'

'If that's what you want.'

'Can I ask your name?'

'Stanley Kuiper.'

Barry said, 'We named you Rabbit, back when we were ordered to hold all questions. You got any problem with that?'

'No.' To Kelly, 'You can ask me anything you wish. All barriers are erased. Those were Pendalon's exact words. Whether I can answer is another matter.'

'What were you – NSA?'

'CIA analytics. Assigned to satellite intel. South and Central America. The most boring job in the world.' Rabbit's voice reminded Kelly of every analyst she had worked with, bland and toneless. Not exactly weak. Just void of any real sense of attachment. Reading the newspaper, feeding intel to frontline troops, no change. 'I spent four years begging for reassignment. And got laughed at.'

'Until Agent Pendalon showed up.'

Rabbit shook his head. 'At first, it was more like a lateral move. She assigned me to their new backroom. The same, but different. She and Mathers and Langdon – he's the link to DOD

– they were putting together a team to serve in direct support to the frontline agents.'

Barry asked, 'How many teams like us does she have out there?'

'You're the first.' He waved his hand, taking in the team, the jet, the action. 'All this only started three and a half weeks ago. Directly after the Morocco incident, Pendalon tried going through local offices, FBI and Homeland. Total waste of time. You're her trial run. Taking direct control. Setting up a new chain of command.'

'Who does Pendalon answer to?'

'I've seen her speaking with just a couple of people. General Skarren, Avri Rowe. That's it.'

Kelly exchanged a look with Barry. Skarren was the newly appointed head of DOD intel and Rowe was the President's Chief of Staff. Her team took the momentary silence as a chance to engage. Pamela Garten, the female agent seated across the aisle, asked, 'So you let this alien tree infect you? Just like that?'

'OK, first of all, it's not an infection. You saw the video. These leaves change into something that only looks like a thread. It's more like a form of energy . . .' He struggled, searching for words.

'You're doing great,' Kelly said.

Barry said, 'So Pendalon came looking for volunteers. And you jumped at the chance.'

'She showed me the same videos, let me read the transcript. I could see the need for someone they trusted to take a look at this from the inside.'

Pamela asked, 'You weren't scared?'

'Terrified.' He shrugged. 'But when it came down to it, I decided, hey, it's not like I was risking such a fantastic life.'

Barry asked, 'So now, what, you can read minds?'

'It's not what you think. Telepathy is . . . different.'

'Walk us through what this means,' Kelly said. 'Play the analyst here. If it's not mind-reading . . . What?'

'More an awareness expansion. I listen and hear at a different frequency.' Rabbit almost smiled. 'If I had known how many doctors and scientists would be prodding me, I might have walked away. I was about ready to do just that, then Pendalon offered me the chance to become part of your team.'

Gradually, all of Kelly's frontline crew joined in. They crowded Rabbit, pressing him with questions. Most of which he struggled to answer. Kelly pretended to follow the conversation, but in truth she had all but disconnected. She didn't understand a lot of what he was saying. In truth, she didn't really care. The fact that Rabbit was talking openly was the key issue, at least for now. She had enough for the moment. The rest would come in time.

She collected her empty plate and cup and slipped from her seat. She walked back to the kitchenette, poured another coffee and began preparing a second sandwich. She had always been a sucker for fresh-baked sourdough.

A few minutes later, the cockpit door opened. Riggs rose to meet the co-pilot, then started back toward her. 'We're forty minutes out. Can I ask what you think of Rabbit's spiel?'

'There's a lot to digest. But I'm beginning to see more clearly why our Mexico ops was so critical.'

Barry nodded agreement. 'Assuming we made it back alive, we'd have witnessed first-hand what this threat represents.'

'Plus we'd have a handle on why those potential operatives couldn't be left in the wrong hands.' Kelly glanced down the plane's central aisle, back to where her team were clustered around Rabbit. 'What do you think of the kid?'

Barry took down a fresh mug. 'A buddy of mine at Quantico was gung-ho army. Did three frontline tours. He liked to talk about their sniper teams. Made them out to be the craziest lunatics who ever walked this earth.'

Kelly nodded, remembering. She had heard the same stories. 'Until the bullets started flying.'

'There you go. Soon as they were out in hostile territory, those guys were the greatest who ever lived.' Barry used his mug to point. 'Rabbit might be infected by some alien tree. Far as I'm concerned, he can talk to daisies on his day off. Long as he's got our back when things go hot.'

EIGHT

Kelly knew something was wrong before the jet stopped taxiing. She waited for the co-pilot to come back and release the gangway, staring through the portal's small window. She turned and told her team, 'Stay where you are. Riggs, on me.'

She descended the stairs and crossed the tarmac to where a lone man stood by a four-door Chevy the color of dried mud. 'Agent Kaiser?'

'Where is everyone?'

'I'm it, ma'am. Sorry.' He offered his hand. 'Jon Alvero, deputy AIC. My boss is back at HQ, arguing his way through the chain of command.'

Kelly liked him already. The office straight-shooter, the calm stable guy who took whatever came at him and did his best. 'Let me guess. Your boss didn't like having somebody he'd never heard of issuing orders he didn't understand.'

'That pretty much sums up our situation, sure enough.'

'Does he know you're here?'

'Absolutely not.' He was aged in his early forties, the skin of his face puckered by some childhood ailment. Dark eyes sparked by a weary humor. 'I'd be forever in your debt if it stayed that way.'

'Fine by me.' She turned and waved to the jet. As her team began off-loading, she asked, 'Do we have accommodations?'

'Oh, sure. I've arranged for you to have the entire floor of an apart-hotel in Santa Monica.' He handed her a printed sheet. 'Great view from the front rooms. Pricey, but hey, it's as close to secure as I could get at short notice.'

'Am I to assume your boss doesn't know about this either?'

Alvero shrugged easily. 'He's already got so much to worry over.'

'I'm very grateful for your help, Agent Alvero.'

'I'm Jon to my pals.' He nodded a greeting to the approaching team. 'Just trying to make fellow agents feel welcome in my home town.'

Kelly handed Jon's reservation sheet to Pam Garten. 'Hire us a couple of SUVs, go settle in. Barry and I will go sort things out at HQ.'

'Good luck with that,' Jon said.

Rabbit said, 'I should come.'

'Really? You're sure about that?'

He nodded. 'In case it's not just a stubborn boss.'

Homeland's main LA offices were located downtown, in the Federal Building on Los Angeles Street. Homeland's primary role on the West Coast was to support ICE – Immigration and Customs Enforcement. Most of their other functions were indirect, as in supporting other federal agencies and fighting the constant bureaucratic turf war. Which, according to Jon, their AIC was very good at. Kelly rode in the front passenger seat, silent and watchful. As they pulled into the underground garage, she was still uncertain how this situation should be handled.

Taking it to Washington meant making noise. Their remit was to stay under the radar wherever possible. Go in, ascertain the danger, arrest those responsible, move on to the next task. She was tempted to ignore Homeland's operations here, just go it alone. But to do so meant revamping their orders.

They exited the elevator and were checked in by the guard/receptionist and passed through the secure entrance. Jon was the same here in ground zero, calm and observant, but removed. A man well used to riding the bureaucratic bull. Getting on with his job as best he could, given the situation. Which was obvious while they were still walking the central aisle. Agents and staffers smirked as they passed, checking out Kelly and her two sidekicks. And all the while, up ahead, a man shouted.

Jon pointed them into the AIC's outer office, where a weathered Latina in her fifties watched them with grim humor. Jon told her, 'Our guests from DC have arrived.'

She gave Kelly a stony inspection, then went back to her computer.

'Have a seat,' Jon said. 'Let me know if there's anything . . .' He saved himself from finishing the empty offer by departing.

Kelly had been seated less than thirty seconds and she already disliked the man ignoring them on the glass half-wall's other side. The AIC was in his mid-fifties, balding and unattractive, face slick with the effort required to shout into his phone. He waved his free arm and strode from wall to wall.

Riggs asked, 'What are we waiting for?'

Kelly did not respond. She felt as though this revealed just how green she was. Confronting a situation that should not be happening.

She glanced at Rabbit, seated to her other side. The slender young man was stretched out, relaxed, observing the show.

Riggs said, 'Let me connect with Cotton. Ask his take.'

The AIC's assistant looked up and met Kelly's gaze. Her shoulders humped in silent weary humor. As in, good luck moving this particular mountain.

Kelly said, 'Make the call.'

Barry spoke for a minute. Two. Then he lowered the phone and said, 'I'm on hold.'

'Maybe we should have just taken off.'

'And have this guy watching our backs?' Riggs started to say something more, then said to the phone, 'Yeah, still here.' Ten seconds, then he disconnected and said, 'Cotton wants us to hold fast.'

'That's it?'

'One more thing. Pendalon says to tell you, "Why bark when you have a dog?"'

Kelly breathed easy.

'You understand what that means?'

'I understand enough.' Kelly watched the AIC continue to rage, but from a safe distance. When the assistant's phone rang, she added, 'Here we go.'

The woman listened a moment, her eyes widening. She rose, cast the three of them an uncertain glance and entered the AIC's office.

Whatever she said was enough to choke off the man's tirade. He studied his aide for a long moment, then locked gazes with Kelly. Furious. But silenced.

He cut the connection, reached for the desk phone. Spoke.

And wilted.

The man's entire body went limp. Face slack, shoulders slumped, free hand slithering across the desk looking for support. He set the phone down like it was made of crystal. Both hands supporting his weight now. Back to them. Immobile. If he heard the assistant ask what was the matter, he gave no sign.

Riggs muttered, 'What just happened?'

Kelly thought she knew but did not respond. She watched through the glass half-wall as the secretary asked her boss if he was OK. The AIC fumbled his way around the desk, slumped into his chair. The secretary asked again, louder this time. He waved one hand, slowly and limp, as though the gesture cost him. Which Kelly decided it probably did.

Her phone rang.

'Kaiser.'

Agnes Pendalon said, 'Your initial targets are two UCLA students, both postdocs in biomedicine.' Her tone was utterly matter of fact, as if she ate blowhard AICs for breakfast every morning. 'They assume they are sufficiently tech-savvy to evade our social media barriers. Your first task is to show them how wrong they are.'

'Understood.' She rose to her feet when an astonished Jon Alvero appeared in the doorway. He gave his former boss a long look, then gestured for them to accompany him.

Agnes went on, 'They have fashioned a dark-web portal with the intention to disseminate the same banished articles and videos that you viewed. We've set up a temporary block that appears as a technical glitch. The instant they are in custody, that portal will vanish.'

As Kelly followed Jon and Barry and Rabbit down the central corridor, heads popped into view, all their former smirks erased by what had just gone down. She saw a considerable amount of astonishment, even some fear. 'You want to know where they obtained the banished intel.'

'That is your first question. Next and far more important is, who do they know that has employed the artifact.'

Kelly entered Jon's office, took a seat, said, 'Artifact. That's your name for the leaves?'

'Or whatever they are.'

'I like that,' Kelly said. 'It suits.'

'Who else has seen the intel,' Pendalon went on. 'Who they are dealing with in regard to next steps. You know the drill.'

'Not yet,' Kelly replied. 'But soon.'

'Let Cotton know of anything further you require. Keep him informed. Every step as it happens.'

Kelly knew her boss intended to close the connection. 'Wait. Rabbit says we're the first of our kind. How many teams total do you have in the field?'

The question froze Jon in the process of reaching for pen and paper. Riggs said softly, 'Nothing in writing.' Kelly watched Jon lean back, wide-eyed, alert, as Agnes replied, 'We have one hammer, care of Army's special ops. What we don't yet have, what we desperately need, are scalpels. People who can think and operate with a surgeon's complete precision. Highly intelligent, dedicated individuals who can take the initiative.'

'Understood.'

But Agnes wasn't finished. 'You, and the teams we hope to model after you, are assigned duty behind the enemy's front line. From the little we have learned thus far, they presently assume they are free to operate. And safe. Your job is to assure them there is no such thing as safety.'

Kelly expected her new boss to disconnect. But when Agnes remained on the line, Kelly decided there would never be a better time to ask, 'How many . . . what should I call them?'

'For the moment, we refer to small numbers like we hope is happening in LA as infiltrations. Larger events are referred to as outbreaks. Unless you can come up with something better.'

'No. That definitely works for me.'

'The answer is four. Four outbreaks in the nineteen days since the missile strike in southern Morocco failed to halt the spread. We have to assume the leaves that were gathered up from those two trees are being disbursed. Which is another reason why we're desperate to act fast and act hard.'

'You're afraid this might explode into something major,' Kelly said. 'A global outbreak.'

'Four outbreaks so far,' Pendalon repeated. 'DC was first, which helped. The alert was clearly defined and so we were able to act almost immediately. Followed more or less the next day by Boston, centered around MIT. We're pretty certain now that Austin and Chicago both were started by the Morocco tree.'

'How did you deal with them?'

'DC and Boston were both the Pentagon's show. Skarren was in charge. I'll give you the details later. For now, his team basically cauterized the wound. And did so with tactics that can only be described as brutal.'

'I can imagine.'

'We are currently in the process of setting up protocols. Defining precisely when and under what circumstances these specialist forces will next be brought in. For the moment, they operate exclusively outside the national boundaries. It's safer that way. In return, they're helping to build our alliances.'

'Why not Mexico?'

'You already know the answer to that.'

'I think so. Yes.'

'Can you be overheard?'

'Roger that.'

'Then I'll say, it for you. Our primary task was twofold. Take down the bad guys. And bring in all newly infested individuals, anyone now joined to the artifact's ranks.'

'That is not happening here in LA?'

'As far as we know, there are no actual . . . how should I put it?'

'Enemy infiltrators.'

'Excellent.' A pause. 'I have noted that. Back to your question.'

'Austin and Chicago.'

'We faced bureaucratic roadblocks. Imagine this former AIC of the Los Angeles office stationed in Washington, then multiply his power base by a hundred. You get a picture of what we were up against. Even after we convinced the entrenched power structure of the crisis, they still treated it like another turf war.'

Kelly watched Riggs and Jon Alvero talk softly. Rabbit was seated a foot or so further back, silent and watchful. 'We don't have time for that,' Kelly said. 'Speed dictated your only option.'

'Right. And it worked. But there were huge problems. Which I don't want to go into. One more thing. Given the mess we've faced in Austin and Chicago, do not under any circumstances rely on help from the local police or sheriffs. They are to be kept strictly outside the loop.'

'Roger that.'

'Find out how far this outbreak has spread. Isolate the carriers. Eradicate the threat before this turns into a whack-a-mole. Make note of anything that might help us operate more efficiently. Get ready for the next outbreak.'

When Kelly cut the connection, Jon Alvero started straight in. 'Tell me what you need. I will make it happen.'

A couple of agents stood further down the corridor, positioned so they could stare through Jon's interior windows and study them. The three people who just shook their world.

Riggs pointed behind her and said, 'Check it out.'

She swung around and watched as the former AIC exited his office, carrying a cardboard box and briefcase, face slack with shock. Kelly asked, 'Who's running the office?'

'Apparently, that would be me.' Jon's nerves showed in the way his fingers danced over the desk's surface, drawing over pen and pad, then checking the motion and pushing them away.

Riggs demanded, 'Who reached out to you?'

'General Skarren, head of DOD intel. He asked if I needed to be put in contact with the White House. I told him no.'

'Probably wise,' Riggs said. 'I'd file the general's offer under "rhetorical."'

Jon nodded. 'My orders are to deliver whatever you want, without question and without delay. I am very good at carrying out orders.'

Kelly was ready for that. 'One secure room, preferably not where we'll be in direct contact with your other agents. Large enough for all of us and our gear. Laptops, secure internet feeds, fully encrypted sat phones.'

Jon made swift notes. 'How long do you need for your ops?'

'No idea.'

'I'm asking because we took over the floor directly below us, used it for a major DEA-led operation. It's empty now. We have another four months on the lease.'

'That should be perfect.'

'Anything else?'

'Two holding cells close at hand. This would be a first-stage location. We probably won't need to keep detainees here for more than a few hours.'

'Not a problem. Our number-one focus here is immigration. We have temporary housing used by ICE agents in the sub-basement. Showers, separate rooms for families, kitchen facilities, the works. I'll have three secure units set aside for your exclusive use.' He must have seen the hesitation in Kelly's features, for he added, 'Agent Kaiser, it's been made perfectly clear there is no ask too great here. Just give me some idea—'

'Say we need to show a reluctant detainee just how serious this is. Someone who assumes they're completely beyond any legal ramifications for their actions.'

'We don't just want to detain them,' Riggs said. 'We want to scare them out of their tiny minds.'

Jon Alvero clearly liked being able to tell them yes. 'I've got just the thing.'

NINE

Connor re-entered the CEO's private office to find Byron
already seated with Jackie Barlow, the in-house security
agent used for highly sensitive personnel investigations.
Why Byron insisted on using Denton for this case, she had no
idea. But her boss had made seemingly bizarre moves in the past,
which in time revealed hyper leaps in logic that had saved them
billions. She disliked how Byron often kept her in the dark about
his motives, but she trusted him. In this business, trust was as rare
as pink diamonds. If he insisted, she would stifle her natural
impatience and wait.

Byron asked her, 'Any update?'

'He wants to speak with Sanjib Gupta. Soon as possible. I'm
pretty sure the timing is a test. Confirm the reality of your stress
over this situation.'

'You checked with Sanjib?'

'His secretary says he is unavailable. No further comment.'

'I'll reach out when we're done here.' He turned to Jackie
Barlow. 'Go ahead.'

'This certainly made a change from the normal background
checks.' Jackie Barlow was a dark-skinned woman in her late
fifties. Trim, precise, the crisp manner of speaking that would
better fit an English teacher. She had worked for NovaCorp since
forever. Jackie was the chairman's in-house security person on all
highly sensitive hires, including prospective board members and
heads of any company NovaCorp intended to acquire. 'Can I ask
why Denton Hayes is under such scrutiny?'

'Absolutely not.'

'OK, so this will be a general sweep. Mind you, this is the tightest
time frame you've ever given me.' Jackie never used paper for her
investigations, or filed records of any work she did for the chairman.
She pulled out reading glasses, set her phone on the table, scrolled
down, said, 'Denton Randolf Hayes, age thirty-two.'

'I thought he was older.'

'Given his background, I'm surprised he doesn't look a hundred and thirty.' She adjusted her spectacles. 'Born in Provost. Product of a truly terrible family situation. Father convicted of meth trafficking when Denton was nineteen months old. Mother arrested twice for selling drugs, charges reduced to misdemeanor possession. She married and divorced three times before Denton's fourth birthday. Relocated each time, wound up in San Fernando. At that point, Denton became a ward of the court, three foster families, then was taken in by a homicide detective, one Randolf Hayes. Adopted two and a half years later. Denton changed his name when he turned fourteen.'

Jackie looked up. 'I found this next part interesting, but I don't know if it applies.'

'Go on.'

'Apparently, his adoptive father instilled in Denton a real love for flying. Father had a private pilot's license, took Denton up every chance he got. Denton earned his own license the same month he changed his name.'

'He became a pilot at fourteen?'

'There's no age limit for private planes. Earned extra money in college and during his summers ferrying planes around the western US. I have photos—'

'No. Continue.'

'Denton never seemed interested in becoming a professional pilot. His real passion was numbers. Went to USC on a full ride, focused on business and accounting, passed the CPA national exams first go. Started with the LA police.'

'We know all this. Skip to what clearly has you concerned.'

'His senior year at university, Denton began an affair with Ryan Stiles, wife of a physics professor and dedicated philanderer. Sean Stiles was twice rebuked by the USC board for relationships with students and threatened with dismissal. Which was when Mrs Stiles filed for divorce. Then the couple entered therapy and reconciled . . .' She hesitated.

'Go on, Jackie.'

'Basically, Denton went off the rails. Became heavily involved in cocaine. He was caught in a sting and arrested for trafficking. His father the cop intervened. Denton's record was expunged, on the proviso that he successfully complete rehab. Which he did.

Went back for his masters in forensic accounting and joined his father's force.'

Byron said, 'This one mistake doesn't mean—'

'There's more.'

Byron sighed.

'Four years later, Mrs Stiles left her husband. She and Denton restarted their relationship within days. Hours. Unfortunately for Denton, the pattern repeated. Ryan goes back to her husband the louse; Denton goes back on the coke. This time, it cost him his badge. He was allowed to resign with a clear record, as long as he did another stint in rehab.'

Byron rose from his seat. Walked to the window. Sighed again.

'After completing rehab chapter two, Denton goes private. Richard's predecessor used him twice.' Jackie looked up. 'I didn't have time to check on whether there was another tryst between him and Mrs Stiles. All I can say is, nineteen months later, he enters rehab a third time. When he came out, Richard's predecessor hired him.'

Connor checked Denton's file. 'He's gone through our regular drug checks. Always shown as clean.'

'With a former cop? Please. He'll show us what he wants us to see.' She pocketed her phone. 'That ends the official part of my investigation.'

'Excellent work.'

Connor looked from one to the other. How they were both waiting. An unspoken signal, a trigger, something. Finally, Byron said, 'Go on.'

'Are you considering this man for a high-level or sensitive position?'

'I can't tell you.'

If Jackie disliked confronting the wall, she gave no sign. 'Well, if you are, I'd personally strike him off my list.'

'Explain.'

'I spoke with a couple of people in the know. This relationship with Mrs Stiles wasn't some momentary fling, older woman seducing the student, followed by a return for some more torrid sex. Denton was in love, and by all accounts, so was the professor's wife. One source claimed they had started talking about getting married. But Ryan and the professor reconciled, like I said, and . . .'

'And what?'

'She broke Denton's heart.' Jackie shrugged. 'Or so I was told.

Indications are that it's at least partially true. Denton has never married. I also haven't found any suggestion of the guy ever having another serious relationship.'

'Interesting.'

'Say just some of these possible downchecks are real,' Jackie said. 'It means you're talking about a guy with a broken personal life and a serious former drug habit.'

Connor waited for her boss to say the obvious. When Byron remained silent, she said, 'You're concerned the guy is hiding something else.'

'There you go.' Jackie looked from one to the other. 'The question I think you need to be asking is, regardless of how good an investigator Denton Hayes might be, should NovaCorp trust him? My primary concern would be that this guy could go off the rails at any minute. Again. Only this time, he holds the potential to harm our group.'

Byron tapped on the window, stopped Jackie's next comment by saying, 'Thank you. Excellent work.'

'There are several avenues I plan on following that should reveal—'

'No.' Byron was firm. 'Thank you. You have given me everything I require.'

'Chief—'

'Drop the investigation, Ms Barlow. That is an order.'

Jackie took that as the dismissal it was. She shot Connor a look of pure caution and left.

Before Connor could voice her own concerns, Byron said, 'I need you to insert yourself into Denton's work. Put everything else aside. Long enough for us to be certain he's doing his job correctly.'

'Can I ask why?'

'Not yet. No. I'm asking that you trust my judgment. A few days at most. If I'm right . . .' Byron faced her. Showed the tension. The fear. 'Daily updates. Hourly. If you discover something, you tell me immediately. Without delay.'

'Byron, I'll risk wasting your time if you can't . . .' Connor stopped when her phone bonged. 'It's a text from Denton. I assigned him a unique tone.' She checked her screen. 'He's requesting an interview with Campion home security. Our file doesn't show coverage, but a number of the neighbors have

Campion planted in their front yards. Denton's hoping to obtain a camera feed off of the incident.'

'Smart.'

'We both know Campion won't give us the time of day.'

'I'll handle it.'

'Maybe this is the one time we should tell him no.'

'I said I'll handle it and I will.' Byron pressed the red button on his phone.

Rachel answered instantly. 'Sir?'

'Get me Janet Campion.'

There followed a pause, perhaps the first Connor had ever heard from the woman in response to a request from her boss. Then, 'Really?'

'Wherever she is, whatever it takes. Anything she insists on, I agree to in advance.'

When he cut the connection, all Connor could think to say was, 'OK.'

'Any reservations you might have about the seriousness of this situation,' Byron told her, 'I assume they have now been put to rest.'

Connor left Byron's office to find Jackie standing by the elevators, typing double-time into her phone. 'Are you waiting for me?'

'That depends.' Jackie stowed her phone. Shifted back three steps, as far removed from Rachel's desk as possible and still remain on the executive floor. Waited.

'I need to get a better handle on Denton Hayes.'

Jackie showed her a professional's bland mask. 'I might be able to help with that.'

'I thought maybe I'd go check out the rehab clinic where Denton went.'

'Emerald Valley Spa.' Jackie nodded. 'That was to be my next stop, until Byron took me off the case.'

'You have a contact?'

'Better than that. I have an in.' Jackie reached into her purse, came out with a bulky envelope. 'The clinician's name is Carla Estana. She agreed to speak with me for a certain remuneration.'

Connor reluctantly accepted the envelope. 'Is this legal?'

'Depends on who's asking, I suppose.' Jackie pressed the elevator's down button. 'I'll call and let the lady know you're coming.'

TEN

T heir first targets were Charles Durrant, thirty-one, and Raja Singh, thirty-six. Kelly had no idea if the two had ingested the power potion. Rabbit assured her he would know. Durrant and Singh lived together with three Siamese cats and a cockatoo in a condo east of Pico. The building was noisy, the neighbors in and out, drinking around the pool and arguing over the outdoor grill. A terrible place for a discreet grab. Kelly set up a rotating one-agent night watch and ordered everyone else to settle in.

Kelly let the team assign her the largest apartment facing the Pacific. She didn't really care about the view and was uncomfortable being treated as superior to the others. But they expected it, so she didn't complain. Her team had the entire eleventh floor, four down from the top. The apartment facing the rear parking lot was designated their on-site communal space and ops center. She dumped her gear, walked four blocks inland to a fresh market, came back, made herself a salad and ate it standing by the front windows. The narrow park fronting the Pacific Coast Highway, the beach and the pier were all illuminated by streetlights that glowed softly in the evening mist.

Los Angeles was three hours behind DC, which put Kelly's body-clock somewhere after midnight. She watched joggers and drifters flitter between the PCH streetlights, and missed Nathan. She rarely allowed herself to peer back like this. But she was exhausted in a way that no simple night's sleep would erase. She had not slept well since Agnes Pendalon had pulled her from normal duties and shipped her off to Mexico. Kelly knew it was a sign of mental weakness, letting her mind relive times with Nathan. But he felt so close just then, as if she could focus on her reflection and find him standing there, half a step behind her, one hand stroking her neck.

She turned away, walked back to the kitchenette, washed her plate and fork. But the motions did little save turn the intimate moment into an argument. In her weary state, she regretted every step she had taken since landing in LA. Nathan would have probably found some way to bind the former AIC to his side. He was a born diplomat – one reason why he had been destined for higher office. Agents fought for the chance to work a case with Nathan Bragg. He did his best to lift up everyone within reach. He took no credit for himself. He rarely lost his temper. He had the finest, purest smile on earth.

Kelly opened her case and changed into one of Nathan's old T-shirts. It was one of the very few personal items she had not given away. She had washed it a dozen times. More. But as she turned off the lights and settled into bed, she could still smell his male fragrance. She wept in helpless longing and eventually slept.

It was always snowing when Kelly dreamed of Nathan. Which was strange since they had never been in snow as a couple. They had planned a January wedding, to be followed by a honeymoon in Aspen. Where Kelly was going to teach Nathan to snowboard. Which she knew he would love. Only there was no wedding, no snowbound holiday, and Kelly knew she would never visit Aspen. Not in a billion years.

But now she dreamed, and it snowed. Which meant Nathan was coming.

The sky wept frozen tears over her loss. As it should.

This particular dream held one difference. A white lumpish mound rested by her feet. Kelly knew with dreamtime's inverted logic that it held the dead drug lord.

Kelly had her arguments ready, in case Nathan intended to criticize her actions.

She looked down at the snow-covered mound and saw again the drug lord's smile. It was a knowing smirk, one that said it all. He probably had other telepaths in some secret cache which he would use as a lever. In return for his cooperation, the Mexican government would ease him into as pleasant an incarceration as possible. And eventually, once time passed and his name had faded from the public's awareness, they would allow him to escape.

Kelly had not let that happen. She knew Nathan would disapprove. And she did not care. Not then, not now. Not even in a dream.

Nathan finally appeared.

He took form within the falling snow, still potent enough to turn mist into a physical form. One that tore at her heart.

He took a long moment to smile at her. Long enough for her tears to form and fall. As always before, her tears became colored gemstones that defied the otherwise white purity of this strange world. Tears that formed a tragically silent tapestry.

Nathan said, 'Don't come looking for me.'

She wanted to scream at him. All the pain building up, all the rage over being left here alone. But it came out as a whisper, the piping of just another fractured heart. 'How can I look? I don't know where you are.'

'There is no direction,' he replied. He spoke in his bedroom voice, low and soft and musical with love. 'Every compass heading is wrong. The target doesn't exist.'

She wanted to deny ever having such thoughts. But just then, facing the man who was gone, she felt the urge. Strong as the pull she had felt when standing beside Nathan's grave.

The desire to search for a bullet that would end this futile quest called life.

She confessed, 'I'm all alone.'

He smiled, gentle as the snow that began swirling between them. Cutting her away from the only future she had ever wanted.

Then he began to fade. Within a pair of breaths, Nathan was nothing more than a dense mist, then nothing at all.

The snow-covered vista was empty of Nathan, of hope. And all that was left was his final whispered word.

'Don't.'

Taking down the two postdocs proved textbook simple.

Kelly's team traveled in a pair of Hertz Buick SUVs, opting to stay with the more faceless rentals rather than the Homeland black-on-black Tahoes. The one vehicle they accepted from Alvero was a white Toyota van with a plumbing supply company's name on both sides and the back double doors. There were two front seats and a vast empty rear hold, with a sliding door on the right side. Perfect for what they had in mind.

They were parked outside the condo complex at a quarter past six. She and Riggs were stationed in the van, with Pamela Garten squatting in the rear hold, seated on a wooden box that had once held a dozen bottles of fine Bordeaux wine. Twice Kelly suggested they share the passenger seat. Garten pretended not to hear. Riggs had started treating Garten as his number two. Kelly thought it was an excellent choice. Garten was razor-sharp, intense, highly focused, an excellent shot with the only weapons they were carrying.

Kelly watched the empty street and wondered if she would ever grow accustomed to guns that fired without sound, or the choices they now had in terms of armaments. From today's fast-acting nerve agents to hallucinogens to highly toxic chemicals that killed almost as fast as a bullet. All of which they were now packing.

She and Riggs discussed several possible ways the takedown might go, depending on how early or late the pair appeared, whether they were alone or together, and so forth. Normal arrest patterns were dependent upon numerous elements that did not apply in this case. Starting with how they could not simply enter the residence. Because they did not have a warrant.

Otherwise, the van remained silent. Kelly hated the quiet. She became helplessly trapped in the previous night's dream and all the dread emotions she was left with. Sorrow, rage, a forlorn lack of hope. Her heart felt so bruised and heavy she wondered if it might simply give up in defeat and stop working altogether.

The hours dragged on. Eight o'clock, nine, rush hour came and went. Finally, Riggs asked, 'What are we missing here?'

Kelly keyed her comm link. 'Who's on the condo?'

'Wyatt here. All quiet.'

It was Pamela who suggested, 'They're postdocs. Work all night, sleep all day.'

Riggs and Kelly said it together. 'Outstanding.'

They laughed, and suddenly everything just felt better. The sun shone, the day beckoned. She was an agent leading a highly capable team on a mission of vital importance.

'There's a Starbucks two blocks down,' Riggs said.

'I'll go,' Pamela said. 'My backside is imprinted with the vineyard's logo.'

But as she slid open the rear door, Wyatt came back with, 'OK, our guys are on the move and heading your way.'

Kelly started to alert the teams, but Riggs was faster. 'All teams, gear up.'

The targets' complex was located on the corner of Roebling and Levering. The two young men wore USC sweatshirts and shorts and sandals. Both chattered while working their phones as they walked.

'They're heading for the In-N-Out,' Riggs said.

'You're kidding, right? Biomed scientists? Definitely vegan.' Pamela worked her own phone. 'Whole Foods is two blocks south, KazuNori Hand Rolls a hundred meters beyond that.'

'Their destination is secondary,' Kelly decided. 'We'll use the In-N-Out parking lot.'

They snagged the parking space directly beside the entrance, earning a long beep from the Range Rover that was also after the same spot. The Range Rover's driver leaned out the window and yelled before burning rubber. Kelly worried the pair might realize something was wrong and bolt. But they were almost a block away and did not look up from working their phones.

Garten exited the van, headed down the sidewalk and joined Wyatt in what appeared to be an animated conversation thirty feet behind their targets. One SUV pulled into the lot and drove further back. The other crawled in the slow lane behind Garten and Wyatt.

Riggs fretted, 'If we miss them, they'll be alerted in full public view. And a nightmare to track.'

Kelly replied, 'First, we don't miss. Second, you're forgetting our little friends.' She lifted the gun she had unholstered and held now in her lap. 'One sign of things going sideways, we shoot and load and bolt.'

Riggs glanced over. 'You OK?'

'First-rate. Why?'

'It's just, you sound, I don't know . . .'

'Go ahead and say it.'

'Angry, OK? You sound mad.'

Kelly leaned back. She sounded like that because it's exactly what she was. Tracking this pair impacted her in the same way as kneeling beside the drug lord in Ojinaga. Only now it was closer to the surface. This pair of postdocs represented the loss she had incurred. The loss she would carry for the rest of her days. Not to mention whatever or whoever was behind this threat.

She had every right to be furious.

Kelly said, 'I want you to handle the first interview.'

Their targets approached the entrance but did not slow. Kelly asked Riggs, 'Who's in our second SUV?'

He checked his rearview mirror. 'Stinson is driving, Ricard shotgun. I think Rabbit's in the back.'

'Tell them to pull forward and block any view from inside the burger joint.' Kelly slipped between the seats and readied herself by the side door. Only then did she realize she could not see a thing. 'Great. Now I'm totally blind.'

But Riggs was ready. 'Five steps and closing. Three. OK, now.'

Kelly said into her own comm link, 'Go, repeat, go.'

She flung the door back as Garten and Wyatt rushed forward, not running, almost casual in their approach. The sidewalk and street Kelly faced were both empty, which meant no one observed the agents gripping the pair and bundling them into the van's rear hold.

Kelly realized she was in the way now, a third wheel in a space cramped by the two agents and the two struggling men. She stepped out, slid the door shut and told Riggs through the open passenger window, 'Drive.'

She walked back to where Stinson had the SUV's motor running. Kelly motioned for Ricard to stay in the passenger seat and slipped in the rear beside Rabbit. Stinson pulled in close to the van's rear as they entered the road.

Twelve seconds. Maybe fifteen. Bang and gone.

ELEVEN

Today

Beverly Flats was once considered the poor cousin of Beverly Hills. No longer. Neighborhoods north of Santa Monica nowadays carried a cachet all their very own. The lots were smaller, the vegetation far less exotic. But imperial palms still lined the streets, and these roads held the same names. Rodeo and Rexford and Canon and Beverly. In bygone days, the city fathers tagged a 'north' in front of the roads to designate their more blue-collar vibe. Nowadays, when a quarter-acre lot with a tear-down house went for two million dollars, such labels were meaningless.

Denton had driven by Ryan's home any number of times. Late at night. His heart shattered, his life in tatters, drunk or stoned or both. Sitting there in the dark. Sick with desire for a future he could never claim.

Today was certainly different.

Back in the early twenties, following the end of the First World War, a group of local businessmen founded Hamilton Home Fire and Life. It remained a regional insurer until the late eighties, when Hamilton gobbled up a trio of other small insurance groups. Then in the nineties, it branched into the growing fields of security for both home and business. But the real transition came in the aftermath of the Great Recession. Two of its largest competitors teetered on the verge of bankruptcy after having invested heavily in the mortgage-finance debacle. Newly appointed CEO, Byron Sykes, insisted the feds swallow all the bad debts and then absorbed both groups. The vastly enlarged corporation took the new name of NovaCorp and had grown steadily ever since.

Private home insurance, small businesses, cars and life – all the better-known types of insurance – were handled by subsidiaries. The name NovaCorp appeared on no standard policy. The parent company only became involved if the policy was larger than a hundred million dollars.

Which made the file on Denton's passenger seat even more of a question.

He drove a Toyota Land Cruiser with the special edition turbo-charged V8. It drank gas like a metal elephant but had the power to tow a semi and possessed an excellent four-wheel drive system. The power was also required because of Denton's other little additions, namely a special locking system, reinforced doors and bulletproof glass. Not all the claims Denton investigated rolled out the welcome mat.

He opened the back and unlocked the three steel cases built into the rear hold. As he pulled on chest-high waders and filled his pockets with equipment, the old guy with his powder-white dog reappeared on the corner. Standing and watching him slip on heavy-duty latex gloves and cross the street. Denton took his time, photographing the scene with his phone. The police tape was strung around three oaks, a pair of ornamental lights marking the drive, and a tall fir that Denton thought was probably a yew though he could not be certain. He inspected the lampposts and trees, searching for any sign of stress, explosive residue, scarring, burn marks.

Nothing.

The closest tree stood just nine and a half feet from where the drive was chopped off. The lampposts were a good three feet closer. Denton had to assume the sharp-edged ditch began where the garage door should have been. Not a leaf was out of place. Not a single scratch on the metal posts.

As he lifted the police tape and entered the crime scene, he noticed the old man had walked over to stand beside Denton's ride. He waved, but the old guy did not respond. Denton turned back to the mystery.

He seemed to be looking at an earthen bowl. Irregular in shape, since it included where the garage had been, the indentation to his left suggested a missing outdoor kitchen/living area. Beyond the depression was a narrow lap pool. The pool's decking and boundary stones were unscathed. The lawn looked pristine, recently mowed, the rear shrubs and flowering plants in perfect order. The pool's water held a few leaves. One dahlia blossom floated on calm display.

'Beyond strange.'

He followed the footsteps of what he assumed were the forensics team and stepped down into the muddy base. The depression was not flooded, as might have been expected. As the detective had said, all the piping was blocked. But the detective proved incorrect on one point. The pipes were not capped. Instead, each had been crimped shut. As though a giant's hand had carefully compressed the ends. Sealing them with delicate care.

The bowl held a few inches of ground-water seepage. Otherwise, there was . . .

Nothing.

From this perspective, the muddy walls looked almost polished. There was no marking that might have been made by a backhoe or some other form of shovel. Instead . . . well, the house was just gone.

TWELVE

Yesterday

As soon as they were underway, Kelly phoned Cotton. But when he answered, she greeted him with, 'Hold on a second.' She leaned forward without lowering the phone. 'Why is the van rocking?'

Stinson, the driver, responded, 'Looks to me like our guests are putting up a fuss.'

She told Ricard, 'Tell Garten to show them her gun. If they kick one more time, shoot whoever is making the most racket.'

Kelly waited until the van went still, then said to the phone, 'Darren, did you hear?'

'You got them both?'

'Piece of cake.'

'Hold on a second.' He muffled the phone, came back, told her, 'Agnes says, soon as you know anything at all, report.'

'Roger that.' She cut the connection and turned to Rabbit. 'Do you want to play a role here?'

He shook his head. 'This is not my gig.'

Kelly was tempted to let it go. Another fragment of enigma about Rabbit. She already had so much going on. But this was mission important. She hardened her voice slightly and demanded, 'Unpack that a little for me.'

'We have two parallel investigations. Yours and mine.' Rabbit folded his skinny legs and swung around so as to point both knees in her direction. 'They might intersect. I hope they never do.'

'Your investigation . . .' When he remained silent, she fielded, 'You're out here in case there are more telepaths on the loose.'

The driver, Stinson, muttered, 'Scary.'

'Correct.' Rabbit watched her through those heavy black-rimmed spectacles. His eyes looked overlarge for his narrow features. 'Until that happens, you don't need to drag me along.'

'I'm not dragging you anywhere. Do you want to be involved?'

'More than anything.'

Rabbit's quiet passion surprised her. 'Why is that?'

'I've spent years wanting to be part of an advance field team. I'm learning so much. Every hour, every second, I'm facing a totally new situation.'

Kelly faced the street. Satisfied. 'You're as much a part of this team as you want to be.'

The Homeland detention area took up over half of the Federal Building's lowest-level basement garage. Beyond the steel sally-port was a narrow parking area with space for six vehicles. Kelly had called ahead, and the parking area and reception/guard station were both vacant. She knew there would have to be some better method for handling such situations, but she remained hopeful they would not be in Los Angeles long enough to require permanent changes.

The two detainees, Durrant and Singh, shouted falsetto protests as they were dragged from the van and more or less carried by two agents each, gripping their upper arms, hauling them down the featureless concrete corridor. They were drawn into an ICE holding cell and their left wrists were manacled to the steel table.

Kelly watched via a one-way mirror from the observation chamber next door. Riggs and Garten stood to either side. Riggs said, 'They screamed like that the entire way.'

'My ears hurt,' Garten said.

'If either of them drew breath, I didn't notice,' Riggs said.

The speaker volume was cut down to a soft murmur. Kelly watched the men rattle their cuffs and yell at the mirrored wall. Barely able to keep her rage under control, she said, 'This is a waste of time.'

Riggs nodded. 'You're probably right.'

'Just the same, we need to try.' She nodded to Riggs. 'Go ahead.'

When he left and the door clicked shut, Garten asked, 'How long do you give him?'

There was a knock on the door to their observation room. Another pair of agents silently slipped inside. Kelly waited until the door closed behind them, then replied, 'Ninety seconds should do.'

Riggs gave it his best.

He entered the holding cell, gently closed the door, motioned for silence. And waited.

'Turn up the gain,' Kelly said.

Their high-pitched screams filled the chamber. 'Lawyer!' Singh sounded like an angry child. 'I know my rights!'

'You are being held under the Prevention of Terrorism Act. Which means no attorney needs to be present until—'

Durrant violently kicked his chair and shrilled, 'Lawyer!'

Riggs stood and watched the two of them pound the table with their free hands and shout in unison, 'Lawyer! Lawyer!'

Kelly observed the two, loathing them and what they represented. 'All right, that's enough.'

She left the observation room, stepped into the central corridor and drew her weapon. She entered the holding call and shot them both in the center of their chests.

The silence was deafening.

She said, 'Load them up.'

During the twenty-minute drive that followed, their two detainees slumbered in the van's rear hold. Garten rode in the second SUV while Kelly accompanied Riggs. She sat with her back on the passenger door, watching the two, coordinating their next steps through Jon Alvero. 'I hope we'll have things in place next time so I won't need to bother you. If there is a next time.'

'First of all, it's not a bother.' Alvero hesitated, then added, 'If there is a second time, maybe I need to know what's happening here.'

'I'll need to run it up the flagpole, but between us, I agree.'

There was no need for all the agents to come along, but her team clearly wanted to be there. And in truth, she felt it might be helpful for all of them to observe the first takedown, be aware of mistakes she was bound to make, ensure the next event was handled better.

The prison for all federally convicted criminals in the greater Los Angeles area was the Metropolitan Detention Center on Alameda. It fit the downtown LA scene like a whitewashed concrete glove. The windows were certainly smaller than the surrounding structures, narrow slits that climbed all seventeen stories of the stone monolith. And the entrances did not show the world a happy welcoming face. The main way in was through bulletproof glass doors, manned twenty-four seven. The lobby was featureless and grim. The visitors would have basically given anything to be somewhere else.

Kelly's team entered through the second portal.

As she waited for the massive sally-port to swing up, she slid through the middle section and gave both detainees the antidote. Which meant they were very groggy, but sufficiently awake to watch themselves be hauled across the cement entry-yard and go through the whole nine yards: registration and fingerprints and photographs and strip search. They remained too confused and frightened to do more than whimper the occasional protest. Which was good, given the stone-faced officers responsible for processing new prisoners.

By the time they were dressed in standard prison garb – cotton drawstring pants and T-shirt and sandals – both men were plainly terrified.

Homeland maintained a separate mini wing for ICE detainees, large chambers for male and female. Directly under that was a maximum-security wing, below ground and windowless. All of these cells were single-use and utterly grim.

Kelly requested two cells side by side, a breach in protocol since normally prisoners who came together were placed far enough apart that they could not communicate with each other. At her request, a guard deposited pad and pencil on the beds before other guards led the two inside. Kelly waited until the men's handcuffs were released, then positioned herself by the hallway's opposite wall. Where both young men could see her clearly. 'You have a decision to make.'

Singh protested weakly, 'You can't do this.'

'You still don't get it. For a pair of oh-so-smart guys, you really are playing like idiots.'

'No! We haven't—'

'Shut up. Your time for fun and games is over.'

Durrant whined, 'Why is this happening?'

'For both our sakes, you'd better know the answer to that.'

'What about our rights?'

'Listen carefully. This is your new reality. Give us what we need, and you're free to go. Refuse, and you enter phase three. You do *not* want to know what that means.'

Singh's legs gave way. The cell was so narrow he collapsed blindly on to the bed. 'This isn't right.'

Durrant protested, 'I'm an American citizen!'

Singh said, 'What took place, what you're repressing, the rowan and the changes . . . it's all real.'

'It's a threat to national security,' Kelly replied. 'Which you both should have realized, if you had taken ten seconds to consider what was happening. But you didn't. And now you are close to becoming classed as terrorists.'

Singh dropped his head into his hands.

Kelly pointed to the pads and pencils. 'Give us the names of everyone you've talked with regarding these highly illegal and dangerous elements. Don't bother with your web activities. That's already being handled. I want all personal connections, right down to casual conversations in your favorite café. Names and full details. What they know, what they're doing with it. Anyone who might have had access to the rowan leaves – that is an essential item. Are we clear?'

Singh moaned, 'This is a nightmare.'

'This is *nothing*. Singh, raise your head and look at me.' She waited until both men were watching. 'You have three hours. If I have any reason to suspect either of you are not giving me your fullest cooperation, you both will effectively disappear.' She gave that a beat, then repeated, 'Three hours. Any longer and we begin erasing your existence.'

Kelly watched as the two steel doors were slammed shut. Met both their horrified gazes through the small wire-mesh windows. Then she turned and walked away.

THIRTEEN

Yesterday

Two and a half hours later, they had everything they needed. Or rather, everything the two men were able to supply.

Kelly left one agent at the detention center, there to shadow the pair in case something else surfaced. The rest of her team shifted to their new office at Homeland. She called Cotton from the road, alerted him to the incoming conference. She would have preferred to make this call from their makeshift HQ in the Santa Monica apart-hotel. But the pre-rush-hour traffic was bad. The trip would have required over an hour. And Kelly wanted to do what Agnes had ordered, which was to report in as quickly as possible.

Alvero was there to greet them and ushered her into the empty chamber. 'Will this do?'

'It's fine. But I doubt we'll be using it very much,' Kelly replied. 'Just the same, you'll probably want to keep it as a dedicated space, in case you need to assign your own team.'

'No problem. What else do you need?'

Trestle tables held more laptops than she had team members. There were chairs for double their number. 'You might want to stick around. Unless you have somewhere else to be.'

'I'm supposed to have the afternoon off so I can cook burgers. My wife and some of her friends are hosting a backyard birthday party for my three-year-old daughter.' Alvero smiled. 'I'd pay good money to stay right where I am.'

Kelly connected six of the laptops to Cotton's confidential video link, allowing all her team to participate and be seen. She positioned Alvero behind and to the left of her own chair. So her superiors would have the option to order him out. She was ready to argue for his remaining in place. But the decision was not hers to make.

Kelly wasn't certain anything she had was urgent enough to bother Agnes Pendalon's evening, DC time, so she had requested a conference with Grey Mathers. But thirty seconds into her report, Grey told her to hold on. Two minutes seated in front of a blank screen was enough for her to become enveloped in a bone-deep weariness. Another silent sixty seconds, she might lose the ability to rise from her chair. She turned to Alvero and asked, 'Any chance of a coffee?'

'Absolutely.' He was already on his feet. 'How do you take it?'

'Black and bitter will do.'

He was back before Agnes appeared on screen, now split so that Grey Mathers was positioned beside her. 'Report.'

Kelly started, 'I'm not sure this is something that requires your attention.'

'Neither am I. And it doesn't matter. We're not setting protocols here. We're feeling our way. We'll grow a formal set of next steps later on.'

'When we have time to breathe,' Grey said.

'We obtained eighty-seven names of people who viewed the pair's materials,' Kelly replied. 'And three further issues.'

Agnes demanded, 'Who's that seated behind you?'

'Jon Alvero is Homeland's new AIC of the LA office. I think he should be involved. We may need his assistance, unless you want to send out more of my original team—'

'No. Absolutely not. Is he aware of the full investigation?'

'Not yet. Up to now, there hasn't been any need.'

Agnes glanced at Jon, asked, 'Have the pair themselves . . .'

'Partaken,' Kelly offered. 'Not yet. Which brings us to how this happened. It seems Charles Durrant had a cousin studying at MIT.'

'Studied, as in, past tense?'

'Right. Apparently, the East Coast Durrant took part in the wooden platform's flight. According to Durrant, his cousin had promised to give them the opportunity. But he has since vanished.'

Mathers said, 'The MIT squad is still in the wind. We think Canada, but we can't be certain.'

Agnes said, 'Intel from our so-called northern allies has not been great. I may want you to go there next. How soon can you finish up in LA?'

'Which brings us to another issue,' Kelly replied. 'And why Agent Alvero is with us.'

Agnes asked, 'Cotton, are you recording?'

'Roger that.'

'OK. Go ahead.'

'Two of Durrant's former colleagues, both postdocs in particle physics related to biochemistry, traveled to Boston. Durrant had intended to travel with them, but Singh became ill. Which was when his cousin offered to come out here. These two postdocs have since vanished.'

'Names?'

Kelly gave them both and waited.

'Grey?'

'Neither are on our list.'

'Add them. How many does that make?'

'From the MIT and UPenn group, forty-two.'

Agnes went on, 'Our best guess is, they're building a new community on land owned by an American Indian reservation. This place is on the Hudson Bay and defines the middle of nowhere. Apparently, there are also treaties involved. Unless the Canadian government receives an invitation, they cannot enter and investigate.'

'The closest paved road ends four hundred and eighty miles away,' Grey said. 'Once the snows set in, this place is cut off. Eight or nine months each year.'

'We're as certain as we can be without direct HUMINT that this has become a major gathering point,' Agnes said. 'Next?'

'Durrant's two missing colleagues are, or were, friends with a Doctor Ryan Stiles. Professor of particle physics at USC. Durrant has no proof. But he was under the impression this professor had . . .'

Agnes finished for her, 'Utilized the artifact. Grey?'

'Another name that is not on our list.'

'We've tried to contact him,' Kelly said. 'Home and office. Nothing so far.'

'Stay on it. Cotton, I want a full work-up.'

'On it, ma'am.'

'Anything else?'

'One more name. Singh has had in-depth conversations with a very close friend of his family.'

'Name?'

'Doctor Sanjib Gupta, head of UCLA Medical School.'

'Not good. This was why you wanted to speak, I take it.'

'That and the missing prof.' Kelly swiveled around, pointed to Rabbit. 'You're on.'

Rabbit leaned forward, cleared his throat, said, 'I'm doing my best to track down Durrant's two missing colleagues, ma'am. So far, I've got nothing.'

'Is that normal?'

'If they have not applied the artifact, yes. I can't access anyone who hasn't become infested unless there is a very specific purpose or course of action. Tracking groups who share a unified intent adds a necessary intensity.'

Kelly said, 'Such as people-smugglers across the border.'

'Yes and no. Remember, we had allies within that group.' He refocused on Agnes. 'Beyond that, inducing sleep is about as far as our abilities go. And in both cases, it helps to have a team accustomed to working together.'

'And if this pair have participated in the artifact?'

Rabbit shook his head. 'That entire situation appears to be in flux. I can only guess here. My team and I suspect they have gained the ability to establish and maintain barriers. Or camouflage. Something.'

'Where does that leave us?'

'We can't find them. We can't be part of their mental processes. We fear they have effectively found a way to cut us out.'

'This is very not good.'

'No. That is, if they have in fact used the artifact.' Rabbit hesitated, then added, 'My gut tells me they have.'

'Stay on it.' Back to Kelly. 'Tell me about this Gupta.'

'He's currently attending a medical conference in San Francisco. Returns day after tomorrow. But according to Singh, before his departure Gupta had dinner with Byron Sykes, CEO of NovaCorp. It could be nothing. Gupta sits on the NovaCorp board. And our research indicates he's also close personal friends with Sykes.'

'So we have to close this loop,' Agnes said. 'Use discretion if possible. But the threat of further . . .'

'Infiltration?'

'Good. I like that.' Agnes made a note. 'Infestation for those who have ingested the leaves. Infiltration for outliers.' She looked up. 'Any further infiltration has to be stifled.'

'Roger that.'

'Darren, how are you on the website and online chatter?'

Cotton's response was calm, measured. 'We've decided to leave the website online and redesign it so it joins with the other Area 51 UFO nutcase social media gathering points. As for Kelly's list, we'll be working through the night. But preliminary indications suggest the two men were having difficulty finding people who treated them seriously. Our take is your group was so successful in cutting out the initial reports that there is nothing to substantiate the men's claims.'

'We had global help on that. Kelly, I want you to treat Gupta as a threat unless you prove otherwise.'

Kelly was ready for that. 'Which is where Agent Alvero's assistance becomes crucial.'

'Use your discretion. Good work, everyone. Remember, our primary focus is speed.'

Kelly and her team drove straight to the apart-hotel. She rode in the back seat, positioned behind Riggs, so her number two couldn't see how exhausted she was. She entered the apartment, dropped her bag and weapons and notes on the table, then stripped as she walked down the stubby corridor and through the bedroom. She showered with the hot water turned up high enough to coax at least some of the weary tension from her body. She toweled off, dressed in Nathan's old T-shirt, then stood swaying by the front window, not really seeing the ocean at all. Dusk painted the scene in shades of copper and ocher. The wind now blew gently off the Pacific, pushing a salty mix through her open window. Happy sounds rose from the street and sidewalk below where she stood. People chattered and laughed. Cars passed with tops down or sunroofs open, the music loud enough to be heard clearly eleven flights up. Kelly felt as though she observed it all from some vast distance. As if she did not belong to such a carefree realm, and never would. She merely visited from a dark and secretive place, one these happy people would never know even existed.

She returned to the kitchen, made herself a fruit salad of everything within reach – orange, apple, raisins, mango, pineapple, banana. Added yogurt, then spread granola over the top. Ate it standing by the counter. Tasted nothing.

Kelly drifted back into the bedroom, cut off the lights and settled into bed. Wanting nothing more than a solid night's sleep. Or two. Gupta was not due back from San Francisco until the day after tomorrow. Agnes needed at least a day to put their NovaCorp plans into place. Her team was on light duty until then. Hoping she could put it all to one side and get a decent night's rest.

It was not to be.

Five and a half hours later, an emergency call blasted her night and sent the entire team racing into darkness.

*　　*　　*

Two seventeen in the morning, the Homeland duty officer woke Jon Alvero. Twelve minutes later, he had confirmed what sounded at first like a crank, a joke, an absurd event that could only happen in LA after midnight. Quarter to three, Kelly and her team were speeding along empty streets, heading north to the Beverly Flats, following Jon into the unknown.

The neighborhood was located behind an upscale outdoor mini mall, down quiet streets where tall imperial palms rose like sleepy sentinels. Attractive low-slung houses alternated with mega-mansions that crowded their neighbors like concrete bullies. When the flashing police lights came into view, Jon pulled to the curb and parked. He walked back to Kelly's SUV and said through her open window, 'Might as well hang back while I have a word with the officer in charge, see if there's actually a reason to wake up the world.'

Riggs observed from his position behind the wheel, 'From the two-step those neighbors are doing, something big has gone down.'

The police headlights illuminated a growing number of civilians moving about and waving their arms. Kelly thought their voices sounded angry, distraught. She asked, 'Where did it take place?'

Jon pointed to an empty lot across the street, now rimmed by yellow police tape. 'That's the address I was given.' He started away.

Rabbit and Pamela occupied the rear seat. The four of them studied the empty space. Finally, Riggs asked, 'Am I the only one who feels like our situation just got kicked up a level?'

Rabbit was the one who responded. 'No. Definitely not.'

The police cordon surrounded a vacant lot. Spotlights from the four squad cars were aimed at nothing whatsoever. Kelly could hear two distinct conversations taking place. One was angry and growing louder by the minute, as an increasing number of confused neighbors insisted that a home had been stolen. They demanded the police do something about it.

The police, on the other hand, were not actually laughing in the neighbors' faces. But the blank stares and empty questions showed what they thought.

Rabbit opened his door and stepped out. He walked forward two steps, three. He stopped a yard or so from the boundary of police tape and just stood there, staring at the floodlit nothingness. Every now and then, he lifted his head like he was sniffing the wind. When Jon Alvero started back toward the car, Rabbit followed.

Rabbit slipped back inside and said, 'Nothing. I've got nothing.'

Kelly addressed the Homeland agent through her open window, 'Why don't you join us? Rabbit, Pamela, scrunch over.' She handed Riggs her phone. 'Put this on the car's system.'

Riggs started her car, coded in her phone, handed it back. 'You're good to go.'

Agnes came on, 'Pendalon.'

Kelly's phone showed ten minutes past three. Just past six in the morning, DC time. 'Sorry to disturb your dawn, ma'am. But we have a serious development.'

'Hold on.' The phone clicked.

Kelly swung around. Alvero was crammed tight against the right door, Pamela scrunched in the middle, Rabbit to her left. No one seemed to mind. Kelly asked Jon, 'Anything useful from the police?'

Before Jon could reply, Agnes was back. 'Mathers, Cotton, you connected?'

All three of the voices held the calm alert Kelly had come to know as standard ops for veteran agents. The clock did not dominate. Sleep was at times just another luxury to savor once the crisis had passed.

Agnes said, 'OK, Kaiser. Report.'

'I'm handing this to AIC Jon Alvero, ma'am. He's just returned from a briefing with the local police.'

'Can the local force hear us?'

'No, ma'am.'

'Go ahead.'

Jon began, 'Ninety minutes ago, Mrs Ryan Stiles returned from—'

Cotton said, 'Wait. Ryan Stiles?'

'Affirmative,' Kelly said. 'Wife of Professor Sean Stiles, the individual under question regarding Durrant and Singh.'

A silence, then Agnes said, 'Proceed.'

Jon described how Ryan Stiles had returned home from an evening with friends to discover her husband missing and her house gone. He described the vacant lot, the absence of any suggestion of violence, the police's desire to treat it as a joke. A nuisance.

When Jon finished, Agnes asked, 'Stanley?'

Kelly needed a moment to realize she was addressing Rabbit, who replied, 'If you mean do I sense anything, the answer is definitely no. Just the same, this makes perfect sense.'

Mathers said, 'I absolutely agree.'

Rabbit went on, 'Professor Stiles is a particle physicist. Someone they want or need. If this gathering is actually taking place up where you've said . . .'

'Hudson Bay, Northern Cree territory,' Mathers said. 'Five hundred miles from a paved road.'

Cotton said, 'Satellite photos show nothing.'

Agnes said, 'Camouflage.'

Cotton asked, 'Of a settlement?'

'Remember the cloud covering after the Morocco strike,' Mathers said. 'The rules of engagement have been permanently shifted.'

Rabbit went on, 'We know they have all the energy they could possibly need. And they can levitate almost anything.'

Kelly was with him, moving in sync. 'But building new homes in the middle of nowhere, that's not something a bunch of relocated physics nerds can handle.'

Agnes asked, 'Cotton, you following this?'

'Enough to be seriously spooked.'

'How far along are you with the list?'

'All eighty-seven names Kelly's team supplied are now under full electronic monitoring. Phones, emails, social media, the works. They sneeze, we know.'

'OK. I want you to start a new search for missing structures.'

'This actually could be very helpful,' Mathers said. 'We've been trying to identify a means for hunting down new outbreaks.'

'Go for homes first,' Agnes went on. 'Look for jokey mentions, police sidebars.'

'Television news that uses this as the evening joke,' Kelly suggested.

Rabbit said, 'Social media sites frequented by the UFO cliques.'

Agnes went on, 'Once you're done with homes, expand to everything. Apartment buildings, labs, the works.'

'On it.'

'Start with the US,' Mathers said. 'When you're ready to go global, let me and Reuben know. We'll do personal alerts to our counterparts worldwide.'

Jon whispered to Pamela, 'This is so big?'

Agnes demanded, 'Who said that?'

'Jon Alvero, ma'am. Sorry.'

'Kelly, how much have you given him?'

'Almost nothing. Yet. But if you approve my next steps, we'll need his help. And to make that happen, he needs to know.'

'You have the green light, when and where. Now tell me what you have in mind.'

Kelly swung further, so as to face Alvero. 'Jon, can you handle the local police?'

'Handle, as in . . .'

'Make their investigation of this house go quietly away.'

He shook his head. 'They're looking for a reason to drop it. Just the same, I'll probably need some help on that.'

Agnes said, 'Find out who is ultimately in charge. Pass their name to Kaiser.'

'Certainly.'

'Kaiser, soon as you have them, let Mathers know.'

'Roger that. We're still left with two potential loose ends. Home security and insurance.'

'Darren?'

'Checking.' Then, 'No evidence that the Stiles residence was contracted to a security company. Home insurance was through a subsidiary of NovaCorp.'

Kelly and Agnes and Mathers and Riggs all said it together. 'Interesting.'

Agnes went on, 'Kaiser, ideas.'

'NovaCorp's first concern will be the potential outlay. Their need to cover a total loss. If we cut them a check, it could stop any investigation before it starts.'

Mathers added, 'It could also give us a lever. Find out what their CEO . . .'

'Byron Sykes,' Kelly offered.

'Right. What he and his board member discussed.'

Kelly was ready for that as well. 'With respect, I think we need to assume they've talked at length. What we need is to ensure the conversation goes no further.' Kelly outlined her idea. And waited.

'Grey?'

'I like it.'

'So do I. OK, Kaiser, make it happen.'

They drove from the missing house to Du-par's in the Farmers Market. The night was quiet, the streets empty. Even so, the deli was more than half full. A waitress greeted Jon by name and shifted two tables together. As soon as they had ordered, Jon said, 'I think maybe it's time I learned what's going on.'

Kelly had assumed this was coming and did not argue. 'Once you know, it can't be taken back.'

Jon studied the faces gathered around him. All of them grim and tight with the secret they shared. 'That bad?'

Barry Riggs said, 'I haven't had a decent night's sleep since they sprang it on me.'

'Roger that,' Pamela said.

'You need to be very sure,' Barry said.

Pamela said, 'A lot of what you'll hear won't make any sense. Explaining won't help.'

'You'll need to carry it a while, see what you're facing on the ground,' Barry said.

'The more you learn, the worse it gets,' Pamela said.

Jon gave it several minutes. Kelly respected him even more for that. How he took them at their word. How he accepted the truth for what it was. 'You're scaring me. That hasn't happened in a while.'

'You ain't seen nothing yet,' Barry said. 'No joke.'

'Still,' he decided. 'I need to know.'

'And I'll tell you,' Kelly promised. She waited while the waitress deposited their pre-dawn breakfasts. 'Soon as we're done here.'

They ate in silence. Jon was one of them now. He might not be aware of the reason, but that was less important than how he had helped them. How he had decided. Frightened and worried. But standing on the cliff's edge. Waiting for her word to jump. Kelly liked him for that.

When they were done, she said, 'One question. Or request.'

'I said it before,' Jon replied. 'Anything.'

'I like you,' she said. 'And I'm glad you've decided to join us.'

He revealed an ancient's ability to smile with only his eyes and repeated, 'Anything.'

'We need to assume NovaCorp will be tempted to investigate this missing house. I hope I'm right; the payment and the threat will be enough to stop that before it starts. But as you heard in my conversation with Director Pendalon, we are now assuming the CEO, Byron Sykes, has heard about our present crisis from Doctor Gupta. So if he decides to pull on this thread and see where it takes him, whoever he assigns to this investigation needs to be tailed.' She gestured to the agents ringing the table. 'You see how small our team is. Agnes made it clear. This is all we have to work with.'

'Involving more of your Homeland agents risks the word of what we're doing here getting out,' Riggs said. 'It can't happen.'

'I can help with that.' He spoke to her but addressed the table. 'Last winter, we arrested leaders of a right-wing group for smuggling. We gave them reduced sentences in return for their members serving in whatever capacity we asked. We pay them. We keep them on a short leash. For something like this, they'd be pretty close to ideal.'

'Any advice on how to handle them?'

'You don't, is the short answer. I'll do this personally. Short and sharp commands work best. Like you're giving orders to a half-wild dog. These are not our friends. They never will be.'

Riggs and Kelly exchanged a look. Then she said, 'I'm glad you're on our team, Jon.'

'Let's get out of here,' Riggs said.

Riggs patted Alvero's shoulder. 'Time to really mess up your day.'

FOURTEEN

Today

Denton took samples of the earth and water from the empty lot, but he was fairly certain that microscopic examination would reveal nothing. He clambered up the side, slipped back under the police tape and was glad to see the old man still standing by his ride. The dog sat by his feet, panting softly. 'Afternoon.'

'You a cop?'

'No, sir, I'm a private investigator.'

The old guy replied, 'The police say nobody but them should enter.'

'I have their permission. Sir, do you live around here?'

'Three doors down. On the left. Been here since it was cheap enough for us to afford our home.'

'My name is Denton Hayes.' He fished a business card from the SUV's rear side pocket. 'I'm a senior investigator with NovaCorp. Could I ask you a few questions?'

The guy took his time checking out Denton's card. 'I didn't see or hear a thing. Slept through the whole shebang.' He used Denton's card to tap his ear. 'Hearing aids. Take these babies out, I'd sleep through another D-Day landing.'

'Just the same, sir.' Denton waved at the empty lot. 'I'm starting off at ground zero. Literally. Anything you can tell me about the house, the family, it would help tremendously.'

The old man studied him a moment longer, then offered his hand. 'Jacob Groate.'

Denton stripped off the gloves, shook hands. 'Very nice to meet you.' He pointed at the little home-security signs planted along the street. 'I see a lot of Campion signs in these yards.'

'They came through here a couple of years back. Offered a major discount if we'd all go in together. Made sense, giving their patrol cars a reason to do regular sweeps. Haven't had a break-in or vandalism since. The fellow who lived here refused to even discuss it. Had his reasons, I suppose.' He gestured at the empty lot. 'And now this.'

'Have Campion been by since this happened?'

'Oh, sure. Back when the cops were doing that thing with the guys in bunny suits searching for clues.'

'Forensics.'

'They checked the adjoining properties. If they found something, they didn't tell us.' He rattled the leash, irritated now. 'Probably too busy laughing with the cops, making UFO jokes.'

'What can you tell me about the incident in question?'

'My wife Emily claims her hearing's perfect. Says there was a soft ripping sound. Like pulling roots from the earth.' He rattled the leash. 'Of course, this is the same lady who claims she's heard the neighbors quarreling. When they were on vacation in Aruba.'

'Sir, I . . . Hang on, I feel like I'm wearing a portable sauna.' Denton opened the rear gate and stripped off the waders. Thankfully, the old man showed no interest in going anywhere. 'Did you know the family who lived here?'

'Husband and wife. No kids. Sure, we knew them well. The guy was a professor of something weird . . .'

'Particle physics,' Denton said. 'USC. That much is in our file.'

'The wife, Ryan, she was a firecracker.' Jacob's eyes sparked. 'And pretty as a sunrise.'

Those words were enough to lance Denton at heart level. 'And the husband?'

'Can't say I thought much of the louse. Look, why don't you stow your gear and come on up to the house. When it comes to bad neighbors, my wife is better at taking out the garbage.' He rattled the leash again. 'Come on, Trinket. Let's go tell the lady of the house we're having company.' To Denton, 'You ever heard a sillier name for a dog?'

'Growing up, my stepmother had two cats. Beau and Coo.'

Jacob was two steps further down the street when he cackled. 'Come around to the back door. We'll be in the kitchen.'

Denton toweled off the sweat, labeled and stowed his samples, locked the car and followed the old man up the street, down the drive, around the house. He found a woman standing in the doorway, whose sparkling gaze matched her husband's. 'Come in, young man. Welcome.'

'I don't want to be any bother.'

'Nonsense.' She was already moving to the counter. 'Would you like a tea?'

He stepped over to where Jacob pushed a chair away from the sunlit table. 'Tea is always welcome, thank you.'

'A gentleman after my own heart. What about a sugar cookie?'

Jacob made sure his wife's back was to them, shook his head, grimaced and swept a hand across his throat.

'Just tea, thank you, ma'am.'

'Very well.' She brought over a tea tray and distributed cups and milk and lemon and sugar. As Emily passed her husband's chair, she whacked the back of Jacob's head.

'Ow. What was that for?'

'Good measure. Sure about that cookie, young man?'

'No, thanks.' Denton waited until she poured the tea and seated herself to ask, 'What can you tell me about Professor and Mrs Stiles?'

Emily sniffed. 'Sean Stiles is a self-absorbed cad. Chases every attractive student who came within ten feet. He's a sex addict, plain and simple. I despise the man.'

Jacob cackled. 'Now tell us what you really think.'

'Ryan is such a good-hearted soul. And so lovely. The times she sat where you are and cried her eyes out. She should have left that man years ago. But every time she started, he'd pour on the charm, play the remorseful bad boy, enter therapy and pretend he'd become reformed. Until the next time.' Emily sipped. 'There was a man in Ryan's life. She never said much about him, other than how much they loved each other.' Emily was too absorbed in recollecting to notice the impact her words had on Denton. 'When things were really bad between her and the louse, she'd let out a few words. How she still loved him. How she wished she could go back and do things differently.'

Jacob said, 'Tell him about that night.'

'It was the strangest thing, that noise. Woke me from a deep sleep. Sounded like, well . . . you'll think I'm silly.'

Jacob rolled his eyes.

'Tell me,' Denton said. 'Please.'

'Like a giant hand was scooping out the earth.' Arthritic fingers made a cup and swept the air. 'I heard these great rattles, a whoosh of sudden wind, then nothing. Just the same, I was completely awake when Ryan arrived.'

This was news. 'Mrs Stiles came here?'

'About an hour later. She'd been at a party. Friends over in Palos Verdes. The poor thing was utterly shattered, I can tell you.'

Jacob said, 'Come back to discover her house had vanished – who wouldn't be?'

'We dressed and trooped up the street,' Emily sipped, rattling her cup as she set it back down. 'I'll never forget that sight.'

'House gone, street totally quiet. Not even a dog barking.' Jacob shook his head. 'Trinket goes crazy when a noisy truck passes. Dog slept through the whole event.'

'Not a soul there except us,' Emily said. 'Only sound was Ryan crying. Poor thing.'

'The police weren't any help,' Jacob said.

'Police.' She made it into a bad word. 'They were horrid. Laughing at her behind her back, thinking she couldn't see how they treated this as the joke of the century.'

'Only reason they didn't try to lock her up as the latest LA nutcase is how the neighbors were all outside by this point,' Jacob said. 'Saying the same things. Insisting the house had been there the day before. Getting angry when the detectives tried to suggest it was some kind of neighborhood prank.'

'I worried Jacob might actually strike one of them, he was so angry,' Emily said.

Denton asked, 'Are you aware Mrs Stiles has gone missing?'

Emily was unimpressed. 'Who wouldn't, the way the cops treated that poor dear?'

'She was frightened by something, wouldn't say what,' Jacob said. 'Wouldn't tell us where she was headed. Only that she'd get in touch when it was safe.'

'That horrid man is behind it,' Emily said. 'Her so-called husband. Some crazy experiment gone wrong. Something. He's poison, pure and simple.'

Denton rose from his chair, then pretended to have a new thought. 'Any idea who held the party Mrs Stiles attended that night?'

Jacob gave another of his old man's laughs. Eh-eh-eh. 'In case you hadn't noticed, that was before the house vanished.'

'Just dotting i's and crossing t's, sir.'

Emily extended a flat hand, clearly taking aim at her husband's head.

Jacob leaned away. 'What's with the slapping business?'

'Just trying to keep you in line.' To Denton, 'Their last name is

Petridis. They both teach at USC. They have a lovely place in Palos
Verdes. She comes from money. We've been out to their place with
Ryan several times. Beautiful home, right on the bluff.'

'Please feel free to call me if anything else comes to mind.'
Denton set another card on the table. 'Thank you for the tea.'

FIFTEEN

Today

Connor was deep into the arid wasteland east of LA when Denton called. 'Did you set up the meeting with Gupta?' No hello, no howyadoin. Connor decided he talked like a cop.

'We're due at his home tomorrow morning at eleven thirty. He can't make it any earlier. He's attending a conference in San Francisco.'

'I guess that works.' A pause, then, 'We?'

'I have been inserted into your investigation. Byron's orders.'

She expected some form of blowback. Angry tirade. Something. But the man remained as contained and steady as ever. 'In that case, we need to work in tandem. Moving in two different directions. Spreading out and covering more ground.'

'I need to know your steps. In advance. I decide where and when I have to be involved.' When he remained silent, she added, 'That's how it has to be.'

He gave that a beat. Then, 'Anything on the security company?'

'Byron is working on that. Personally. Just FYI, it's a huge ask. The year before last, NovaCorp tried to acquire Campion. It wound up in the courts. Byron's team fought dirty. They lost.'

'You were involved?'

'Not personally. The acquisition was handled by my former boss.'

'OK. Changing the subject, I have a possible lead from the detective's best friend. Chatty neighbors. Who in this case were also friends of the missing lady. Ryan Stiles attended a party the night of the—'

'Call it an event.'

'Good. Event works. The party ran late. She came home to find the home gone. Her husband missing. She woke up the chatty neighbors, Jacob and Emily Groate. Who heard nothing, by the way. Emily claims to be a light sleeper. She had no idea anything was amiss until they were standing on the street, waiting for the police.

Who have not made friends in the neighborhood. A lot of snide jokes, a good measure of disbelief.'

Connor liked this open discussion of items she would otherwise know nothing about. No hesitation, no sign of holding back. She liked that a lot. 'Where was the party?'

'Palos Verdes.'

'What can you learn from people living ten miles away from the event? Ryan was there *before* it happened.'

'She has to be somewhere. I'm thinking she's too smart to leave an electronic trail. Which means she has to be off the grid.'

Connor saw her turning up ahead. 'I should be back in the office by mid-afternoon. Call the instant you have something to report.'

Denton drove down Rexford to Whole Foods and bought an early lunch of pastrami and avocado on whole wheat. Ate it watching the traffic and mentally reviewing everything he had learned.

Or, rather, he did until the Buick SUV pulled up tight beside his door, angled so he could not drive away. A second Buick blocked his rear. Very professional.

A stunningly attractive woman in a slate-grey suit rose from the rear seat. Then Denton corrected his first impression. She might have been beautiful, except for the load of weary rage she carried. The woman walked around the front of his ride and tapped on his passenger window with a leather wallet holding a Homeland ID. He unlocked the door and watched her slip inside. She was aged in her early thirties, strong features, gaze to match her suit. 'Kelly Kaiser, Homeland. And you're Detective Denton Hayes.'

'Not anymore, Agent Kaiser. Not for years.'

'Even former officers bleed blue – isn't that what they say?'

'I hope I never find out.' Denton set his water in the cup holder and rewrapped his sandwich. 'What can I do for you?'

'May I ask what you learned from Mr and Mrs Groate?'

'Nothing I assume you don't already know.' He took his time cleaning his hands on a fresh napkin. 'Can I take another look at your credentials?'

She handed over the wallet.

Denton gave the ID a careful inspection, passed it back and went on, 'Ryan Stiles went there straight from discovering her home had vanished. She had apparently been at a party. I assume you've confirmed this?'

Kaiser shook her head. 'Answers first, then questions. That OK with you?'

'Mrs Stiles was harassed by the police, according to both Groates. She claimed her husband was missing with the home. She also stated that she was in serious danger, and she has since vanished. Which apparently suits the LA police, who can now ignore the whole affair.'

'You spoke with the officer in charge.' It was not a question.

'Sure. Celeste . . .' He made a pretense of searching his pockets for his notepad.

'Jones.'

'Right. Detective Jones sounded embarrassed by the incident. Especially with the UFO nuts and lower-tier news hounds swarming.'

'Do you often handle residential claims, Mr Hayes?'

'You already know the answer to that.'

'And yet here you are.'

'Waiting to hear why Homeland is involved,' Denton replied. 'Wanting to finish my lunch.'

'You were called off a much larger investigation in . . .'

Denton sat. Waited.

'Phoenix, isn't that correct? And flown here by corporate jet. Taken straight into the office of . . .'

Denton remained silent.

'The NovaCorp chairman and chief executive officer, Byron Sykes. Who has apparently taken a personal interest in a missing house.'

Denton did not respond.

'Mr Hayes, our government is officially requesting that NovaCorp drop its investigation into this case.' She drew a buff envelope from her jacket's side pocket. 'NovaCorp's total exposure is two point seven million dollars. This is a certified check for three million. You are to consider this as payment in return for your closing this inquiry. Now. Today.'

He made no move to accept the envelope. 'That is not my decision to take.'

'My card is in the envelope. In case you or your chairman need to contact me. Which I sincerely hope will not happen.' She set the envelope on the console between them. 'Please inform your chairman that any hint of continuation in this matter will result in NovaCorp losing every federal contract it currently holds and being refused the option of bidding in the future.' She opened her door. 'Thank you for your time.'

But as she rose from the car, Kaiser leaned back down, studied him intently. 'I'm going to have trouble with you, aren't I?'

'I can't possibly imagine how, ma'am.'

'We'll see.' She hummed a sour note. 'Enjoy your sandwich.'

SIXTEEN

The spa was located fifty-five minutes from downtown LA. Connor climbed through Newhall Pass and entered the San Gabriel mountains, winding higher still, then took a narrow country road heading west. This section of Antelope Valley was desert-dry and empty. She passed a few trailer parks baking in the heat, the surrounding scrubland filled with derelict cars and other signs of a hard life. After that, fifteen minutes of nothing, until she rounded a sharp bend and entered a pristine myth.

The change from desert scrubland to Emerald Valley Spa was shocking. The location was a bowl-shaped depression in the high desert, one rimmed by imperial palms and framed with hibiscus, oleander, birds of paradise, and other blooming shrubs Connor could not immediately identify. The buildings were modern and low-slung, and looked very expensive. Terracotta walkways crisscrossed the immaculate lawns. Hummingbirds swooped and dived. It was as perfect an idyl as money could create.

During her drive, Jackie Barlow had texted directions and confirmed the meeting. Connor parked in the lot designated for the Renaissance building – the spa's name for their rehab center. Behind the building sparkled an Olympic-size pool. Heat created wavy lines over the pavement. Connor texted the number Jackie had given her, then waited with the engine running and the a/c on high.

Ten minutes later, a stocky Latina with a heavily seamed face stepped through the doors. She waited in the shade as Connor approached.

'Doctor Estana?'

'I only have a few minutes. Your contact mentioned a payment, yes?'

Connor handed her the envelope and observed the woman's complete lack of nerves, remorse, anything. Up close, the face clearly showed scars from a very hard life. Connor wondered at the road that had brought this woman here, treating rich addicts in the middle of California's high desert.

Carla Estana slipped the envelope into the pocket of her clinic jacket. 'This way.'

The building was a lie.

That was Connor's clearest impression, walking into the front lobby. Everything appeared bright and welcoming. But there was an electronic lock on the front door and a calm-faced receptionist who could have bench-pressed Connor's BMW. Another guard sat behind a desk inside an office with a glass wall fronting the foyer. A pair of giant modern-art posters dominated the side walls. It took Connor a long moment to realize both said, *One Day At A Time*.

'I need your ID.' Estana passed it to the guard, then, 'Face the guard, please.' The man lifted a computer camera, shot her picture, tapped on his keyboard, then passed a visitor's badge to the doctor, who said, 'Wear this and remain with me at all times. Your badge does not open any doors, so don't stray. Do not approach or attempt to speak with any of the patients.'

'Understood.'

She nodded to the guard, who hit a button. The door to Connor's left chimed.

Estana led her down a spotless hall, the few patients they passed all dressed in cotton jumpers and sweatpants bearing the spa's logo. Through a large commons room, then a cafeteria nearly empty at mid-morning. 'You want a coffee, or use the facilities?'

'I'm good, thanks. How much does this place cost?'

'Two thousand a day, which covers all basic treatments. Special therapies run between one-fifty and five hundred an hour.'

'Wow.'

Estana halted midway down a residential hall, used her badge to unlock the door. 'In here.'

She locked the door behind them, then used the badge a second time on an interior keypad. When the pad chimed, she said, 'The monitoring system is now cut off. If anyone asks, you intend to make an intervention and are here to inspect the facilities.'

Connor said, 'Denton Hayes.'

'Are you recording?'

'No.'

'Let me see your phone.' Estana inspected it, handed it back, said, 'He's been a patient here. Three times.'

Connor accessed the corporate system on her phone and drew up Denton's photo.

Estana barely glanced at it. 'That's Denton.'

'So . . . He uses cocaine?'

'I can't say about now. But that particular addiction was what brought him here.'

'How long has he been using?'

'I can only tell you what he said in therapy. You know about his relationship with Ryan Stiles?'

'A little. She broke his heart.'

'She wrecked his life. At least twice, possibly a third time as well. The first visit, Denton was young and healthy and determined. He struggled through a recovery that everyone hoped would be his one and only. Some drinking followed his first release from here, some light drugs, some wild weekends. But he stayed relatively clean. You know what happened next.'

Connor inspected the room, taking a moment to collect her thoughts. The chamber could have easily been a junior suite in some posh five-star resort. Floor tiled in what was probably marble. Contemporary rug, matching wall-hanging, comfortable furniture, huge bed. All in muted pastel shades. 'Ryan Stiles re-entered his life.'

'Correct. They restarted this highly destructive relationship. She again returned to her husband. Denton began another downward spiral. And continued until he was arrested. The LA police gave him the choice. Public dismissal, arrest, prison. Or graduate from rehab a second time. Go clean. Stay clean.'

'How does a cop afford this place?'

'We have a relationship with local and state law enforcement, as well as higher echelons of the state government. Part of a secret agreement the spa holds with the state's water board.' Her voice was as flat as pounded tin. No emotion, no guilt over disclosing confidential information. Not even impatience. 'Denton Hayes successfully completed the program. Again. We signed off. Again. He left. I was fairly certain he'd be back. I'm sorry to say I was right. And it won't be his last visit here either. Unless, you know, he doesn't survive the next time she forces him to crash and burn.'

'What makes you so certain?'

'Because in the three times he's entered rehab, Denton never confronted the true reasons for why he came in the first place. He attends counseling sessions because he must. But he never reveals anything of a personal nature. He refuses to discuss Ryan Stiles. In this manner, he resembles a certain kind of patient we occasionally treat. Stars in particular, but others as well. They have built pain into their lives so deeply they can't let go. Actors use this as a foundation for their roles, drawing upon it, refusing to see how it wrecks them when they're off camera. Denton is like that, only different. He rebuffs any efforts to help him confront what Ryan has done to his life because he still loves her. He hopes they might be able to get back together. Which would be the ultimate disaster, in my opinion. I fear he won't survive another dose of that woman's venomous affection.'

Connor walked to the windows. Swept back the gauze drapes. Looked out over the green lawn, the brightly colored flowerbeds, the two ponds whose surfaces sparkled with gemstone brilliance in the desert wind. 'When was the last time he came?'

'Three and a half years ago. I expect him back any day now.' There was a soft buzz. The clinician pulled her phone from the jacket of her white coat, glanced down and said, 'I have to go.'

Connor waited until the doctor had led her past the front guard, taken her visitor's pass and opened the front door to say, 'You like him.'

Estana hesitated so long that Connor feared the woman was not going to respond. Instead, she released the door and stepped into the dry desert heat. 'What makes you say that?'

'You do,' Connor said. 'You like him a lot.'

Estana breathed through pursed lips. Shallow breaths. Then, 'It must be nice, having a man love you like that. Despite the shattering pain. I always thought Denton belonged to a different era. When knights accepted the agony of unrequited love. They saw it as merely a component of their life, their world. A pain without end. Actually, an end in itself.'

Connor nodded slowly, but not to the woman's words. Instead, she watched as Carla Estana revealed hints of her own past, the lines creasing the skin around her eyes. Old scars deepened by the harsh light. The semi-permanent pain she herself carried.

Estana continued, 'These knights, they took a scarf, a pin, a talisman. And went off in search of a quest as great as the loss they were destined to carry unto death.' She blinked and shuddered through a hard breath, and drew Connor back into focus. 'I did not press Denton any harder than I did because of this, Ms . . .'

'Connor.'

'If a man of honor chooses a course that is wrong in today's world, and yet has held sway for centuries among good men, who am I to declare he must change? I can offer, but I must respect his decision to refuse. Even if I know, even if I am deeply worried, by what another encounter with that woman will do to him. I hate the prospect of seeing Ryan Stiles destroy him. Which she will. Denton deserves better than that.'

SEVENTEEN

Denton drove east on Santa Monica, pondering next moves. Whenever the traffic slowed, he glanced at the envelope on his central console.

As he passed the invisible boundary separating Beverly Hills from West Hollywood, Denton realized he had picked up a tail.

Two blocks further, he found a parking space in front of a coffee shop. He cut the motor and went inside. He stayed by the entrance, his back to the front windows, and watched via the side wall's mirror as the tail banged through a yellow light and burned rubber making the turn. Denton assumed it was circling the block. Four minutes later, the vehicle reappeared and slipped into a space three down from his own. Denton pretended to sip from a cup someone had left on the neighboring table and placed the call.

'RHD Ramparts. Detective Jones.'

'Denton Hayes, Detective. Do you have me under surveillance?'

'Why on earth would I want to do that?'

'I figured it wasn't LAPD. This tail does not appear to be professionals. But I wanted to check.'

'You're sure this is happening?'

'Yes.' He related the past few minutes. 'They're sitting curbside, motor running.'

'I hate amateurs worse than a rash. What's the ride?'

'Black Dodge double-cab pickup.'

'Definitely not one of ours. You get the plates?'

'Yes. But maybe it's best you leave this alone.'

'Because . . .'

'By any chance, have you met an agent from Homeland named Kaiser?'

'Now, that's interesting. The answer is right after you and I spoke, I got called into a meeting with my lieutenant, the division captain and two deputy chiefs. All this brass together in one room. Guess why.'

Denton breathed. 'They're pulling you off the case.'

'Correction. As of half an hour ago, there never was a case.'

'Interesting.'

'No signed complaint. The lady in question, Ryan Stiles, gave false contact details. And has since vanished.'

'Should you declare Mrs Stiles a missing person?'

'We have to wait forty-eight hours if the individual is over eighteen. By which time the paperwork on this one will most likely have been circular filed.' A pause, then, 'Where are you now?'

'Joe's Coffee on Santa Monica. Before this happened, I was heading to NovaCorp.'

'OK, tell you what. Keep heading east. I'll have a black-and-white do a standard in-car check on their plates.'

'Does this mean you're staying on this?'

'Don't talk stupid. Of course not.' She thought. 'You know the Rhythm Room?'

'The jazz club. Love the place.'

'We've probably seen each other, then. I'm usually there at least once each week. You want, shoot me a text.'

'I'll ask who's playing.'

'Place starts bouncing around ten. Look for a lonely lady at one of the front tables.'

Denton was in the chief's outer office when Connor arrived, texting at hyperspeed as she walked. She said, 'Give me a second.'

'Take your time.'

'Can't. Byron is waiting.' She studied him, his legs straight out, arms crossed over his chest, chin down. 'What are you doing?'

'Thinking. Taking a breather. Planning.'

Byron Sykes appeared in his doorway. 'All good moves.' He motioned them inside. 'Bring them with you.'

Denton rose. 'I think Rachel should join us.'

'Really? Why?'

Denton spaced out the words. 'Just in case you are correct.'

Connor was impatient to tell Byron what she had found out in the desert spa. Press him a second time to let this guy go. Whatever lay behind Byron's fears and concerns, they needed to send this semi-broken player down to the seventh floor. Bring in the first team. Get the party started. But apparently it would all have to wait.

Soon as the door shut, Denton asked, 'How often is this room swept?'

Byron looked at his PA, who replied, 'Twice each month. The entire floor.'

'The last time was . . .'

She clearly disliked not knowing something. 'I can call security.'

'No.' Byron and Denton both. Then Denton said, 'We'll assume it's OK. But this needs to be the last time we meet here.'

Byron did not show any surprise. 'I assume there's a reason behind your caution.'

In response, Denton set an envelope on the table. He relayed his conversation with Agent Kelly Kaiser. The offer of three million dollars. The warning. The tail. His call with the LA detective, the news the LAPD investigation had officially been closed. Four minutes, start to finish.

When he was done, Byron asked, 'Did your contact with the police call you back?'

'She did. Two items worth noting. First, Celeste had a black-and-white check the tags. The plan was to set up a routine stop, see who was in the truck, get their pictures on their dash cam. Ten seconds after the officers keyed in the license number, though, the pickup wheeled away and vanished.'

Byron nodded. 'Second?'

'The pickup belongs to a well-drilling operation based in Fresno. The detective's contacts in the Organized Crime division say the company is a known affiliate of the Inland Army, a right-wing group with ties to the meth trade and several biker gangs.'

Byron's response was calm. 'You are right to be cautious.'

Connor felt like every word out of Denton's mouth was challenging her intention to have him taken off the case. She had the distinct impression of being introduced to a different Denton Hayes. On the surface, he was the same quiet and introspective individual, carrying years of hazardous baggage. Only now she wondered if indeed it was all a mask. Letting people see what they wanted and dismiss him. Because . . . Why?

She had no idea.

It was almost reassuring to hear Rachel say, 'Excuse me. I don't understand what is going on here.'

Denton kept his gaze on Byron. 'Let's assume for the moment that my meeting with Kelly Kaiser and then picking up a tail are not simply a coincidence.'

'Not a chance,' Byron agreed, tapping the envelope holding Kaiser's check.

'Which suggests Homeland is now using a right-wing group with criminal ties to track me. And the police system has assets at the highest level who are dialed in, feeding intel to Homeland, keeping this totally off the grid.'

Connor asked, 'What exactly is "this?"'

'That's the question we need to answer,' Denton replied, still addressing Byron. 'Unless you want me to cease and desist.'

'Absolutely not,' Byron replied.

'Is there anything else you can tell us about what raised your alert level?'

Byron's response was a slow breath, a moment of reflection, then, 'When do you meet Sanjib?'

Connor replied, 'Tomorrow at some point. His secretary called an hour ago, asked to shift our meeting to the medical school.'

'Given the new surveillance, I don't think that would be wise,' Denton said. 'May I make a suggestion?'

'Go ahead.'

'Have Rachel call Sanjib, tell him the meeting will no longer be necessary.' He slid a cheap phone across the table toward Byron. 'After that, use this burner. Text Sanjib and ask when his plane lands. Don't use your name. Use something else as an ID.'

'"Grateful patient,"' Byron said. 'He'll understand. But I don't need your phone. Jackie Barlow in Security supplied me with an encrypted satphone for emergencies.'

'This isn't an emergency yet, but it could become one very soon,' Denton said.

'Agreed.' Byron turned to Rachel. 'No notes. No diary entrances. No records. From this point on.'

Denton suggested, 'Rachel should perhaps serve as our cut-out.'

Rachel said, 'I have no idea what that even means.'

'I'll explain later,' Byron said. To Denton, 'I'll say one thing; the rest needs to come from Sanjib. This isn't about a missing house. It never was.'

Denton pointed to the envelope. 'And this check isn't about covering our losses. This is making sure we both understand the importance Homeland attaches to our looking the other way.'

Connor latched on to the one point she fully understood. 'Sir, if Homeland's threat is real . . .'

'It is,' Denton said. 'Count on it.'

'Our current work on federal contracts totals well over three hundred million dollars.'

'Balance that against the entire company going up in smoke. I personally don't see much of a choice.' Byron turned to Denton. 'Next steps. Go.'

'I understand you want Connor to stay involved.'

'Something this momentous, it's essential to have a second confirmation.'

'In that case, we require cover stories, something strong enough to hold up if or when Agent Kaiser looks our way. For myself, I need to be assigned a case that keeps me totally outside Richard's orbit. My boss is too detail-oriented to let me operate freely. His leash is too tight.'

'I know just the thing.' Byron said to Rachel, 'Call Camila Suarez. Tell her I'm assigning our top investigator to her issue. And give Denton the file she sent up.' When Rachel left the room, he asked, 'And in regard to Connor's involvement?'

Denton looked across the table. If there was any humor to his gaze, Connor could not see it. 'The only option I've come up with is, she and I start a torrid affair.'

'What? No!'

'I'm definitely open to an alternative.' Denton was already rising from the table. 'I'll go make contact with my new boss.'

Connor remained seated as Denton rose. 'I need a private word.' When the door clicked shut, she continued, 'I went out to the rehab clinic that treated Denton. Three times.'

Connor took Byron's silence as permission to go on. She started with the security agent's concerns. The bribe. The conversation with the clinician. The warning. The clinician's view of Denton being a knight out of his proper time in history.

Byron remained silent, watchful. Which only opened the door wider to Connor's growing concerns. 'Here's a guy that is borderline fractured. Barely holding his life together. Everything boils down to his connection to this woman. Ryan Stiles. The same woman who's at the center of this mystery investigation. We're telling him to go find the woman who could destroy him? How could that possibly make sense?'

Byron did not respond.

'So now we have an agent from Homeland Security telling us to back away. She threatens our company with losing a major portion of our annual revenue and profits. And not only do you tell him to continue, but you order me to go along with this absurd notion of being his new flame? Really? Byron, I admire you more than just about anyone I have ever met—'

He broke in. 'What are your next steps?'

She leaned back. Took a breath. Tried to shift her fears and frustrations to the back burner. 'Meet Sanjib in secret. Followed now by Campion. Which we really shouldn't be doing, not after Homeland's warning. But to break off at this point—'

'Hold that thought.' He buzzed for his PA. When Rachel entered, he handed her the Homeland agent's card. 'See if you can get the lady on the phone.'

Rachel dialed on the conference phone, spoke, nodded.

'Put it on speaker,' Byron said. Then, 'Agent Kaiser?'

'I was hoping I wouldn't hear from you.'

'Two quick items and we're done.'

'Go ahead.'

'First, I accept your request. The investigation into the Stiles missing home is hereby officially closed.'

'Glad to hear it.'

'Second, I have gone to considerable trouble and expense to make an appointment with Campion Security. As you may know, last year we made a failed hostile takeover attempt. There is considerable bad blood. They have reluctantly agreed to this meeting. If I cancel now, there is every chance it will raise red flags over there. They might become curious enough to start looking into the missing house themselves. Asking the very questions you are telling us to drop.'

Kaiser was silent, then, 'The purpose of this meeting is . . .'

'Denton wanted to see footage from the neighborhood's security cameras. Interview their head of security and the first responders.'

Another silence.

'Hello?'

'When is the appointment?'

Rachel replied, 'Day after tomorrow. Seven thirty in the morning. The only time she would agree to.'

'I will meet your man in the Campion headquarters lobby. Tell Hayes to be on time.'

The line went dead.

As Rachel hung up the receiver, Byron checked his watch. 'It's now a quarter to five. I will meet you here in precisely twenty-four hours.'

Rachel said, 'Sir, you're scheduled to attend the grand opening—'

'Cancel it.' He turned to Connor and continued, 'I did not enlist Ms Barlow to investigate a man I did not know. Most of what she told me, Denton's boss has twice used as ammunition to try to get him fired. I needed to know if there was anything else.'

She breathed around her continued sense of disconnect. 'I am totally at a loss here.'

Byron rose from his chair, walked to the outer window, studied the LA skyline for a long moment, then said, 'We are circling back to what Sanjib told me. Which I don't want to go into, because it may well taint your own observations. My closest friend and ally on our board insisted that the investigation be handled by someone with Denton's specific traits. These same personal characteristics that have raised your and Ms Barlow's red flags. In effect, Sanjib has insisted that the core issue, the construct that could well threaten our company's very existence, can best be understood by someone with Denton's background. More than that will have to wait. I am well aware of the risks. But Sanjib . . .' He swung around. 'If you still feel as you do now tomorrow afternoon, I will stop everything. The investigation, Denton's involvement, his access to the executive level. The works. For the moment . . .'

'What could possibly happen in twenty-four hours to change my mind?'

Byron nodded. 'That is precisely the question I need answering. Now get to work.'

EIGHTEEN

Connor walked along the security division's main corridor, still uncertain what she should say to Jackie or how she might put her concern into words that made sense. Even to herself. The security division's ceiling was forty-six feet high. The central chamber housed a concrete cube whose walls were laced with a spiderweb of electronic shielding. This structure formed the headquarters of NovaCorp's surveillance and online security ops. Four satellite divisions based around the country employed almost a thousand mostly young, mostly would-be hackers. They monitored clients and their online operations, and fed a constant stream of intel and alerts to the home office team.

Most of the cube's staffers considered Jackie Barlow and her focus on human intelligence, or HUMINT, to be dinosaurs. Dead and gone, only Jackie didn't know it yet. What Jackie thought of this, she never said. Connor had worked with her on several occasions and considered the woman to be tops in her field.

She knocked on Jackie's open door, walked in, seated herself and waited.

Jackie took her time. Finished typing, then slid her keyboard to one side. Clearing the decks. She rose and walked over and closed her door. Came back, pulled over a second visitor's chair, sat down. So close their knees were within an inch or so of touching. Letting Connor know in the strongest possible terms that she was not alone in this.

What Connor thought was, *I was right to come.*

Connor said, 'I need your help. I hate asking. Especially for this.'

'What if I went ahead and said yes in advance?'

'Don't speak too fast. You haven't heard what this is about.'

'Just the same. Yes.'

Connor breathed deeply. Felt the tension she'd carried from Byron's office gradually ease. 'I'd always thought we'd become friends. You know. Someday.'

'Let's make that now,' Jackie said. 'Tell me what's wrong.'

So she did. Just laid it out. From entering Byron's office that morning to now.

Midway through the telling, Jackie pulled over a yellow legal pad and pen and started writing. Connor protested, 'Byron says no records. He even told Rachel not to make notes.'

Jackie kept writing. 'This helps me think. I'll shred it soon as we're done.' She rolled one finger. Continue.

When Connor was done with her telling, the only sound was Jackie's pen, drawing arrows, making circles around words Connor didn't feel any need to read.

Then, 'So. About your ask. I see five immediate tasks. Maybe six. Starting with me checking in with Byron, making sure he's OK with me being involved.'

'Call him. Now.'

Jackie reached for her desk phone, dialed, waited, then, 'Rachel, it's Jackie Barlow. Could I please have a word . . .'

She hung up.

Connor asked, 'What just happened?'

'Byron instructed Rachel that in case I called, I needed to contact him via his and my encrypted phones.'

'He mentioned something about that.'

Jackie swiveled her chair around, used her thumbprint to open a safe set in the side wall's credenza and pulled out a different phone. 'A couple of months ago, I set Byron up with a next-gen satphone. Automatic encryption of all calls and texts. At the time, it was a just-in-case sort of move.'

Jackie tapped it awake, scrolled through the speed-dial numbers, touched one. She watched Connor as it rang, then, 'Sir, it's . . . Yes, she's here now . . . Very well. Thank you . . .'

She set her phone on the corner of her desk. Took a long moment. Then, 'He agrees in advance to whatever you and I decide. And he said we needed to hurry.' Jackie wrote the word on her pad. Began drawing a star around it. *Hurry.* 'Where were we?'

'I have no idea.'

'Next steps.' She looked up. 'Denton's right. Your best bet moving forward is for you two—'

'Don't say it.'

'To start an affair. It doesn't have to be love. My job is to spread the word that NovaCorp's Ice Queen is melting.' Jackie almost managed a smile. 'I'll call it lust at first sight.'

'Is that what they call me? The Ice Queen?'

'Of course not. Doesn't matter. Will you please pay attention?'

'I'm trying not to. Denton Hayes. Me.' Connor shuddered.

'Moving on.' Jackie flipped back to her first page. 'You need to completely separate what people see from what you're actually doing.' Jackie reached into her open safe, pulled out another phone, this one still in bubble wrap. 'Here.'

The polished black surface was utterly featureless. 'It's heavy.'

'Compared to older models, this one is feather light. You're holding the very latest satphone. Automatic encryption. Untraceable. Number's taped to the back. I'll give you mine and Byron's.' She set another on the desk. 'This one's for Denton.' Jackie waited while Connor stowed both in her purse, then went on, 'Next, your day job. I'll work on this with Rachel. We'll drown you in new work, tell your staff it's all from Byron, very urgent. Won't take you more than a few minutes each day.'

'Great.'

'What about your new flame's day job?'

'Don't call him that. Byron's already got him working on something with Camila Suarez.'

Jackie leaned back. Studied her intently.

'What?'

'I've heard about this. What Suarez has become involved in has crazy written all over it. I wonder if Byron thinks they're linked.'

'What is it?'

'Let Denton tell you. I've only gotten snippets from my crew.' Another smile. 'I can already see the sparks flying between you two.'

NINETEEN

Denton took the stairs down two levels and entered the hushed arena of money central. The actual traders who handled the tens of billions in NovaCorp's care occupied three raucous floors directly below this one. Denton had several pals among the traders. He loved the explosive energy that dominated the trading floors. It was unlike anything he had ever known. Even more powerful than the steady low-key tension of the police stations.

The twelfth floor was so quiet he thought he could almost feel the electric friction, like an energy that pulsed a thousand times per second, blanketing the air he breathed. It held the hushed intensity of a chapel dedicated to the creation of wealth.

The research division dominated the central bullpen. The private offices rimming the outside walls housed the investment division's six directors. Denton had heard conflicting opinions about Camila Suarez. To some, including almost all the traders who answered directly to her, Camila was brilliant, mercurial, lightning fast in her decisions, fiercely protective of her people. She was also responsible for a greater share of corporate profit than any other investment team. Her detractors – and there were many – claimed she was dictatorial, ruthless and prone to fearsome rages. She was not in her office when Denton arrived. Her PA, a slender young man with a bow tie and nervous tic, told him to wait.

Ten minutes later, she strode in. Camila wore a short khaki skirt over muscular legs and tested the fabric's limits with each impatient stride. Pale cream jacket, matching silk T-shirt, simple gold necklace and Cartier tank watch. She was hawk-faced with short-cropped dark hair and a predatory gaze. 'Hayes, right? Inside.' The pneumatic spring kept her from slamming the door, but she gave it her best. 'I just came from the chief. Byron says I'm supposed to trust you. I am totally against having you become involved. This could be the biggest investment project NovaCorp's landed in years. Of course it has to be vetted. But I need someone who gets what we're doing here. Not a former cop.'

'You want this checked out by a senior investment executive,'

Denton offered. 'Somebody on your floor. Or your rep on the board. I understand.'

'He tells me you hold the power to green-light this move or squash it dead. His words.' She looked ready to strike him. 'I don't like it and I don't like you.'

Denton saw no need to respond.

'He told me about your accounting background. That means nothing to me. Zip. Zero. Nada. You're a pest. Nothing more. Involving you risks millions. More.'

Denton gave it a beat. Then, 'Did it help any, your venting like that?'

'Some. A little. Not enough.' She reached for the doorknob. 'Let's go.'

As they entered the elevator, Denton said, 'I need to take my own ride. I'll be going straight on to another appointment.'

Camila's only response was to stab the button for the basement garage. She did not speak until they exited the elevator. 'Where are you parked?'

Denton pointed. 'Black Land Cruiser.'

Her skirt snapped tight with each angry stride, *thwock, thwock, thwock*. She beeped the car lock to an Audi A7. She opened the driver's door, called out, 'Try and keep up.'

As they left the garage and headed west on Sunset, Denton's disposable phone chimed. Connor started in with, 'I have a new satphone. Soon as we meet, so do you.'

'Excellent. Any update?'

'I agree in principle to your plan, with one caveat. You have one day to prove beyond reasonable doubt all this is worth the risk. Byron's timeline.'

Denton nodded to the sunlit windscreen. A fixed target could work in their favor.

'Denton?'

'Three things. First, we need to have dinner at the finest restaurant in Palos Verdes.'

'That's easy enough to identify. Harder to make happen. The place is called Mar'sel. Hugely expensive. Impossible to get a last-minute reservation.'

'Can Byron help?'

'I'll ask. Why is this important?'

'We need to be seen. But not tracked. An exclusive restaurant won't allow watchers inside.'

A pause. Then, 'Same question. What will be doing that can't be traced?'

It was Denton's turn to hesitate. He heard a soft echo to Connor's words. Which meant she had put him on speaker. Someone else was listening in. He started to ask who that might be. Then decided it was his turn to trust her. He said, 'There's a family named Petridis – husband and wife both teach at USC. No idea what departments. They live in Palos Verdes. I need you to find and download recent photos, send them to this number. Then contact them on their home number. Say tonight we'll be eating at that restaurant – sorry, I don't remember . . .'

'Mar'sel.'

'Mention my name. Tell them I have information for Mrs Stiles.'

A longer pause. Then, 'Three things?'

'We need a signal. Either of us can use it, or Byron and Rachel—'

'And Jackie Barlow. She's involved with Byron's OK.'

'I know her. Good. *Parti Pris*. You know the term?'

'I'm a lawyer, Denton. Of course I know.'

Legally, the term meant a firmly held prejudice or opinion that tainted the outcome. 'There's a second definition. Very ancient. In old French, it means to grasp the hidden agenda. Take firm hold of the secret danger.' He paused. When Connor remained silent, he went on, 'The very instant one of us uses that term, everything changes. The team gathers. We move into high gear. We go on the attack.'

Connor said slowly, '*Parti Pris*.'

'Whatever it takes,' Denton said. 'We're closing in. We need all the help we can get.'

Connor cut the connection and sat staring at the phone. It rested on the corner of the desk between them, gleaming dark as an oblong jewel. The sound quality, even on speaker, was incredible. Denton's voice had come through amazingly clear. Full tonal effect, no distortion, almost as if he had been there in the room with them. She said, 'I don't get it.'

Jackie frowned at the silent phone and did not respond.

'Does that sound like a guy on the edge to you? Somebody barely holding things together?' When Jackie remained quiet, she demanded, 'Well, does it?'

'He sounds like a cop.'

The chair could no longer hold her. Connor rose and started pacing. 'I don't like going into this with so many questions. How am I supposed to trust a guy I can't get a handle on?'

Jackie waited until Connor reached the far wall and started back. 'The last three years I was on the force, I worked as liaison on a couple of major busts. The guys who worked undercover, they had this way of talking. Not just calm. Their manner with us, calm doesn't even begin to describe them. They were totally, utterly . . .'

'Tell me.'

Jackie grasped the air before her face. 'Like they had this ability to be rock solid. So tight and together, the things they faced on the street couldn't get to them.' She nodded to the phone. 'That's how Denton sounded.'

'Together. Solid.'

'I know that goes against what I've been saying. Just the same . . .' Jackie watched Connor make another circuit of her office. 'Do you know guns?'

'Not even in theory. No guns.'

'OK, Lipstick Taser then.' She offered a tight smile to Connor's blank expression. 'My two kids are Minion crazy.'

'And Minions are . . .'

'Girl, you have got to get out more.' Her smile was a trace more defined. 'Maybe this thing with Denton—'

'Don't you *dare* start down that road.'

'You know, listening to him there, I actually felt better about the whole deal. Whatever it is.'

'Glad one of us feels that way.' Connor gave up on the pacing. Walked back over, picked up her purse and the phone. 'I better go start on the mystery man's requests.'

'And I'll start passing the word our lady is head over heels in love. Or something.' Jackie was still smiling. 'You be sure and give Denton a big hug from me.'

TWENTY

Camila Suarez's destination was a fifties-era bungalow located a few blocks off Pico Boulevard, in a distinctly blue-collar residential area. When Denton rose from his Toyota, traffic from the elevated freeway formed a constant soft thunder. He watched as Camila Suarez approached a woman standing in the home's side doorway. Neither of them looked his way. The woman was similar to Camila, yet very different. NovaCorp's executive was tougher, more dynamic, far more refined. The woman in the doorway was rail thin and very tense. She stood with arms wrapped around the base of her ribcage. Her hair was unkempt and going grey.

Denton had no problem with Camila's simmering anger. Before the courts had intervened, and then in two of his foster homes, Denton's early childhood had been marred by adults who had manipulated each other into almost incoherent fury. As young as five or six, Denton had come to realize that some adults actually *wanted* this. They *enjoyed* it. By then, Denton had developed the quietly observant mask he still wore. He also found his means of escape through numbers. He assumed his teenage passion for flying came from the same desire to escape. Not to mention the sense of control, taking responsibility for the machine and his own life, flying through open air – so many reasons to love planes. But not even his first solo flight could compare to his passion for numbers.

Numbers were clean, precise, trustworthy. People might manipulate them, use them for creating myths. But numbers themselves never lied. Search hard enough, and they would whisper the truth. Denton still found a special delight in uncovering the twisted falsehoods. Numbers remained his friends.

When Camila finally turned and gestured him forward, Denton decided this was why he instinctively liked her. She was at heart a numbers person. She sought the truth. Just like him.

'This is my sister, Sofia.'

'How do you do.'

The woman refused to unwrap her arms or even glance his way. 'Is this absolutely necessary?'

'I've already answered that.' When Sofia remained in the doorway, blocking their path, Camila snapped, 'Do I even look the slightest bit happy with this situation?'

'Then send him away.'

'I've told you three times. The company's chief executive *ordered* me to make this happen. If you want our money, this guy is going to ask his questions. Now get out of the way.'

But as the woman reluctantly stepped back, Denton told Camila, 'This isn't what you think.'

'Oh, really.'

'Whatever your project is, my being here has nothing to do with giving it the green light.' He kept his gaze on Camila but directed his words at both women. 'This is about something much bigger.'

Camila took a wide stance, planted fists on hips and replied, 'I don't believe you.'

'You have no reason to. Yet. But listen carefully to the questions I need to ask, and you'll see.'

His words released a fraction of both women's tension. Enough that he was allowed into the kitchen and granted a seat at the dining table. Denton accepted a glass of iced tea he didn't want and waited until Sofia was seated beside her sister to say, 'I need to call Byron.'

'You're just going to bounce into the chairman's office, have a little afternoon chat?'

'Yes. May I?'

She glanced at her sister, said, 'Go ahead.'

Denton used his burner phone to call Rachel, who answered so swiftly that she could easily have been sitting there with one hand hovering over the phone. Waiting for him to reach out. 'Yes?'

'Does Byron have a secure means of contacting me?'

'He does, yes.'

'Can Byron call me back on this number?'

'Hold, please.' She was back almost instantly. 'Thirty seconds.'

Denton set the phone on the table between him and the two women. When it rang, he put it on speaker and said, 'Sir, I am here with Camila Suarez and her sister.'

'Can they hear us?'

'Affirmative.'

'Is this line encrypted?'

'No, but this is a burner that is only used by us and Connor.'

A pause, then, 'Go ahead.'

'In order to obtain what we need from Ms Suarez and her sister, it's necessary to reveal at least part of why I'm here.'

Byron took longer to respond, 'You realize the risk this represents?'

'I think so.'

'Camila, you there?'

She leaned closer. 'I am, sir. Good afternoon.'

'Every question you insist on asking carries significant consequences. To you and your family.'

Sofia's tension became electric. 'What type of consequences?'

'Who is that speaking?'

'My sister. Sofia.'

'Listen carefully. The safest way forward is to grant Denton what he needs, then forget this ever took place.' The line went dead.

Sofia's stress level lifted her voice a full octave. 'What is going on here?'

'Byron is worried about an event carrying such a high level of threat that it could push NovaCorp into bankruptcy,' Denton replied. 'The only reason I'm here is to determine whether Camila's project is tied to this greater risk.'

'My son has nothing to do with anything like this!' Sofia pointed at the kitchen door. 'I want you and your dangers out of my house!'

Denton remained utterly shielded from the woman's ire. 'I need to ask your son just a couple of questions – three at most – and I'm gone.'

Before Sofia could argue, Camila told her sister, 'The only way you are getting paid is by letting this happen.'

'Don't you *dare* threaten me.'

'I'm trying to make you see reality. I've got the cash in my trunk, Sofia. And the only way it's entering this house is for you to let Denton ask his questions.'

Sofia took up the same position as when they first arrived. Holding tight to her fears by gripping her arms around her middle. 'What now?'

'Tell me about the son.' Denton opened the file Rachel had given him and pretended to search for the boy's name. 'Goyo.'

'Goyo is Spanish for Greg. He insists we use the English name now. Since last week.'

This time, when her sister went silent, Camila said, 'Greg is . . . special.'

'In what way?'

'Depends on who's talking,' Camila said, watching her sister now. 'But the issues are definitely mental.'

Sofia muttered, 'You always make it sound like your nephew is retarded.'

'I never use that word,' Camila said. 'Not once. Not ever.'

'Greg is a genius. I've known it since he started talking.'

Camila did not respond.

'The problems I've had, dealing with a system that refuses to look beyond the obvious.' It was just the two sisters now. Repeating a conversation they'd been having for years.

Camila said, 'We finally got him into a school that focuses on special-needs teens.'

'Thanks to Camila,' Sofia said. 'I always thought it was a good move. Until last week.'

'The changes you've recently seen in Greg weren't connected to the school and you know it,' Camila replied.

Denton asked, 'When did these changes start?'

Another long look between sisters, then Camila said, 'Eleven days ago?'

'About then,' Sofia agreed.

'Change how?'

'Greg started living in what was my home office. I work part-time for a bank's call center. Whenever I walked in to start my shift – middle of the night, daybreak, it didn't matter – he was there using my computer, working on this data stream. I didn't even know what that meant before this happened.'

Camila said, 'End of last week, Sofia shows up in my office with two buy orders.'

'Greg insisted. It wasn't a request. It was, "Do this or I run away."'

'Which was the only reason I agreed to do a mock trade,' Camila said. 'The kid was beyond crazy.'

'Don't use that word.'

'Well, that's what it was. Crazy in the extreme. Going totally nuts when you asked him to stop with the silly notions. I came. I saw it for myself.'

'You saw one tiny fragment of what I'd been living through for days and nights.'

Denton said, 'You did the mock trade. Then what?'

'The timing and results were exactly what Greg said. Then he came up with another trio of instructions. This time, I made real trades.'

Denton asked, 'What was your return?'

'A hundred and thirty percent.' Camila continued to watch her sister. 'In twenty-eight hours.'

Sofia said, 'Then he did it again. Handed me these little notes. Words and numbers I didn't understand.'

'That was another crazy thing. How this kid was using the Nasdaq symbols for companies, the current trading range, where we needed to go long or short, the precise timing of our trades. All of it.' Camila pointed to Denton's file. 'Which brings us to the latest item. And why we're sitting here.'

'It's perfectly reasonable for us to gain from this,' Sofia said.

'Nothing about this is reasonable,' Camila replied. 'Your son has gone from being cocooned inside a silent world all of his very own to negotiating for a commission with NovaCorp.'

'You really brought us the money? All of it?'

Camila shot Denton a glance. 'I told you. It's in the car. Two hundred and fifty thousand dollars.'

'I need to see it.'

'Sofia—'

'Now, Sis.' She pointed at Denton. 'You want me to let this stranger speak with my boy, it's payment in advance.'

The two sisters remained locked in mutual glares for a long moment, then Camila rose. She shot Denton a look. As in, *See the trouble you're causing me.* 'I'll be right back.'

When it was just the two of them, Sofia said, 'Camila and her company are going to make a fortune off my Greg. And she still makes me beg. Like we don't deserve part of what's been happening here.'

Denton had the distinct impression she was not addressing him. 'What else can you tell me about your son?'

She eyed him with distaste. Turned away. Denton thought that was all he was going to get from her. Then she said, 'Greg is a very special individual. The world wants to fit him into their tight little square hole. And he won't go. He'll *never* go. So they do their best to push him to the side and ignore him.'

Denton remained silent.

She continued to address the empty doorway. 'Greg has always been quiet. And extremely observant. But because he doesn't like to talk, it's easy to ignore just how gifted he is.' A pause, then, 'Greg loves puzzles. Diagrams. Riddles. He takes things apart, studies them, then walks away. Sometimes he puts them back together, but only if he's interested in something. His attention is total.'

Denton asked, 'What about his interest in the markets?'

'Stocks, bonds, futures, currencies . . . commodities. I didn't even know what that word meant until last week.' Sofia looked at him. A nervous woman, years of dealing with a nearly impossible situation etched into her features. 'Three afternoons a week, I take him to the local community center. He meets with friends he's known online for years. They're fascinated with e-games. Greg likes to play, but his real interest is in how they're put together. They meet and they talk and sometimes they play, sometimes they break into the game's structure. All you see on the screen is this flow of numbers and symbols.'

Camila entered, carrying a battered leather valise. Denton lifted one finger, motioning for silence. 'What happened eleven days ago?'

Sofia nodded, intent on him now. As though she'd waited all this time for someone to ask that very question. 'The answer is, I have no idea. But he became a lot easier to deal with. More focused on the world outside his latest puzzle. More *engaged.*'

'And he started on the markets.'

'That very afternoon. Talking with his online pals, his other games and puzzles totally forgotten. Like they never existed. Now I have to order him to eat, go to bed. Mornings, I wake up, he's already there. Working his screens.' Her fingers began a nervous dance. 'I'm so worried this thing might consume him. Just burn him up.'

Denton rose to his feet. 'Can I please speak with your son?'

Behind the kitchen, the rear of the house was dominated by a glassed-in garden room. Translucent blinds covered all the windows, casting the interior in a murky twilight. A young man was seated with his back to the door. Before him, a table ran the length of the room. On it were three laptops with the most brilliant screens Denton had ever seen.

'Adamant Custom Workstations,' Camila said. 'Fourteen thousand dollars a pop. Compliments of NovaCorp.'

'Oh, please,' Sofia said. 'Like you were so happy to give him the equipment he needed.'

Camila demanded, 'Exactly when did I become the bad guy in this picture?'

Sofia huffed but did not respond.

The screens held running streams of graphs and data. News alerts ran at the bottom of two screens, moving so fast that Denton had difficulty reading the words.

The bespectacled young man was dressed in T-shirt and boxers. Rubber sandals. Pale limbs, the skin white as bleached bones. Long fingers typed at hyperspeed. Dark hair fell over eyes that flittered from one screen to the next.

'Greg, darling, there's someone—'

'Did they bring it?'

'The money? I haven't had time to count, but—'

'Wait.'

His fingers moved like pale spider-legs, flying over the keyboards. Then he stopped typing and scribbled on a pad by his elbow. He tore off the page and reached behind him. 'Hi, Aunt Camila. You need to go long on all three. And the futures market for silver is about to tumble. Go short. Big as you can. Do it today.'

Camila stepped forward, cast Denton an uncertain look, then took the page. 'What size for the longs?'

'Big as they let you. Hold for forty-four hours. Sell. Silver starts falling tonight. But it's a temporary shift. The rumor they're chasing is bogus. This time tomorrow, get out.' He continued to watch the electronic rivers. 'Is Father back yet?'

'He called twenty minutes ago. He said to tell you everything is arranged.'

'Are you packed?'

'Mostly. Greg, honey, are you certain—'

'You agreed. The moment Father returns, we move.'

Camila asked, 'What's going on, Sis?'

'She can't tell you.' The head came up, like a feral beast tasting the shadowy air. 'Here he comes. Go get started.'

Denton watched as Camila walked to the windows facing the drive and pulled open the drapes. 'What on earth is your husband driving?'

'I have no idea. Terrance said we were going to need a bus, the biggest he could rent on short notice. Greg found him a Mercedes. It cost us a fortune. Which is why the money . . .' Sofia looked at her son, who was in the process of closing down his workstations.

'Every time I ask Greg what on earth is going on, all my son will tell me is that I need to wait with the questions. I don't even know why we're running. Greg won't say. And his father is no better. Four nights back, Terrance went through his own version of what has happened to my son. Ever since, the two of them have been laying down tracks.'

The boy kept stacking his laptops and winding the cables. His motions deliberate. Almost solemn. 'Hurry, Mother.'

Denton watched the narrow woman hesitate, her features twisted in fear. Then a man's voice called her name from the front door, and she slipped from the room.

Denton addressed Greg, or started to. 'Can I ask—'

The young man interrupted him. 'One question. Just one.'

It was Denton's turn to taste the air. Sofia stepped back into the doorway. Watching. Denton asked, 'Will NovaCorp survive?'

Greg stopped. He turned his chair so as to face Denton, looking at him directly for the very first time. He smiled. 'That is the right question.'

Denton heard Camila respond with a sharp intake of breath. He asked, 'And the answer is . . .'

'With you involved, maybe. Probably.'

'When will we know for certain?'

'That's another question. Sorry.'

A tall man, an older and stronger version of his son, appeared in the doorway next to his wife. 'We're ready.'

Greg asked, 'Do you have a burner you can give me?'

Denton hesitated, then passed it over. 'The number's taped on the back. I'm supposed to be given a satphone with encryption.'

'Let me have that number soon as you can.' Greg pocketed the phone.

Terrance checked his watch. 'Son . . .'

'One moment.' Greg continued to smile at Denton. 'Will you take advice?'

Denton took his time. Angling for a handle on this kid who was definitely not a kid. Or showing any of the signs of a special-needs teen. The calm, the intensity, the focus, the certainty . . .

He said, 'Absolutely.'

'When someone approaches you and mentions the word "threads," pay careful attention.'

Denton was still trying to shape the young man's words into

some form that made sense when Greg rose and handed his father
a shopping bag full of cables. He hefted the laptops and followed
his father from the room. He paused in the doorway and said,
'Remember, Aunt Camila. Hold the buys for forty-four hours
and not a moment longer. And your silver contracts have to be
covered tomorrow afternoon. Don't let your traders be fooled by
the market. What they think they see is a myth.'

Denton remained standing there as three voices exited the house.
There was the sound of doors slamming and a diesel engine starting.

Camila stood by the side window, the drapes pulled aside,
watching as her family disappeared into the sunlit afternoon. 'I don't
understand. They didn't even bother to lock up.'

Denton continued to study the empty table. 'You need to report
to Byron the very instant you're back. Phone Rachel from the road,
make sure he's there and ready to listen.'

'What do I tell him?'

'Everything that happened, everything that was said. From the
moment we showed up.' Denton headed for the kitchen. 'We're all
done here. I have to get to my next appointment.'

'Wait!' She followed him back through the house, her former ire
utterly vanished. 'What if he asks for your take on all this?'

Denton beeped open his ride, stood in the westering sun,
welcoming the heat. This pressure on his body, the dry, acrid taste
of another hot LA afternoon, anchored him to the earth. 'Tell him
I'll be in touch as soon as I have something definite. But my gut
tells me that we don't have a week.'

TWENTY-ONE

Connor noticed the tail a block after leaving NovaCorp. The cherry-red pickup followed her west, weaving in and out of traffic. Big, oversized tires, darkened windows, that rack of ridiculous lights across the cab's roof. Like they wanted her to know she was being tracked. Like they didn't care if she was frightened. Like they were bulletproof.

As Connor pulled into the Palos Verdes resort's parking area, she watched the cherry-red pickup peel away, turn a corner and disappear.

By the time she entered the restaurant, Connor had left scared behind. She was angry.

Mar'sel was a jewel in the crown of the peninsula's top boutique hotel, the Terranea. Connor had heard about the place for years but never managed to snag a table. She followed the hostess through the main dining room, out to the broad flagstone terrace with its jaw-dropping views over the cypress groves, the rooftops, the Pacific.

Denton was so intent on his phone he did not notice her arrival until her shadow fell over the table. He jerked to his feet, pulled out earbuds, held her chair, said, 'You look lovely.'

So far, so good. She declined the waiter's offer of a drink, and when they were alone, she said, 'I'm pretty sure I was followed.'

Denton nodded. 'That fits the pattern.'

'What pattern is that?'

'I'll explain. First, I want you to see something.' He used a napkin to clean the earbuds. 'Sorry, these are my only pair.'

'Oh, please. How could I possibly be bothered by your earbuds when we're supposedly starting a torrid affair?'

'Was that a joke?'

'No. Well, maybe half of one.' She fit the earbuds in place. 'What am I seeing?'

'This is a video of a TED Talk given eight days ago by Professor Sean Stiles. Before you watch this, I need you to understand who he is. I've met the man a couple of times. I've also researched him. Extensively.' Denton spoke without inflection or shame. As if it was normal for a professional investigator to track the husband of a woman he loved. 'Professor Sean Stiles has no sense of humor whatsoever. His colleagues and wife describe him as somber. Pompous. Pedantic. Too handsome for his own good. He is also a notoriously sloppy dresser. Despite this, he holds some kind of magnetic draw when it comes to young female students. His colleagues scorn him, both for his string of barely suppressed scandals and for how he has never, in their opinion, had an original thought. He makes his mark through reworking other people's ideas. Polishing them. Adding a few missing elements. Some of his enemies consider him little more than a thief with degrees. It's apparently a pattern found in many second-rate academic minds.'

'What am I supposed to be watching here?'

He tapped the screen. 'Take a look.'

Professor Sean Stiles was dressed in a black knit shirt, midnight-blue gabardine slacks, tasseled loafers so polished they reflected the overhead spots. Freshly styled hair, immaculately groomed. He stood to one side of a circular stage, surrounded by steeply banked seats. Every seat visible on the screen was taken. Beside him was a movie-sized white screen, displaying seven lines of very complex mathematical symbols.

Sean began, 'These equations represent some of the most challenging issues currently breaking the heads of mathematicians and theoretical physicists. Over the past five or six years, a vague whisper-campaign has swept through the halls of our top universities and think-tanks. People in the know are suggesting we've taken these issues as far as we can. Unless there is a new Einstein-size breakthrough, we will never resolve them. From where we stand today, they will remain impenetrable mysteries.'

The man was, in a word, arresting. He was beyond handsome. Connor had met several film stars, and in this first glimpse, she was certain the professor held that same sort of incredible draw. Dark hair, cleft chin, tall . . .

Magnetic.

'There is only one point on which all of my colleagues are in unanimous agreement. And that is, I am no Einstein.' He released a brilliant smile in response to the audience's laughter. 'What I may be able to do here is ask a *different* question. What if it's not our level of mathematical knowledge? What if we already know enough? Instead, what if it's a question of our perspective?'

The man Connor watched was dynamic. Cheerful. He *connected*. It was a rare gift, this ability to make everyone in the audience feel like he spoke directly to them. He shared their space. That was how Connor felt.

'Some of our greatest progress has come through challenging assumptions. The earth is not flat. Nor does the universe rotate with our planet at its center. Nor is it held up on a collection of giant elephants, balanced on the head of a universal pin.' His face replaced the equations, offering a gigantic version of his smile. 'We only have time to challenge one assumption today. And here the audience says, "Hallelujah."'

'So why don't we look at the concept of duality? It's as good a place as any to begin, since it dominates so much of our thinking. Right–left. Light–dark. Newtonian gravity versus quantum.' He momentarily lost his smile. 'Life or death.'

He continued, 'So much of what we see, how we think and feel and measure, comes down to this core biological and mental component of the human makeup. But what if duality did not exist? How would we see the world and all these supposedly unanswerable questions?'

The seven equations flashed back on the screen as Sean said, 'You can't simply erase this issue of duality and work in a mental vacuum. You need a replacement concept. And for this I propose . . .'

A new image shone on the screen.

'We have recently identified several stellar systems containing seven suns with planets in what appear to be stable orbits. We class these as hierarchical systems, where four central stars hold to a pair of inner enclosed loops, with three more stars in a tertiary loop further out. Their combined orbits look something like . . .'

The series of interwoven loops looked as complex and precise as a stellar clock.

'So how do their planets maintain stable orbits? Some astronomers claim it isn't possible. They insist we can't draw such a conclusion from one glimpse at one tiny point in time. So I've spent the past few sleepless nights working out their orbit, showing this is indeed not just possible, but happening.'

A massive equation replaced the orbiting suns – hundreds and hundreds of symbols.

'Please feel free to check my math.' He paused for laughter as the equation was replaced by an even more complex mobile image.

Only now there were four small silver orbs included in this stellar dance. 'This is the system described by my calculations. Here we see four planets orbiting the central binary systems, with elongated shifts every two hundred years as the other suns come within range. Stable and yet not stable. Imagine life on such a planet. Sunlight is constant. There is effectively no night. Once every six hundred and fifty years, the suns gather and the heat intensifies. Seas boil, life withers, unless this planetary life form has adapted to spend several decades every cycle far underground. Ditto for their water supply. Ground water vanishes. But if their primary sources are very deep, the surface temperature is a temporary issue. One they have learned to live with.

'And gravity. In each six-century cycle, there is a forty-nine-year gap. For this period, all seven suns are close enough to impact the planet's gravitational system. Gravity varies day by day, even hour by hour. The residents living through their underground phase experience variations in their weight and even the direction their bodies are pulled. Seven suns they cannot see compete for their attention. And then it passes, their world stabilizes, and they return to life in the open. On a world where there is no night.'

The seven equations returned to the screen. 'What would that mean in terms of how they view such issues as these . . .'

Connor hit pause and removed the earbuds. 'All right, I've seen enough.'

Denton stowed away his gear. 'Tell me what you thought.'

'Obviously, you wanted me to see that it's not the man you described.'

'Right.'

'I'm assuming you're going to tell me this is also part of a pattern.'

'Excellent.' He motioned to the hovering waiter. 'Let's order, then I'll explain.'

Connor let Denton order for them both and approved his choices. One plate only. Filet of halibut roasted over an open fire. California asparagus. White wine redux. Saffron rice. A glass of Sauterne for her, water for the gentleman. Connor rarely allowed someone else to choose her meal. She was very into food, loved taking her time, inspecting every item and combination of ingredients on the menu. But not tonight. She could feel an immense pressure growing, drawing her into the flow of events. She needed to remain focused on what was out there. Tracking her to the restaurant, changing a professor she already detested into an altogether different man.

Not to mention coming to terms with a colleague she suspected she did not know at all.

While they waited for the meal, and then as they ate, Denton gave her a very detailed account of his afternoon. From standing in Byron's outer office, reading the file Rachel supplied on Camila Suarez's nephew. Going to the young man's home, the conversations with Camila and her sister, and the single question he was allowed to ask.

Denton described his sense that all these impossible events were somehow tied together. By the time he finished, Connor had the feeling that she was finally with him. Walking step by step with this man toward answers. Sharing the hunt. *Trusting* him. Which went against everything she had previously learned about Denton Hayes. Just the same, as soon as the waiters had removed their empty plates and they declined the offer of dessert, she asked, 'What is your take on this?'

He nodded. The slight movement gradually becoming a motion that took in his entire upper body. A subtle rocking in place, timed to his words. 'Have you ever heard of fractal patterning?'

'Sorry, no.'

'It's a type of mathematical structure. Incredibly complex. Basically, it refers to a form where the core pattern is constantly repeated. Every part of the fractal is made of the exact same design. Zoom out, move in, any and every segment represents the whole. Fractals surround us in so many aspects of the physical universe. And no one knows why. Some quantum physicists believe it is a fundamental component of the physical universe at the smallest levels. They believe fractal patterning contains the key to combining the four fundamental forces.'

'OK, so . . .'

'Remember what we discussed with Byron. This investigation is not about a missing house.' He continued with his tight rocking nods, a mere fractional movement. 'I think the only way we can solve this is by looking beyond the singular events.'

'Finding the repeating pattern,' she said. 'I get that.'

'We start looking for tiny unexplained elements that appear over and over. Then moving out. Seeing how they might represent a bigger issue. The unseen threat, one so big it frightens Byron and sends us on this wild goose chase.'

She stared at the growing darkness beyond their candlelit idyll, so strong a force it even swallowed the Pacific.

Then Denton pushed back from the table. 'Heads up,' he said. 'It's time for act two.'

TWENTY-TWO

Denton didn't think the couple who took up station on the bar's last two stools looked anything like academics. Kostas Petridis was a ham-fisted bear of a man. His eyebrows grew upwards a full inch, as though they were magnetically drawn to his unkempt iron-grey hair.

The woman seated next to him, Professor Eleni Petridis, was an elfin princess. Long dark hair silvered with a few delicate strands. Eyes like grand opals, far too large for her delicate face. They remained intimately focused on each other as Denton rose from his table and walked to the men's bathroom.

Just the same, ninety seconds later, Kostas lumbered in and started washing his hands in the sink next to Denton.

Denton said softly, 'Ryan was right to run.' When Kostas glanced worriedly at the stalls, Denton said, 'They're empty. I checked.'

'You think this or you know?'

'We don't have time for that.' Denton set a handwritten note on the sink's edge. 'The number to my new satphone.'

'How on earth should I be able to contact a woman I last saw at our party?'

'In that case . . .' Denton started to retrieve the slip, but Kostas was faster, snatching it away. Denton told him, 'Memorize the number, destroy the paper. Nothing stays written down.'

'Do you know what is happening?'

'What has she told you?'

'Nothing. She says that is the only way for us to stay safe.'

Denton nodded. 'Tell her to destroy her old phone, credit cards, all IDs. Stay off the grid. When she's ready, she should call. I want to help.'

Kostas shifted over, started the hand dryer. Kept his voice down to where it was almost completely drowned out. 'And you? You will stay safe?'

Denton left the bathroom, returned to their table, told Connor, 'We should go.'

They returned to both cars and headed north. Connor thought they made a strange sort of procession, her black BMW following Denton's Land Cruiser, and behind them one or more trackers. She had no idea if they were actually being tailed. All she had to go on was how a pair of headlights had pulled from the road leading to the resort as they passed. She was fairly certain the same headlights were still there, holding steady two cars back. She felt threatened, and the feeling made her mad all over again.

She had agreed on their heading to Denton's basically because the alternative was far less appealing. There was no way in heaven or earth she was going to invite Denton Hayes to spend the night in her apartment.

But the closer they came to his tiny home, the more she regretted her decision.

The location was nice enough. Sunset Boulevard circled the northern side of Santa Ynez Lake, then swept down the canyon before dead-ending into the PCH. She knew this area well. There was a parking area just off Los Liones Drive she used every other week or so. Los Angeles had a number of such semi-secluded areas, but the Topanga State Park and Temescal Gateway were her two personal favorites. Both had trails leading up semi-steep slopes that rewarded hikers and joggers with great views and the crisp, spicy air of pine- and eucalyptus-forested slopes.

His home was off Tramanto, a steep road on the northern boundary of Pacific Palisades. The area used to be called Castellamare, but realtors effectively erased that blue-collar name as the builders continued their high-value creep north.

Three silent blocks later, Denton turned right into a narrow, downward-sloping alley and stopped by steel garage doors. As Connor waited for them to open, she wondered if she was making a terrible mistake.

She followed Denton down to the garage's far end. Denton parked between two vehicles draped in specialty canvas covers. He rose from his vehicle and pointed her into the adjoining space. Connor found it odd how a simple studio apartment would possess two highly coveted underground spaces by the elevators. She cut the engine and popped the trunk.

Denton hefted the simple leather valise she used as her go-bag and pointed to the steel door marked *Stairs*. 'You mind walking?'

'Not at all.' She detected a subtle change in her host. A solemnity, so weighty it cast a shadow over them both. Connor wondered if it was somehow tied to her being in a home he had probably once shared with Ryan Stiles.

He walked the stubby first-floor corridor and stopped by a door facing the street. 'You know about my former drug use.' It was not a question.

'Yes, Denton. I know.'

He stepped back, allowing her to enter first.

The studio defined a grim bachelor's life. IKEA furniture. Bare walls. Awful puce-colored shag rug. Bed crammed against the wall opposite his kitchenette. Connor struggled for some polite way to tell him she was not staying here.

'I keep this place as a reminder,' Denton told her. 'The life I'd have if I let myself fall back into that dark pit. Not just drugs. The sorrow. The empty days.'

'I don't understand.'

'This is where I lived during the worst times. I keep it as a reminder of what I'm doing my best to leave behind.'

He motioned for her to step back into the corridor, locked the door and headed back down the corridor.

This time, they took the elevator.

Denton pressed the button for P1, then applied an electronic fob attached to his keychain. They rose four floors, then the elevator opened into a private foyer. 'This is where I live.'

The foyer's pale marble floor was framed with alternating blocks of onyx and blue granite. Denton used the same fob on the double doors' electronic keypad. The main room was grand and high-ceilinged, the furniture very sparse. A single painting above the fireplace was almost swallowed by the otherwise empty walls. 'Ten successful investigations. Ten commissions plus my pay. I've almost paid off the mortgage. Once that's done, I furnish.'

'I don't understand.' Connor set down her valise and walked to the glass wall opposite the entrance. A broad patio opened to the jaw-dropping view of rooftops and, far below, the moonlit Pacific. 'Why keep this a secret?'

He joined her at the window. 'Old habit. I let people see what they want to see. You know about my time in rehab?'

'I went there.'

'Carla is still expecting me to show up?'

'Any day now.'

She watched his reflection in the glass. Denton seemed both sad and stoic, like he was reknitting the mask he showed the world. 'People see this, it's all too easy for them to think I've started dealing.'

'That almost makes sense.'

He pointed to their left. 'There are two guestrooms. Make yourself at home.' He headed for the corridor opening to their right. 'I'm going to bed.'

TWENTY-THREE

Kelly and her team spent the afternoon and evening making their first written report and putting things in motion. Sanjib Gupta's wife became suitably freaked by the agents' silent presence, staking out her house, tracking her every move. She phoned her husband six times, growing ever more strident when he refused to return home early, insisting he had to deliver the conference's closing address. Darren Cotton and his team had full access to the Guptas' phones and emails and fed abbreviated recordings to Kelly. She and her team listened as the recently released postdoc, Singh, phoned in an exhausted panic and related what had happened. When Gupta responded, the doctor sounded both weary and resigned.

Cotton's team also maintained close electronic surveillance on Denton Hayes. As per the NovaCorp CEO's promise, Hayes was pulled off investigating the missing home. He was then sent on some in-house job, one regarding a concern the CEO had over a sizeable investment opportunity. Information was patchy, as the phone Denton used remained silent. He did not access his corporate or personal email accounts. Kelly was not particularly concerned. While she had been seated in Denton's ride, her team had fitted the Land Cruiser with a tracking device. This proved especially important when Denton spotted the team Alvero had put in place to trail him. After Denton called the detective formerly responsible for the missing house, Jon's team was ordered to stay well back. Still on him, but at a distance. Their report confirmed what she was seeing on the laptop's screen. Denton traveled to a private residence with Camila Suarez, a senior member of NovaCorp's investment division. They stayed for just under an hour, long enough to confirm the house belonged to Camila's sister and brother-in-law. While this was happening, they listened via Byron's in-house phone as Denton's boss, NovaCorp's head of investigations, complained loudly to the CEO over Denton being assigned yet another case over which he had no oversight.

Kelly was prepared to close that particular segment of their operation. Except for one loose thread.

Connor Breach, NovaCorp's head of legal, had been a sidebar issue until that afternoon. Her connection to Kelly's investigation had been considered indirect at best, like a shadow cast over a moving target, but not the target itself. On the weight of her being present at several of the meetings, Kelly's team had inserted themselves into her phone. Soon after, Connor communicated with Denton Hayes and mentioned joint conversations with the company's CEO. Following that, she had headed up to Antelope Valley. Which proved to be the turning point.

Darren Cotton's team broke into the rehab center's confidential files and learned Denton Hayes had been there three times. Again, in itself not something of major importance as far as Kelly's team was concerned.

But by this point, the questions were mounting, like a subtle itch inserting itself into Kelly's brain.

She contacted Jon Alvero, requested another team to tail Connor Breach. When the attorney parked somewhere, they were to attach a tracking device.

Then the lawyer lady had gone straight from this jaunt into California's high desert to a meeting with the CEO, followed by dinner at a swanky restaurant in Palos Verdes. With none other than Denton Hayes.

At which point Kelly told her number two, 'The coincidences around these two are mounting.'

Riggs was not convinced. 'This is a highly successful corporate attorney. You ask me, she's interested in getting personal with a co-worker. She knows the guy has a past. She wants to enter whatever this is with her eyes wide open.'

Kelly was not convinced. 'All of this just happens to take place right at the same moment we show up? My gut tells me something more is at work here.'

'Such as?'

'I have no idea.'

The agents not tracking Mrs Gupta and Rabbit were gathered in the apartment serving as their ops center, watching as Riggs said, 'Given everything we've faced so far, gut feelings work for me.'

Kelly checked the wall clock. It was almost eight at night, and she had been hard at it since two the previous morning. She rose to her feet, unkinked her neck and said, 'Soon as we've collected

Doctor Gupta and extracted what we need, we return to Denton Hayes. We add Connor to the mix.'

'Unpluck them both feather by feather,' Riggs agreed. 'Just to be certain.'

'One person on rotating night watch,' she said, starting for the door. 'When Jon shows up, assign him one of the unused apartments in case he needs a place to crash. Somebody come get me when it's my watch. Everyone get some rest.'

Kelly entered her apartment and decided the shower could wait. She settled into bed feeling strangely happy. Sharing their disembodied mission with Jon Alvero, putting successful ops in place regarding the head of UCLA Medical School, fitting together coverage on other potential risks, all this went a long way to anchoring Kelly. This was her new reality. She and her frontline agents were a vanguard force, seeking to halt an alien invasion. Her boss in DC approved of their work. Her team was made up of excellent and highly trained individuals. What was more, they were with her.

Kelly dreamed of having the magical ability to weave order from threads of chaos. Her power was so great she might have drawn the rainbow overhead into her tapestry, except for how a persistent tapping drew her away.

She opened her eyes and realized someone was knocking on her door.

She rose to her feet, padded into the living area, then stopped. If it had been one of her team, they would have phoned her first. She moved at an angle to the front door and placed a hand over the eyehole, wondering if someone was about to shoot and cost her a finger. The knocking continued, faster now. Kelly looked through the spyhole and saw Rabbit.

She unlatched, unlocked, asked, 'What time is it?'

'I don't . . .' He pulled out his phone, said, 'Quarter past six.'

'And?' When he just continued his childlike bounce, shifting from one foot to the other, she demanded, 'Rabbit, what is it?'

'Diyani says it's happened.'

She pulled him inside, locked the door. Moved to the kitchenette and started the coffee machine. 'And Diyani is . . .'

'Remember the group we rescued in Mexico?'

It felt like years ago. Longer. Eons. 'The woman who cried when she touched your face.'

He nodded. 'She's become the head of the group. Or maybe spokesperson is better.'

She watched the coffee drip. Wished she could bark a command, force the machine into a higher gear. 'Because of her relationship with you?'

'No. Well, I can't say . . .' Rabbit smiled. 'OK, maybe.'

'You old Romeo. So, they're now all serving as part of Pendalon's team?'

'Not directly. Not yet. Right now, it's more like they're backing me up.'

'Agnes must be doing backflips.'

'She's pleased, no question. They've been given apartments on an Air Force and NASA base in Maryland. A whole building has been set aside just for them. Unlimited access to base shopping. After what they've been through, they're in heaven.'

'And they're working together to . . .'

'All this is trial and error. But Agnes and the others are worried about this possible new barrier. Actually, this was your guy's idea.'

She poured herself a mug and a second for Rabbit. 'Darren Cotton is working with your team?'

'Sort of. Is there any milk?'

'Sorry. I don't. Ditto on sugar. Or sweetener.' She shrugged. 'Take it like medicine. I do.'

He sipped, grimaced, set the mug aside. 'Darren heard Agnes talking with Grey about this barrier thing. You know, what I mentioned when we were at the missing house. He asked if it was permanent, or maybe just a temporary fix. Which nobody had thought of before. Because if it was temporary, he said we should put teams on rotation. Go twenty-four seven, round the clock, watching in case they popped into view.'

'That is actually a very good idea.'

'Right. Especially because it worked.' There was no smile now. 'Diyani is certain there's been a new infestation.'

'Where?'

'Right here. In Los Angeles. Under our very noses.'

TWENTY-FOUR

Connor emerged at a quarter past seven. She had slept deeply and felt both refreshed and confused. This level of calm was not her normal response to strange circumstances. Particularly when it came to men.

Denton stood by the kitchen's center console, slicing fruit into two bowls. Coffee simmered in a fancy machine behind him. A mug and pitcher and sugar bowl awaited her arrival. She asked, 'Why didn't you wake me?'

'No need. Gupta's flight doesn't land for another two hours.' He used the paring knife to indicate the bowls. 'I can make you a frittata if you like.'

'Is there yogurt?'

'In the fridge. Plain and vanilla flavored. Coffee?'

She was already moving. 'Absolutely.'

'I make it strong. There isn't any sweetener. Sorry.' He smiled. 'When I left yesterday, I wasn't expecting my first-ever houseguest.'

She poured a mug, added milk and leaned against the counter. 'I'm honored.'

He passed her a bowl and began sketching out his plan for the morning. Her only question was regarding transport. They had to assume the watchers were still in place. Not to mention the possibility of trackers having been attached. Which meant neither of their vehicles could be used for the airport run. When Denton assured her that was taken care of, she did not press.

He waited until she had finished eating, then asked for his new satphone. Connor returned to her bedroom, emerged and, at his request, hit the speed dial for Byron. As she listened to him offer their boss a summary of the previous evening's events, she wondered at this sudden level of calm trust. Given the wreckage of her former relationships, not to mention her drunken recluse of a father, trusting men did not come easy. Byron was a rare exception. And now, apparently, Denton Hayes. A man who defied all the evidence she and Jackie had gathered. Connor poured herself a second mug as

Denton backed up, apparently at Byron's request, and summarized his meeting with Greg Alderton. Denton listened a moment, then gave a more detailed account of the TED Talk given by Professor Sean Stiles, the utter disconnect it represented to the man Denton had made it his business to know. Then came his super-fast meeting with the couple in Palos Verdes probably sheltering Ryan Stiles. Denton finished with their plans for the morning, using the safe anonymity of LAX's arrivals terminal as a means of contacting Sanjib Gupta. A brief pause, then Denton thanked Byron for his time and cut the connection. He stood there, cradling her phone in both hands, frowning at the sunlit glass wall.

'What is it?'

He shook his head. 'I feel like we're missing something important.'

There it was again. *We.* Including her with the ease of, well, a partner. Connor drank from her mug and considered what that signified. Denton Hayes was not the only one who had spent a lifetime perfecting the habit of working alone.

He glanced at the wall clock, then faced her. His eyes remained clouded by what he could not identify. 'We'd better get ready.'

When they left the apartment, Denton wore a very upscale jacket; Connor suspected it was a silk and wool weave, mostly slate-grey but with pale-blue undertones. Striped shirt, elegant tie, gabardine trousers, loafers that looked Italian. Gold watch. She tried for a light tone. 'You dressed up for me. How nice.'

He hit the elevator button and smiled. 'You know, I was just thinking it'd be great to do that. Dress up and take you somewhere for real.'

Connor gave herself a mental *Wow*, as in she had no idea how to respond.

When the elevator doors closed, Denton said, 'About our ride.'

'I'm sorry . . .'

'Today, going to the airport.' This time, his smile only touched his gaze. 'Did I say something wrong back there?'

'I actually can't answer that.'

'Spoken like an attorney.' He faced the doors. 'After the police showed me the door and I did rehab to stay out of jail, I spent a couple of months drifting. I had to find work; otherwise, I knew the lure of old habits would be too strong. My dad had a friend; he owned a local delivery service, nineteen trucks, sub-contracted with FedEx and DHL. He became certain someone in-house was skimming. Couldn't figure it out. Afraid if he made noise, he'd lose trade. I discovered he was right, identified the culprits, had friends in the white-collar crimes division pretend like they had put it all together.'

The doors opened into the basement garage. Denton walked over to the left-hand vehicle draped in the canvas cover, and said, 'He paid me off the books. With this.'

Connor actually felt like the moment deserved a huge *ta-da*. Underneath the cover was a work of art. 'We're driving *this*?'

'You know it?'

'Know it? This would be the pin-up on my wall, if I went in for that kind of thing.'

He liked that. 'I don't believe you.'

'What, a girl can't be a petrol head? That's the exclusive domain of guys in T-shirts and badly spelled tattoos?' The steel-grey exterior shone in the garage's harsh lighting, a sculptured jewel with saddle-leather interior. Connor traced her hand down the passenger side, feeling the waxed polish. 'What is this, the eighty-four?'

Denton laughed, perhaps for the first time. At least that she had heard. 'OK. Now I'm really impressed.'

She kept going mainly because she liked how much pleasure he took from this conversation. Like her confessing to a passion for vintage BMWs was enough to unlock another portion of his secret world. Like she cared. 'The E24 was the world's fastest four-seater. Inline six, fuel-injection with four valves per cylinder, reinforced chassis, most powerful brake system in production. Spent the entire decade winning every touring car championship in Europe.'

He studied her from the car's other side. Finally, 'Let's go for a drive.'

For their departure, Denton slipped on a cloth cap and dark Wayfarers and asked her to duck down into the passenger footwell. The engine purred like a contented hunting cat as he started from the garage. 'You OK down there?'

'Long as it's not all day.'

'I see just one team, a cherry-red chromed-out beast.'

'They tracked me yesterday.'

A slow rumble up the incline, stop at the intersection, hard left, then, 'OK, they're out of sight, no interest in following us. You can come up now.'

Denton slipped down to the PCH and headed south. The BMW was a glorious beast of a ride, growling its way through the morning traffic, leaping forward when it had the chance. Connor had always loved cars and speed and the freedom she felt on almost any open road. As if she could outrun her worries, her stress, even her loneliness if the day was fine enough. 'Someday you have to let me drive this.'

'You can drive now.'

'Thanks, but no. I want to save that pleasure for a ride without a destination.'

'Speaking of which, you've met Gupta before, right?'

'Several times.'

'It may be better if you approach him.'

'Whatever you say.' She turned her face closer to the open window and watched the sparkling Pacific flash in and out of view. The wind was a cool morning wash of salt and diesel. They stopped at a light, and she breathed in fragrances from the car's interior, wax and saddle soap. 'I wish we could just forget all about the mysteries and the mess, just drive on down to Mexico.' When Denton did not respond, she looked over and found him watching her, smiling. 'What?'

'I was thinking the exact same thing.'

'No, you weren't.'

A car behind them beeped. Denton refocused on the road and gunned the engine. 'For a lady who knows all my dark secrets, you sure are treating me like . . .'

'A friend.'

He shot her another smile. 'Something like that.'

They didn't speak again. There simply wasn't room for planning or anything else that might stain the moment. When it was time, Denton took the LAX off-ramp and climbed the escarpment and joined the airport traffic. 'Terminal Three, right?'

'Yes.'

The main Los Angeles airport was designed as a giant oval. The terminals rose like concrete pearls around its outer rim, while the interior held office buildings and freight terminals and control tower and parking. Denton entered the T3 deck, took his ticket, and climbed the ramp, circling higher and higher. 'I'd like to park where there's an empty space to either side. The top level will mean the car's baking hot when we get back, but if it's OK . . .'

He jammed on the brakes. The car halted midway into a parking space.

There in front of them stood a woman. Lovely, fragile as a wounded bird, exhausted and weeping.

Denton said, 'That's Ryan.'

TWENTY-FIVE

B y the time they needed to leave for the airport, Rabbit and his team were no closer to identifying the new outbreak's precise location. Kelly had a growing list of questions she needed answers to, starting with how they searched for people they could not actually name. As soon as there was a free moment, she intended to start breaking the mysteries down into bite-size fragments.

Kelly wanted her entire team – those not holding surveillance on the Gupta residence – present for the LAX takedown and whatever came next. Jon Alvero offered to meet her at the terminal, saying she would need his help with airport security. Riggs drove the first SUV. Pamela Garten occupied the front passenger seat. Kelly and Rabbit took the back.

Kelly could see the inability to identify the new target had severely stressed Rabbit. Which was not necessarily a bad thing. Once they were underway, she opted to ease into her questions with something personal. 'Can we go back to what we were talking about in my apartment? It's OK if you don't want—'

'I don't mind. Ask away.'

'Is it hard for you, being away from Diyani like this?'

'Yes and no.' He swung around, not quite facing her, and leaned against the other door. 'We're not in constant contact, if that's what you're thinking. Diyani has her world, her life. Just the same, we're together.'

'I can't imagine what that's like.'

He shrugged. 'I've never been in love before. So I don't have any real basis for comparison. But I get the feeling . . .'

'What?'

'I remember how my parents were. They were a great couple. Totally in sync with each other, right to the end. When Dad's cancer returned and he passed, my mom just fell apart. The defining element of her world was gone; her life was over.' Rabbit pulled off his glasses, rubbed the bright red spots on his nose. 'If I was pressed to make an analysis, I'd say Diyani and I have a new level of openness. It's totally different from what my parents had, but somewhat the same. We feel intensely close in a way that the physical distance doesn't really matter. Well, of course it matters. But not like . . .'

'You're not really apart,' Kelly said. Hurting over where this conversation had gone. But liking it just the same.

'That's it exactly. In the ways that matter most, we're together.' He used both hands to settle his glasses back in place. 'I think my mom and dad had that at some level. What happens now is just more defined. Or complete. I don't know how I can say it any better.'

'You're doing just fine,' Riggs said. 'Although I'm not sure I'm ready to have my ladies know what I'm thinking.'

'That's your problem right there,' Pamela said. 'Ladies. As in, the plural variety.'

'Variety,' Riggs said, bouncing his hands on the wheel. 'That's the key word, all right.'

'You're a piece of work,' Pamela said, smiling. A little.

'Oh, and you have this oh-so-perfect little love life?'

'There's nothing little about my lovers, and don't you forget it.'

Kelly sensed Rabbit shared her appreciation over how the conversation had steered away from the deeply intimate. 'Thank you so much for sharing.'

'I've never talked about this before.'

'I doubt anyone has. At least, to outsiders.'

'You're not that. None of you are. Not to me.'

Riggs responded with, 'Nice to have you on our side.'

'It means the world,' Garten agreed. 'Especially now.'

Her team.

Jon Alvero was parked in the restricted access zone outside the LAX terminal. Riggs flashed his lights and Jon signaled for the uniformed airport security to remove the cones and let them in. When they were parked, Jon greeted them with, 'Gupta's flight has been delayed half an hour.'

'Good.' Kelly had spent the remainder of the journey planning next steps. 'Is there somewhere we can have a quiet word?'

'Not inside.' Jon frowned at the terminal's entrance. 'The man in charge of airport security is not our pal. And he's waiting on the other side of those doors. Ready to mess with our morning.'

'Then let's do it here.' Kelly signaled for Rabbit and Barry to join them in the lead SUV. She then told Pamela and the rest of her team, 'Head inside out of this heat. Somebody grab me a Starbucks. Black.'

When Barry fired up the engine and turned the a/c on max, Jon said, 'I'm in regular touch with the outside crew tailing the two NovaCorp employees.'

'And?'

'Denton Hayes and Connor Breach are still in his condo. Half an hour ago one of the crew slipped inside the garage, confirmed both cars are still there. Not a peep out of them.'

Kelly pushed aside all the unanswered questions about those two. Everything except the immediate needed to wait. She took out her own phone, called Cotton and told Barry, 'Put this on speaker.'

When Darren came on, she said, 'Jon's with me. We need to talk next steps.'

'We're not talking Gupta.'

'Not unless it's necessary.' To Jon, 'This is Darren Cotton, leader of my team's other half.'

'The better half,' Darren said.

'Careful there, sport,' Riggs said.

Kelly told Jon, 'Darren and Rabbit have developed a new approach to identifying possible outbreaks.'

'Outbreak?' Jon said. 'You told me, but I'm not . . .'

'A launch of new telepaths,' Rabbit said. 'Not a lone transition like Professor Stiles. A new group.'

'And this group happens because of a tree that doesn't exist any longer—'

'Leave the details of how it happens for later,' Kelly said.

'Else we'll be here all day,' Riggs agreed. 'And you still won't understand.'

'New outbreak,' Jon said. 'Got it.'

'This new infestation is here. Los Angeles. We're still working on identifying exactly when and where. We should have something definite by the time we finish interviewing Gupta.' Kelly offered a swift summary of what she had in mind with the medical school chief. She finished with, 'I see two options. Everybody else, chime in. If we're lucky, once we identify this new group's location, we make a sweep, bring them all in together. If not . . .'

'You need my help,' Jon said. 'My team.'

'Your agents,' Kelly corrected. 'This isn't something we can hand over to your semi-tame goat brigade.'

'Of course not.' He frowned. 'What should I tell them?'

'You see for yourself how hard it is to come to terms with the new reality,' Riggs said.

'Not to mention the need to keep everybody in the know totally silent,' Rabbit added.

'Which is why I probably shouldn't tell them anything at all.' Jon offered another of those smiles that did not grow beyond his gaze. 'They've seen what happens to agents who don't jump when you bark. I think we can be assured of their cooperation.'

TWENTY-SIX

Connor thought Ryan Stiles was stunningly beautiful. The woman standing by the parking garage's side wall also looked exhausted and frightened, which added considerably to her age. Even so, Ryan held herself with a dancer's poise, seemingly ready to rise on to her toes and leap away at any moment. Tall and slender, auburn hair streaked with gold, eyes that appeared to change color in the poor lighting. Her shading was Scandinavian, her appeal timeless. Connor felt a twinge of something; she was almost tempted to call it jealousy. Not to mention a deep and abiding sympathy for Denton. That brief moment was all she needed to imagine the young and impressionable college student, literally overwhelmed by this somewhat older woman. Her timeless beauty, her magnetic appeal, her desperate need for a good man. Ryan Stiles drew him in and they fell in love, and then, when Denton was at his most vulnerable, she broke his heart.

Connor asked, 'What is she doing here?'

'That is half of the question we must answer.' His voice sounded utterly cold. Not angry so much as clinical. 'The other half is even more important.'

Connor listened closely but heard no hint of everything that had come before. The only evidence of fractured love was there in front of her, on Ryan's exhausted and tear-streaked features. 'How did she know to meet us?'

'Exactly.' Denton cut the motor but kept on the car's lights, aimed at the woman who had twice wrecked his world. 'Ryan being here is the answer to Byron's question.'

Connor glanced over. In the indirect lighting, Denton's face was calm and emotionless as a kabuki mask. 'Will NovaCorp survive?'

He nodded. 'I suspect Byron wasn't just asking about our company.' Denton pointed at the woman standing in his headlights. 'Her presence is the answer.'

'Which is . . .'

'All business. All governments. All the foundations underpinning our culture. All this is threatened by the impossibility of Ryan Stiles standing in this precise spot. Waiting for us.'

When Ryan started toward the passenger door, Denton remained motionless. Watching. Intent. So Connor rose from the car and said, 'Hello, Ryan. I'm Connor.'

'The lawyer. Hi.'

'How did you know I am an attorney?'

But Ryan wasn't listening. She leaned down and looked through the open door, every move dislodging more tears. 'Hello, Denton. Can I come in?'

'That depends. Will you tell us what is going on?'

'All I know,' Ryan replied. 'All I can put in words.'

Denton glanced at Connor, nodded once, then went back to inspecting the concrete wall in front of them.

Connor slipped into the rear seat as Ryan said, 'It's so good to see you again.'

Denton did not reply.

Ryan went on, 'Thank you for warning Kostas Petridis.'

Denton waited until Ryan closed her door, then said, 'Tell us what you know.'

'Two weeks ago, Sean started working on a new project, or concept . . . something. He spent hours talking on the phone and zooming with a contact at MIT.'

'What was his name?'

'Ranjib Singh. He has a relative doing postdoc work in microbiology at USC. I've met him at some university function. Ranjib called the Petridis home number this morning. He said a man would be stopping by. And he would save my life.'

'How did Ranjib know to reach you? You've been in hiding.'

'I asked the very same question. He said answers for things like that needed to wait until I was safe.'

'What happened next?'

Ryan tightened the distance between them. 'Why are you being like this? Why are you so cold?'

'Answer the question or get out of the car.'

When Ryan's only response was to drip tears, Connor asked as gently as she could, 'What happened after that, Ryan?'

'Ten minutes later, less, this man showed up. His name is Greg

Alderton.' Ryan saw Denton jerk in response to the name and asked, 'You know him?'

'Go on,' Denton said. 'What else?'

'Greg gave me very exact instructions, starting with how I needed to meet you here.' She swung around so as to face Connor. 'He's waiting for you in the arrivals hall. There's a news kiosk by the security gate. You need to meet him in . . .' She glanced at her watch. 'Nine minutes. He was very precise about timing.'

'I'm supposed to meet him alone?'

'Denton needs to do something else. Greg will explain.' Another glance at the watch. 'You should hurry.'

'How am I supposed to know this man?'

Denton was the one who replied, 'He's tall. Late teens, early twenties. Chalk-white skin. You can't miss him.'

'I don't like doing this on my own.'

'Just the same.' Denton glanced in his rearview mirror. 'You should probably hurry. And Connor.'

'Yes?'

He shifted in his seat, coming as close as possible to facing Connor straight on. '*Parti pris.*'

TWENTY-SEVEN

When Kelly entered the terminal, a bullish, unattractive man was arguing with her agents. Pamela broke off and walked over, handed Kelly her coffee and declared, 'That guy is being a total pain.'

'Larry Grazer, head of LAX security,' Jon said. 'Former LAPD.'

This was no time for niceties, and Kelly was already pressed by the issues beyond confronting Gupta. She walked over and stopped within inches of his face. 'Chief Grazer, I'm Kelly Kaiser. I believe you know Agent Alvero.'

'I'll need to see some ID.'

'Not happening. You've already wasted all the time we can give you.'

He was a craggy-faced bulldog in an ill-fitting navy jacket. 'You got some nerve.'

'No, Chief. What I have is a very restricted timeline.' She held up her phone. 'Our target is a reluctant witness in a case that goes all the way to the White House. Say the word, and I'll have the President's Chief of Staff personally tell you exactly what he thinks of your giving us a hard time.'

'You don't want that to happen, believe me,' Jon offered. 'Remember my boss? He tried what you're doing. And he's gone. We're talking, what, Guam?'

'He's not here, which for the moment is all that matters.' Kelly waggled her phone. 'What's it going to be?'

Grazer's face grew even redder, but all he said was, 'Where's your target?'

'Arriving on American from San Francisco. Delayed.'

Pamela was checking the overhead screens. 'His flight just landed.'

'You're making an arrest?'

'I already answered that. Pay attention. We are escorting a reluctant witness from the premises.' Kelly pocketed her phone. 'And one way or the other, we are moving. With or without you. We need your decision. Now.'

* * *

Larry Grazer did not speak again until he had badged them through security and they were approaching the gate. 'This is totally against protocol.'

Kelly let Jon Alvero reply, 'Say the word, Chief. I'm sure Agent Kaiser would be more than happy to arrange for a call you never want to have happen.'

Grazer watched as Kelly's team fanned out, setting up station around the jetway's entrance. 'Can you at least tell me what in blue blazes is going on? I mean, it is my airport.'

'Certainly.' Kelly showed her team an open palm. Wait. 'With or without your help, everyone in this area is going to take a giant step away from the doorway leading planeside. That includes the ground crew behind the desk.' When he looked ready to argue, she moved in close a second time. 'Do please let me know if you feel inclined to make trouble. I'm happy to have someone higher up the food chain clarify the situation to your boss, who I assume is . . .'

'Airport director,' Jon offered. To Grazer, 'She means what she says.'

Pamela motioned to the ground crew opening the jetway portal. 'Plane is about to disembark.'

'Time's up,' Kelly said. 'Back away now.'

'See, that's why I love working with the feds.' But Grazer did as he was instructed.

Kelly told Riggs, 'Clear the area.' She stood front and center, Jon at her side, while agents moved passengers and staff alike.

As she started down the jetway, however, Rabbit moved up alongside and asked, 'Something's come up. Maybe. I need to call Darren Cotton. It's urgent.'

Kelly wanted to stop, question, possibly even shift gears. But events were pressing her forward. Eyes watched on all sides. Hostile gazes. She handed Rabbit her phone. 'Hit one on speed dial.'

Two ground staff, the flight's entire cabin crew and their co-pilot were all gathered by the plane's door. Kelly badged them, then left Pamela to speak the proper words. 'Where?'

'First class, seat three C.' Riggs tracked her every step. 'That's him.'

Dr Sanjib Gupta already had a leather valise by his feet, and his jacket folded neatly on top of the briefcase in his lap. He was a narrow, handsome man in his late sixties, silver-haired and trying hard to remain calm. 'Doctor Gupta, I'm Agent Kaiser with Homeland Security. Will you come with us, please?'

Only then did he look her way. 'Most certainly.'

TWENTY-EIGHT

Connor took the stairs down four levels and joined the crowd and waited until the light halted traffic along the terminal's main thoroughfare. The heat was blistering but welcome, because it anchored her to the immediate world. The noise and the traffic and the planes rushing overhead might not have been enough. The heat definitely helped.

She entered the terminal's cool wash thinking about the face Denton had shown his former lover. He had offered Ryan a clear declaration that the door was slammed shut on another dose of their on-again, off-again relationship. He had revealed nothing more than a cold, hard response to old temptations, and a grim determination not to reopen old wounds.

Connor knew it was ridiculous to feel so pleased.

Denton Hayes could very well be dark and dangerously close to the edge. Just the same, Connor was increasingly certain that Denton had just answered the age-old question: could someone truly change?

What was more, Connor found herself liking this new guy. A lot.

She was so involved in her internal dialogue that the young man's approach went unnoticed until he said, 'You're almost too late.'

Greg Alderton stood a trace under six feet. His face and arms were chalk-white and frail-looking. His eyes were a startling green and shone with electric brilliance.

'You're Greg?'

'Of course.' He pointed to the news stand up ahead. 'We need to get where they won't see us.'

She remained where she was. 'Don't you want to know my name?'

He kept moving. 'Doesn't matter. You'll never see me again.'

As soon as it was just the two of them in Denton's car, Ryan started talking. She offered a scattered summary containing few complete sentences. Starting with the drastic changes in her husband. Or, rather, as she insisted, her ex. Ryan described the new way Sean had started behaving, as if none of their tragic problems had ever existed. As if they were not just husband and wife, but friends. How everything was different now, and Ryan would only understand what that meant by agreeing to do it herself. Take the step. Bond with the leaf. Or thread. Sean had called it one thing, then the other. As though the two were interchangeable.

Ryan said this was when she finally decided she could wait no longer. The reasons and the excuses, nothing worked. She was divorcing the man. She told Sean, expecting argument, pleas, the same mess she had been through before. Instead, he simply said that he hoped she would change her mind. In time.

Ryan had then phoned her dearest friends, Kostas and Eleni Petridis, and agreed to speak with a divorce lawyer coming for dinner that night. It was only on the drive over, that final conversation echoing in her mind, that she wondered if perhaps Sean had not meant that she would change her mind about them. That he was actually more concerned that she accept and use this leaf. Or thread. Whatever.

She arrived at the Petridis home and met the lawyer, who had showed up early so they could have a private chat. She set up an appointment for the next day. She endured the dinner. She went home.

Only there was no home to come back to.

She phoned the police, then retreated to the home of neighbors. Later, when she returned to stand in front of the empty lot, Sean phoned. Their final conversation lasted seconds. He said Ryan was in grave danger and needed to disappear.

After enduring the police questioning, she fled to Kostas and Eleni. Waiting for what, she had no idea. She had begun to wonder if it was all some sort of ruse, just another of Sean's wiles. Until Denton met Kostas at the restaurant and confirmed the danger.

Then nothing, until that very morning. When a tall bone-white young man showed up at the Petridis home. And refused to leave, even when Kostas said he was calling the police. Just standing there on the doorstep, smiling and saying he needed to speak with Ryan, and that it was a matter of life or death.

Greg Alderton then met with Ryan for five minutes. Less. Long enough to tell her that she had to be here. This exact time and place. Because Denton would be there to rescue her—

'That's not what he said,' Denton said. Speaking for the first time since Connor had left for the terminal. 'I'm not here for you, Ryan. I never will be again.'

'Denton . . .'

He felt as if he had spent two years practicing the words. Preparing himself for this moment. Not cold, not hard, not anything. Calm and resolute. 'Those times are over. There is no us and there never will be again. Now tell me what he actually said.'

She dripped silent tears as she fumbled with her purse, coming out with a folded paper napkin. 'He said to give you this.'

TWENTY-NINE

Denton unfolded the napkin and stared at the leaf.

The sight pushed Denton far away from the space his body occupied. He raised his gaze, able to look directly at Ryan for the very first time. There was no such thing as objectivity between the two of them. The flames were too potent, their ardor a force that would remain a part of him unto death. But now was different. The past he had built around her absence was no more. She would never again occupy a space in his present life.

Hers was a special beauty, at least to him. Even now, from this safe perch, Denton felt the way her gaze, her closeness, her every breath sparked the air with pixie dust. Her body was slender and feminine and lithe and strong, a magnetic combination. Ryan drew glances from virtually everyone who spotted her. Male, female, young, old – they all wanted to see more. To *know* her. Her face was almost perfect and yet very alien. Her eyes were the color of sunlight through a dawn mist, grey and blue and gold. Her hair matched this remarkable blend, reddish gold and naturally streaked. The porcelain purity of her features defied age and time both.

Ryan said, 'It becomes, I don't know . . . a golden thread is what he said.'

Denton remained intent upon her and also this leaf. And studying himself in the process. Realizing that he was moving on. No longer a part of whatever she declared was their current emotional state. He heard himself ask, 'Who said that? Greg?'

She nodded, wiped her face, said, 'He was such a weird guy. I'd have called the whole thing nuts. Except this was exactly how Sean described it. A leaf that became . . .'

'What?'

'A transit point. A portal to tomorrow. He used a different term every time he described it. Pushing me to do it. Join him in this. Whatever it is.'

'I'd say for once your husband told you the absolute truth.'

Ryan said softly, 'Ex-husband.'

Denton had spent years wanting with desperate urgency to hear

Ryan speak those words. Now, though, he felt her voice pluck gently at the space over his heart, searching for a way in. 'We can assume Sean told you the truth because this is the only possible explanation for how he went through such a transformation. And did so basically overnight.'

'How can you be so calm about this? So detached?'

Denton used his response to redirect the conversation, away from the intimate, back to the leaf. 'Because this is the second time I've confronted the impossible. Greg Alderton, who it's claimed has special needs, managed to produce a series of stock-market instructions that netted NovaCorp huge profits. He'd never shown any interest in the markets until ingesting the leaf.'

Ryan's expression shifted. Gone was the tragic plea of a woman in love. She became almost funereal. Resigned. Her voice deepened. Softened. Scarcely a whisper. 'You're going to do it, aren't you?'

He had known this was going to happen. The very instant she had set the leaf there between them. His entire being was focused on whatever this leaf represented. 'I am. Yes.'

'Greg said I could do this with you. If I wanted.'

He had no idea how he felt about this. But it was her decision. Not his. 'And?'

In reply, she opened her door. The tears gone with the hope. 'Goodbye, Denton.'

'Wait. What do I do?'

She hesitated a moment, as if tempted to walk away. Leave him without any direction as to next steps. Then, 'Greg said he hoped we'd feel a bond, a link, something. But I don't feel anything except . . .' A flicker of the old yearning. 'Tell me what to do.'

'No.'

'Please, Denton, I need—'

'Ryan, stop. Either you want to do this, for yourself alone, or you don't.'

She nodded once, resigned. 'Focus on the bond. Ingest the thread. That's all I know.'

He watched her shut the door and start away. Ryan crossed the concrete expanse, then paused at the stairwell. She might have started to turn back, give him one last look. In the end, though, she entered the stairwell and disappeared.

Denton stared at the empty seat beside him and wondered if

he should have handled it differently. He decided a more polite closure was simply not possible. No matter how much she might have deserved better. But all that was in the past. Ryan was lost to his present and his future.

Denton picked up the leaf. And in that instant . . .

THIRTY

Connor reluctantly followed the young man across the terminal and into the news shop. When they were positioned in the rear corner, she demanded, 'Why are we here?'

Greg found that humorous. 'Saving your life isn't enough?'

She started to reply that she doubted anyone was in LAX with her murder on their mind. But Greg did a boneless slide to the counter, where he bought a bag of salted cashews and a Smartwater. He returned to where she stood, opened the bag with his teeth and offered it. 'Want some?'

'I want to know what is going on.' She felt enormously exposed. If they were indeed in danger, their position was all wrong. The shop was brilliantly lit. Ceiling cameras covered every square inch. Beyond the long open front, people moved in a constant swirling tide. 'This is insane.'

'We won't be here long.' Greg ate a few of the nuts and rolled his eyes with pleasure. He smiled at her. 'I don't get out much.'

She watched him tilt his head back and empty the little bag into his mouth. 'Answer my question or I leave.'

He was still chewing as he walked back to the counter and bought another bag. He returned, caught sight of her growing ire and sighed like an exasperated teen. Greg drank some water, then used the bottle to point at the portal through which all arriving passengers passed. 'The friend of your boss – the doctor.'

'You mean Sanjib Gupta?'

He shrugged. 'His plane arrived a while ago, right?'

Connor took two steps forward, far enough to scan the arrivals board. The delayed AA flight from San Francisco did indeed now read as *Landed*. She moved back to where he devoured the second bag of nuts. 'So?'

He drank more water, then said, 'You're not here to meet your contact. If you do, you'll be arrested and put in jail.'

'On what charges?'

'Doesn't matter. It's not going to happen because we've met.

You're here to see the enemy.' He drew Connor back another step, until her shoulder touched the glass-fronted refrigerated cabinet. 'Here they come.'

The entire arrivals hall paused in mid-stride. The bustling, chattering crowds, the multiple phone conversations, the happy reunions . . . All attention turned toward the dark-suited parade. Connor's breath froze as Sanjib Gupta was politely marched through the arrivals entryway, across the hall and out the closest exit. Agents formed a phalanx around the medical school director, as they would a high-powered dignitary. An attractive hard-faced woman and a gangly young man in civilian clothes brought up the rear.

Connor took one step forward, far enough to watch as the crew approached a trio of SUVs, one black and two bland, where more dark-suited agents waited in attendance. Almost instantly, Greg touched her arm. 'Step back.'

She did so, following him over to the side where they were blocked from view. 'What's the matter?'

'The woman. That's her. The enemy.'

'She can't see us. Far as I could tell, she didn't even look our way.'

'The guy with her. He's like me.' Before she absorbed the full implication of what he said, however, Greg relaxed. 'OK. They're gone. We need to talk.'

She was shaking as she followed him from the shop and entered the neighboring Starbucks.

Greg asked, 'You want something?'

'Same as before.' Connor was glad at least her voice remained steady. 'I want to know what's going on.'

'Coming right up.' He sounded impossibly cheerful.

She watched him step into the orders line and seated herself. The danger was gone, at least for now. But seeing a NovaCorp board member and distinguished surgeon marched through the airport like a criminal, not to mention Greg's flash of warning, brought home her sheer vulnerability.

Two days ago, she was in a job she loved. Everything well defined, the risks bound by rules and laws. Now the world had shifted into something new. A state where the invisible held dangers she could not define, much less identify.

One question, though, Greg could not answer. Connor had to decide this for herself.

Did she want to stay involved?

For the first time in her entire life, she was tempted to play the ostrich. Stick her head into the corporate sand. Pretend the entire episode had never happened. Hope it would all simply flow on past and leave her untouched.

As if in confirmation, Greg returned to her table with an overly rich concoction of coffee and caramel and whipped cream and ice. He seated himself, drew on the straw and hummed with happy pleasure. He took a folded paper from her pocket and set it on the table. 'Give this to my aunt.'

'Who?'

'Camila Suarez. She's in investments.'

'Of course. Denton met with her.' She opened the page, saw a series of symbols and dates and numbers. 'What is this?'

'Aunt Camila knows. Tell her to go all in tomorrow. First thing. Soon as the markets open. Pull all funds out on noon the next day. Not a minute later.'

'What about my answers?'

'In a second.' Another pull on the straw. 'We get five percent of her take, like we agreed. And tell Aunt Camila I need a way to contact her safely.'

Connor reluctantly drew the satphone from her purse. She handed it over. 'The number is taped to the back. I'll set up one for your aunt.'

Greg slipped it into his pocket. 'Thank you very much.'

The words sounded oddly formal. As though he rarely spoke them. As though any such conversation was not often part of his days. She asked, 'Now will you tell me what's going on?'

'Anything I say won't help. There's only one way for you to understand. When it's time, Denton will show you what needs to happen. If he doesn't, we'll get word to you through another means. But we think it will be Denton.'

Her heart skipped a beat, the sort of response to hearing a guy's name that a lovestruck teen might make. She hoped her voice sounded stable as she demanded, 'What does Denton have to do with all this?'

'A lot. And that has to wait. Along with all your other questions.' Her face must have shown a rising anger, because he added, 'We're involved in things where words just don't work. You must have already seen that for yourself.'

'*We* are involved.'

He grinned. 'You want answers? When the time comes, take the step. It's the only way you'll ever understand.'

'That's it?' She watched him rise to his feet. 'What step are we talking about?'

'More questions that have to wait. I need to go meet Denton. You should stay here a while longer. Have a sandwich. Something. So they don't see us leave together.'

'I'm supposed to just waltz on back to NovaCorp?'

But he was already gone.

THIRTY-ONE

Sanjib Gupta towered over the world. He would have been close to seven feet tall if he had stood fully upright. But he held to a slight stoop as he followed Kelly's team out of the plane and down the jetway. He placed each foot down carefully, moving forward with the somber grace of an aging stork.

Because of his height, Kelly directed Gupta into the front passenger seat. Riggs settled behind the wheel. Kelly and Pamela Garten took the rear. She could have driven, but Kelly wanted to focus exclusively on the man. Kelly watched Rabbit settle into Jon Alvero's ride, still working her phone, then asked Gupta, 'Where shall we take you?'

'I have a choice?'

'Most definitely. That is, assuming we don't need to waste time, Doctor Gupta. You're going to answer my questions, give me what I need, and I will effectively separate myself from your existence.'

'Permanently?'

'For both our sakes, and in deference to your family and your professional standing, I fervently hope so.'

'In that case, please take me home.'

Once they were underway, Kelly said, 'You have heard from the two postdocs, Durrant and Singh.'

'Several times.'

'Tell me what they said. Start with your initial conversation regarding the topic that is now deemed a state secret,' Kelly said. 'To the very last detail.'

Gupta basically repeated what Darren had offered. It was more or less the same information she and her team had received from Grey Mathers, back before they left DC. Only Gupta distilled the issues with the ease of a professional lecturer. Kelly knew he left out details and did not care. When he was done, she asked, 'What have you told your wife?'

'Nothing. Yet. That was going to be a difficult conversation. We were planning a trip to Lake Tahoe next weekend. I decided to wait until then.'

'Very wise. Now tell me exactly what you shared with Byron Sykes of NovaCorp.'

For the first time, Gupta hesitated.

'Yes?'

'What I said and what he actually heard may be quite different.'

Riggs offered a soft huff, while Kelly and Pamela exchanged a tight smile. 'Understood.'

'I told Byron everything I gained from the two postdocs. Or tried to. I also shared with him both the manuscript and compiled video clips. Byron wisely refused to accept a copy. He was far more aware than I of the potential risks involved. Something I should have seen as inevitable, given how the information has effectively vanished. In any case, I now realize Byron's decision was by far the smarter move.'

'You have the document and video with you now?'

'I do.' Gupta passed back a memory stick. 'This is my only copy. After my wife's first call regarding your agents, I erased everything. Laptop, phone, tablet. Gone.'

'Give me your phone.' She passed it to Pamela. 'I need to be absolutely certain, Doctor Gupta, that you have learned the necessary lesson.'

'I most certainly have.' A pause, then, 'You frightened those two young men to death.'

'Better than the alternative,' Kelly replied. 'You understand what I mean by that, yes?'

'All too well.'

She watched Pamela work through the phone's document and video files, deleting as she went. Kelly asked, 'Have you spoken with either Connor Breach or Denton Hayes about these matters?'

Gupta frowned. 'I don't know either of those names.'

Those were the last words spoken until they pulled into the drive of Gupta's Bel Air residence. Pamela handed back his phone and the doctor rose silently from the vehicle. Kelly stood by the rear door and watched as he stork-marched up to where his wife stood in the front entryway.

As soon as the door closed behind them, Rabbit slipped into the seat Gupta had occupied and announced, 'I think we have something.'

THIRTY-TWO

Denton had no idea how long he sat there. He tried to look away, check the car's clock, but even the eye movement was beyond him. Ryan's departure and the conflicting emotional storm had become reduced to mere shadows. He was still totally aware, totally free to choose. The draw he felt was unlike anything he had ever known. The desire was very real. The *certainty*. More potent than the hunger he'd experienced at the very height of his cocaine addiction, when it held the power to literally blind him.

The instant he picked up the leaf, it dissolved. Or morphed. Something. In its place was a thread, shimmering gold.

The act was as natural as taking his next breath. And as necessary. Just the same, he held back, wanting to see this clearly. This instant before the actual juncture.

It seemed to him that the bond was already in place. The initial stage of this union had happened. Ingesting the thread made it fully real. A permanent link to whatever came next.

There was everything that had brought him to this point in time and place. Thirty-four years and several lifetimes of tragic errors.

Absorbing the thread opened him to everything that came in the new now. That was the only way he was able to put the sensation into words. The new now.

Just the same, he knew a fleeting regret that Ryan had refused to take this step as well. See what lay beyond the transition. Then the thought and the emotions simply faded, lost to the growing certainty of moving into something *more*.

He cupped the softly illuminated thread to his face . . .

And breathed.

The shift was as subtle as midnight whispers between lovers.

Just the same, the transition was seismic. One moment, reality was composed of Denton Hayes, a man defined by solitude and loneliness. The next . . .

His concept of individuality was being extended to include . . . what exactly? Denton struggled to fit this new awareness into words.

At one level, he was precisely the same man. He had still been shattered by love, struggled with cocaine addiction and now did his best to maintain an existence without either.

Just the same, there was a new dimension to consciousness, to *life*.

He was joined now to others. People he had never met – most of them, anyway. But they were there; of this Denton had no doubt whatsoever. They watched. They waited. And they hoped. That he would be able to shrug off his past, move beyond his boundaries, and . . .

Wake up.

As soon as he recognized the message for what it was, he was filled with a sense of desperate urgency. He was not merely welcomed. He was needed.

The longer he focused upon this new orientation, the more he felt removed from everything that had come before. The past and the baggage were still there. But it was partly shoved aside in order to make room for the *new*.

He spoke the words aloud, the only way he could be certain they were correctly shaped. 'What do you need me to do?'

The answer was a blast that literally flung him into action. He had to rent the largest vehicle the airport agencies had on offer, then get to the private air terminal. Lives hung in the balance.

Denton sprang from his BMW and bolted across the parking garage. The elevator was for mere mortals; Denton flew down the stairs, bouncing off the concrete walls at each turn. He threaded his way through arrivals traffic, into the hall, and selected the rental agency by the simple fact that it was the only one without a line.

All the while, a crowd of the unseen shouted what he could not hear.

Hurry.

THIRTY-THREE

At Jon Alvero's suggestion, they drove the six blocks to the Bel Air Hotel and parked in a corner of their front drive. Jon badged the parking attendant, then joined the others clustered around the open windows of Kelly's ride.

Kelly told Rabbit, 'OK, let's hear what you have.'

The young man replied, 'There's something happening here.'

'What does that word mean – "something?"' She could see that Rabbit struggled to fit his magnified awareness into words that made sense. So she spoke with a calm that was light years from what she actually felt. 'We're on the same side here. I believe you. The same goes for all our team. We know we're entering territory where the words don't fit. All we ask is that you try to shape this into something we can all grasp.'

Rabbit nodded slowly in time to her words, then offered, 'We've been hunting for the location of this new infestation.'

'We, as in you and your DC crew.'

'Right. But we weren't getting anywhere. Then it hit me and Diyani, right at the same moment. They're on the move.'

Kelly liked how Jon Alvero and her agents had shifted inwards, forming a unit as solid as a wall. All attention, all gazes, every aspect of their unit, focused on this guy it would be so easy to call a stranger. An outsider. They trusted him. 'So they're moving location. And this is making it hard for you to track them.'

'Exactly. And one thing more. We're almost positive they're splitting up.'

For the first time working with Rabbit, she felt as if they were almost in sync. Not quite to the point where she could follow what he wasn't saying. But close. 'So you focused on one person.'

Rabbit nodded. 'We tried to identify a leader. The guy on point – isn't that what you call them?'

Riggs offered, 'Smart.'

Kelly asked, 'And that's given you a location?'

'Not at first. This guy, he's all over the map. Or so it seemed to us. But we're pretty sure we've identified a link to the others.'

Pamela asked, 'How many others are there?'

'This is where it gets confusing.'

Barry actually laughed. 'What do you call it up to now?'

'OK, more confusing.' To Kelly, 'There are a *lot* of them. Forty, maybe more. Only not all of them are, you know . . .'

'Bonded. Infected.' Whatever.

'Exactly. There's a core group of maybe seven. Then all these others.'

Jon said through the open window, 'So they're like, what, families?'

'That's what we figured. Diyani is certain some of the core group have problems. Maybe physical or mental, or both . . . We don't know what it is, exactly. Only they need help to get around, maybe even stay alive. Becoming linked hasn't changed that.'

'Back to the central issue as far as we're concerned. Have you managed to find us a target?'

'We think we have two. The main group went to a center of some kind. All we can say for certain is that they feel safe there. Diyani was the one who identified it. Darren is trying to find us the address. Which is kind of hard, because Diyani sees a building, a place. Not exactly where it's located. We know it's in Van Nuys. And it's a very particular kind of structure. She's working with Darren on that now.'

'And the leader?'

'Right. He went to the airport. We're pretty sure it was around the same time as us.' Rabbit held up her phone, which showed a very attractive woman's photo. 'This is Connor Breach.'

'NovaCorp's head of legal. So?'

'She met him in the terminal.'

Kelly felt her personal zone freeze solid. 'You saw her?'

'I don't see *anything*. But I'm almost positive she and the guy watched us leave with the doctor.' Rabbit wiggled the phone. 'This woman, she's come through the clearest. Why, I have no idea. But I think maybe . . .'

'Tell us.'

'Ever since this guy arrived at the airport, he's being protected.'

Riggs asked, 'Like what, he's shielded from view?'

Rabbit shrugged. 'I have *no* idea. But yeah, it feels kind of like that.'

Kelly added another dozen questions to her mental list. For later.

When events stopped moving at warp speed. 'So you tracked the woman.'

'Right. She definitely came through a lot clearer.'

Riggs said, 'But she's not one of them.'

'I'm pretty sure she's still standing on the periphery of all this. Anyway, Diyani and I were both positive she's connected to your investigation through NovaCorp. So I asked Darren for a photo. She and the guy were in the terminal. He left. We're pretty sure she's still there.'

'And this leader?'

'Gone. Smoke in the wind. I'm certain we're blocked by some kind of shielding. Diyani feels the same.'

Kelly's phone chimed. But when Rabbit held it out to her, she said, 'Give it to Jon.'

Alvero listened briefly, then lowered the phone and said, 'OK, Darren Cotton has come up with something we can use. Soon as Rabbit said some of the team had physical or mental issues, I thought maybe this was going to be the place. It's an adult day-care center in downtown Van Nuys.'

'How far?'

'Ten minutes away, if I hit the lights and siren.'

Kelly rose from her car. Faced the weary group coming off surveillance duty on the Gupta residence. 'If you want, you can head back to Santa Monica, grab some Zs. You've earned it.'

'You kidding?' This from Ricard. 'We came all this way; we want in on the dance.'

That was the response she'd been hoping for. 'Pamela, you and Ricard take two others and head back to LAX. Once you're there, split up. Make a quick sweep of Terminal Three, just in case they're still there. But one other thing can't wait. Soon as you arrive, someone has to check out the private air terminal, in case the lawyer is trying to set up a secret getaway.'

'I'll handle that,' Garten said.

'Rabbit, have your team continue trying for a fix on this lone target and the lawyer. Soon as you have something concrete, feed it to them. Jon, tell Darren what we've just heard. Ask him to start the sweep of all Terminal Three's security camera footage immediately. Focus on this attorney, Connor Breach. And through her, try to get a fix on this guy on point.'

'Which means wrangling with the security chief again.' Jon actually smiled. 'It will be a pleasure.'

'You need to let that chief know that one whiff of trouble from him will result in scorched earth as far as his career is concerned.'

Rabbit said, 'Maybe I should go with them.'

'No, you ride with me. If we can grab the main group in Van Nuys, that guy playing lone ranger will be easier to nab.'

Carey Sutton, head of Van Nuys Adult Day Care, was a heavyset woman in her fifties with a cheerful, capable air. She wore a beige ankle-length skirt and matching cardigan. Reading spectacles dangled from a silver chain around her neck. When Kelly showed her badge and explained why they were there, Ms Sutton replied, 'I've been wondering when somebody would show up.'

'In that case,' Kelly replied, 'I'm talking to the right person.'

'Not really,' Sutton replied. 'On account of how I don't know a thing for certain.'

'That makes two of us.'

'Well, what do you know – an officer of the law who offers honesty to the little people.'

'I try to, and little people is not a term that exists in my book. What exactly is your position here?'

'I run this place. Sort of.'

Kelly liked how she finished so many sentences with a hint of humor. The smile remained fixed in her gaze, despite everything that surrounded her. The center was in desperate need of repainting and repair. They stood in the front foyer, facing doors that opened into two identical chambers, large and linoleum-tiled and each holding a dozen or so adults. All of them were severely disabled. Several of the overhead lights were out. One window was cracked. Somewhere in the distance, three male voices shrieked. Another cackled almost as loudly. A woman sang a tuneless dirge. Kelly asked, 'Is there somewhere . . .'

She pointed to a tattered sofa and trio of hardback chairs by the reception desk. 'Here works as well as any. My office is the eye of a hurricane. Besides, the only people who understand what we discuss are my staff. And they're all too busy to care.' Another glint of a weary smile. 'That is, now that the crew you're probably interested in have taken off.'

Kelly felt a weight settle in her chest. 'They're gone, then.'

'Little less than an hour ago. Just upped and vanished about fifteen minutes after they showed up. And their families, by the looks of things. I had the distinct impression they used this as a staging area.'

'What makes you say that?'

Carey settled on to the sofa with a sigh, as relaxed as an aging cat. 'Oh, you get to know the people and their families. It's part of the job. Today I watched them come in – this huge group of people who know each other for reasons that are not what you might call happy. Yet here they are, laughing and hugging and talking like families heading out on vacation. Then piling into a very nice, very new bus. Mercedes, I think. Expensive.'

'Did they mention where they were going?'

'Somewhere safe. That's all they said.' She fiddled with the chain holding her spectacles. 'Which was a bit insulting, I must say.'

'Why is that?'

'We are exactly what you see.' Carey gestured to the rooms beyond the open doors. 'We provide a safe haven for adults with profound intellectual and/or physical disabilities. My staff are mostly highly trained professionals who could earn double working elsewhere. We're here because we care. Our job is to make them feel welcome. And safe.'

Kelly glanced at Rabbit. He stood by the exit, staring at nothing. Frowning in concentration. She asked Sutton, 'What can you tell me about this core group?'

She did a little bounce, once, twice, then levered herself back to her feet. 'Come with me.'

She led them through the left-hand door and across a room containing nineteen adults, none of whom even glanced their way. They were supervised by two clinicians in white; solid and capable people with voices that held both affection and iron-hard discipline.

They left by way of the rear exit and walked down a broad corridor. Carey Sutton unlocked the door to a smaller room with six long wooden tables, each holding three or four computers and as many hard-backed chairs. 'Many of our guests would tear this place apart, given half a chance. Four times each week, we host various groups in here. Most come for remedial training and require almost one-on-one supervision.'

'But this group is different?' At a nod from the director, Kelly pressed, 'Any specifics you can offer would be enormously helpful.'

'They come here three afternoons each week. One o'clock to five, sometimes six. Four young men, three women, all in their twenties. Two have the sort of physical disabilities that keep them in wheelchairs. I suggest they are also geniuses when it comes to math and numerical logic. But it's hard to tell. Only two of them are comfortable conversing with someone outside their crew. That includes their families. Or rather, it did. Two seemed almost totally incapable of speech. Before.' She pointed across the empty room. 'They came, most with a guardian, and they gathered in the far corner. Sometimes they used our computers, but mostly for backup. They all brought laptops. This was their social time, the only such contact beyond their families that most had.'

Kelly felt Rabbit press in closer, heard him ask, 'That changed?'

'"Change" is too easy a word. The difference was seismic.' The center director now shared Rabbit's distant frown. 'The session before they vanished, a gentleman came to see them. He was brought by one of the families, which is the only way he gained entry. These people, my crew, they fawned on him. I can't describe it any other way. Even the ones who don't communicate verbally – I actually saw tears. He didn't stay long. A few minutes. Then he left. Poof. Gone.'

Kelly felt a conflicting sense of excitement and electric dread. The weight of moving too slowly. The despair of remaining one step behind. She told Riggs, 'Ask Cotton for a photo of the missing professor, Stiles.'

'I have it,' Rabbit said and passed over his phone.

Carey Sutton's eyes widened. 'That's the man. Who is he?'

'Another individual we would very much like to interview. I'd rather not say anything more.' Kelly passed the phone back to Rabbit. 'When was he here?'

'Eleven days ago.' Definite. 'You know what happened to them?'

'We think so. Yes.'

'Will you tell me?'

'Ms Sutton – Carey – for many reasons I can't go into, it's important that I do not divulge what we suspect.'

Rabbit said, 'It's better if you don't know. For you, your staff and all your other guests.'

She studied them a moment, then decided, 'Honesty like that will take you a long way in my book.'

'Back to your core group. When they returned after this gentleman's visit, how soon did you notice the changes?'

'Oh, right from that very first moment.' She pointed to the rear corner. 'They met back there, same as usual. But now they clustered around just two laptops. Even the ones who rarely communicated were *involved*. And something else. Something you rarely see among the people who use our facility. They were happy. Excited. It infected the adults as well. The family members gathered by the rear wall, listening and taking part. Which is another rarity. How everyone was taking part.' Her smile turned sad. 'I even heard laughter.'

Then, on a hunch, Kelly told Rabbit, 'Show her the young man at the airport.'

Carey's eyes widened. 'How utterly astonishing.'

'You know him?'

'That's Goyo Alderton. Or Greg, as he insisted on being called after meeting with that man. This name change irritated his mother Sofia no end. She is such a nervous, protective . . .' Carey leaned in closer to the phone. 'Where was this taken?'

'Los Angeles Airport, Terminal Three.'

She blinked. 'I am utterly flummoxed.'

'What is it about the photo that surprises you, Ms Sutton?'

'Greg normally served as the crew's spokesperson. Which was ironic, because he was without question the shyest individual I've ever met. Strangers terrified him . . .' She studied the image. 'I am rendered speechless.'

Kelly motioned for Rabbit to stow the phone. 'Can you tell me anything about where they might have gone?'

Carey straightened. 'Strangest thing. Greg's father was the one driving that bus. While they were loading their cases in the back, I spoke with a young girl, maybe seven or eight. She said she wasn't supposed to talk, but she wasn't the least bit happy about what was taking place. The child didn't understand why she couldn't call her friends, or why they had to leave. But her brother had told them they had to run away. She said it wasn't fair.' She stared out the front window. 'She said Greg had made enough money for them to all go far away. I asked where they were going. Somewhere cold, she said. And she hated the cold. I think she said Canada. But right then, an adult rushed over, yelled something, grabbed the child and pulled her away.' Carey shrugged. 'I'm sorry I couldn't be more help.'

*   *   *

By the time Kelly left the center, an idea was taking hold. It was very vague at first, not even clearly an action. More like Kelly was coming to terms with the need for a next step. For the very first time, she felt able to identify what was missing from their investigation. This in itself she took as a very good sign.

If she was right.

If she was willing to do what was required.

The afternoon heat was an oppressive weight. Even so, Kelly stood by the first vehicle, studying the center. So involved in defining her next step that she could ignore the nearly blinding sunlight.

'Kelly, you OK?'

'Thinking.' A long breath. 'We need to check out the Alderton residence, and we need to report in. Can we arrange for the other cars to hear my conversation with Agnes?'

'No problem.'

Three minutes later, they were underway. Two minutes after that, Agnes came on the cars' speakers. Kelly heard herself break down the morning's activities into proper segments. Gupta, the new infiltration identified now as seven individuals with various disabilities, their connection to the missing professor, Rabbit's inability to locate their so-called leader, her meeting with the center director, Greg Alderton meeting with the attorney at LAX. She thought she probably sounded subdued, but for the moment she could not bring herself to care.

When she was done, Agnes asked, 'Stanley, are you there?'

Rabbit was seated in the rear seat next to Kelly. He leaned forward, as if proximity to the radio was required. 'Yes, ma'am.'

'This group of seven. Tell me about this supposed ability of theirs to remain undetected.'

'It's the same problem we've had with Greg Alderton. We only know he was in the airport because of the woman there with him.'

'Connor Breach,' Kelly supplied. 'NovaCorp's top in-house attorney.'

'We think she's not actually joined with these others,' Rabbit went on. 'For the group themselves, the barrier they're hiding behind feels to us like a mental fog. But we think Darren Cotton came up with a significant idea – that their shielding method may not be totally constant. Which is why we've set up an around-the-clock search.'

Kelly was seated behind Riggs, who was driving. She shifted

over further, tight against the side door. Compressing herself into a smaller space. When Rabbit was finished, she said, 'With respect, ma'am, there's another key issue we need to address.'

'I'm listening.'

'Professor Stiles clearly targeted this group of seven individuals,' Kelly said. 'Why them? He certainly didn't just pull their names out of a psychic hat.'

Rabbit offered, 'Ma'am, I think she needs to know everything.'

Agnes hesitated, then said, 'Very well.'

Rabbit said, 'The infestations in Austin and Chicago both started with a group just like the ones we're seeking. And several of the Washington—'

'We're not certain of DC, beyond one individual,' Agnes said.

But Rabbit was persistent. 'The individual was a pre-teen with behavioral issues, son of a Secret Service agent. Added to that is the Vice President's daughter, who previously had spent years in and out of trouble.'

'To the point of self-harm,' Agnes added.

'We also think a Congresswoman traveled with her family, including a niece with severe mental issues.'

Agnes said, 'We've started monitoring similar groups in other cities.'

'Nineteen,' Darren added, speaking for the first time. 'More every hour.'

'We know savants are drawn to the artifact,' Rabbit said. 'A desire so intense it dominates their lives. We also know the other types of person commonly drawn to the artifact are in a semi-broken state. Emotional crisis, mental imbalance, something. Even a desperate hunger to escape an utterly boring existence. Like me.'

But Kelly's attention was snagged by something else. 'They are *drawn*.'

'Correct. Afterwards, they are at least partly healed. They also work in tandem. Their abilities grow exponentially.'

Riggs said, 'Like what, a hive mind?'

'I don't even know what that means. But maybe. Yes. In a way.'

Kelly said, 'You don't like that term. Why?'

'Do I look like I've lost my individuality? I'm connected. But we're not a unit. Just the same, what I can do, how I see, it's . . .'

Riggs suggested, 'Amplified?'

Rabbit nodded with his entire body. 'That's it exactly.'

Riggs pulled up in front of a fifties-era tract home. 'This just gets weirder by the minute.'

Kelly could feel the suffocating heat radiating through the glass by her cheek. 'Back to this latest group. Do you have any idea what might be their focus?'

'They were into math and computer logic,' Rabbit said. 'Which means algorithms. Which means . . .'

'What?'

'Their former spokesman serves as the guy on point. Only now he has the collective mental strength of six more minds backing him up.' Rabbit pointed at the silent house. 'The core role of algorithms in artificial intelligence is to determine patterns. Fractal patterns. Trends. Taken far enough, these calculations can predict. Not what an individual will do. But the *probability* of collective actions.'

Agnes snapped, 'We're moving into the realm of untested theories.'

'Sorry, ma'am,' Rabbit replied. 'I think this is as real as it could possibly be.'

For the third time that day, Kelly felt the voices recede. *The guy on point.* Rabbit's words resonated so deeply that she shivered.

Kelly asked Riggs to handle the search of the Alderton residence. She remained seated alone in the lead vehicle, the a/c on full, cocooned in her very private world. *Guy on point.* The concepts formed a silent dirge. She knew now what needed to be done. And she was going to do it. There was no argument, no defiance of the weight pressing her forward, strong as the afternoon's heat.

It all came down to motive.

If she was going to do this thing, change her life forever, it needed to be for the right reason.

It seemed to her that Nathan took shape in the sunlight beyond her window. He remained so much a part of her and yet forever gone. Silently urging her to make use of the quiet moment.

Kelly pulled out her phone and called Nathan's parents.

While in university, Kelly had lost her father to heart failure. Then, eleven months later, her mother was felled by a single massive stroke. That first visit to her beloved's home, Nathan's folks had adopted her in all but name.

Jerry Bragg was a retired Marine colonel, hard as nails but with a heart made to invite in a young woman who refused to admit how lonely she had become. Jerry answered as he always did. 'How's my darling girl?'

'Missing him. So much.'

'Soon as we're finished chatting,' Jerry told her, 'I'll pass you to the missus. These days, she's always ready for a good cry.'

'Better not. It doesn't look good if I break down on duty.'

'I hear you.' He waited through a few shared breaths, then asked again, 'How are you, Kelly?'

'Depends on the day. I wanted to tell you, I've been named to lead a task force going after the bad guys. The ones behind Nathan's death.' She breathed around the wound caused by naming her fiancé. Then, 'The situation is a lot bigger and more complex than him going south on an inspection tour.'

'Hold on a second.' There followed the creak of floorboards, then the soft double click of a door being shut and locked. 'What can you tell me?'

'Right now, not a lot. But soon.' She took the hardest breath of all, then confessed, 'I'm pretty sure I know what needs to happen. And it scares me, Jerry. So much.'

'I don't recall hearing this from you before.'

'I've never really been frightened by the thought of dying.' She closed her eyes, then forced them open again. The dream image of Nathan's snow-covered form and the final whispered warning were too vivid. 'But I'm terrified of taking the wrong step. And doing so for all the wrong reasons.'

'Putting your team in danger,' he offered. 'Not being aware of how wrong you were until the bullets are flying.'

She huffed, clenched, fought to maintain control. 'That most of all.'

'Which is partly why you're such a good agent, Kelly girl. The best Nathan ever knew.'

'He told you that?'

'Several times. That was how he described you, between the time he fell in love and the day he brought you home. Then you and I first met, and I knew my boy had you pegged.'

She wiped her face. 'I can see what I think is the right way forward. But everything is so tainted by the lies I tell myself to keep going without him.'

'That's not the issue, though, is it?'

'Sorry, I don't . . .'

His voice did not rise in volume. But there was an iron-hard quality now. A commanding officer facing the prospect of taking his troops into deadly harm. 'Can you identify that one single next step?'

'I think so. But I'm not sure.'

'Sometimes you can't be certain. When that happens, and it's time to act, you go with what evidence you have. The intel at your disposal. The orders you've been given.' A pause, then, 'Do you trust your team?'

'They're the best there is.'

'And they're with you?'

'Yes. Definitely. Scared like me. Worried. But with me every step.'

'There you go. Fear is a good thing sometimes. Useful. Sharpens your awareness. Increases response speed. Helps clarify the issues you might otherwise ignore. But you can't let it control you.'

Kelly watched her team emerge from the house, a slow straggle of hunters with no sign of prey. 'I'd better go.'

'You'll call me when the dust settles?'

'The very instant.'

'Good luck, daughter. And good hunting.'

THIRTY-FOUR

A s Kelly's team approached their vehicles, two phones rang.

First Jon's, then Kelly's. The LA Homeland AIC watched Kelly through the vehicle's sealed windows, growing ever more somber the longer he listened. Kelly met Jon's gaze and listened as Pamela's report crystallized her own next step. She told Pamela to stay on the line and rose from the vehicle.

Jon listened to Kelly's summary, then confirmed, 'The LAX security chief wants to know if our investigation has anything to do with fast-acting nerve gas. Apparently, that's been used in the private air terminal. I told him we were investigating.'

Kelly nodded slowly but not to Jon's words. Pamela Garten's report chopped away any reason Kelly had to hold back. All her reservations were gone. What had started as a hunch was now an utter certainty.

Kelly lifted her phone and told Pamela to meet them back at the apart-hotel.

'There must be something more I can do.' Pamela sounded utterly defeated. A good woman and better agent brought low through no fault of her own.

'There is,' Kelly replied. 'But not at the airport. We're all done there.'

'I mean, something I could have done better.'

Kelly knew argument was futile. The woman would not understand until everything was laid out. 'We'll meet at the hotel, debrief, and you'll see you handled it as best as anyone possibly could have.'

'What a total mess.' Jon waved his phone in frustration. 'The chief just sent me footage from the terminal's security cameras. You won't believe it.'

Actually, she would. 'Forward it to Darren. Ask him to splice it together and make something we can show Agnes.' She turned to Riggs. 'Let's head back to Santa Monica.'

'You haven't asked what we found in the Alderton house.'

'I don't need to.' She slipped back into her seat. 'I know now the answers we're after aren't here.'

As they pulled into the apart-hotel's parking lot, Cotton called to say Agnes and Mathers wouldn't be available for another hour and a half. So Kelly went for a run.

It was a miserable outing. Her mood matched the fierce afternoon heat. The prospect of what lay ahead was just one more barrier to push through. A mile and a half down the narrow park, she stopped and leaned against a tree, wishing she could just erase it all, forget the doubts and the hurt and the absence, just for a moment. Instead, the shade only granted the dreamtime snowfall a stronger ability to defy the California heat. She swiped her face with both hands and sprinted away.

Why had he come as he did, with the dead drug lord prone in the snow between them? All these plans, the reasoning, the intention . . . Was she lying to herself? Was she in truth merely looking for her own way out?

None of this would probably plague her so, had Nathan not spoken as he did. Her dead fiancé's final word chased her back down the park and into the hotel. Through her stretching and shower and dressing and salad and coffee, she could not get that awful, softly spoken warning out of her head.

Don't.

Kelly briefed her team first. She owed them that.

When she was done, they responded with the silence her words probably deserved. The ops room's computers showed the faces of those back in DC. Mirroring the emotions that surrounded her. Concerned. Confused. Struggling to come to terms with what she had said.

Then Riggs asked, 'Are you sure?'

'I am. Yes.'

Before anyone else could give voice to all the reservations Kelly felt, Pamela said, 'You're right to do this.'

Jon Alvero breathed a quiet, 'Whoa.'

'Our present tactics, all the power we hold, it isn't working,' Pamela said. 'I've just witnessed this first-hand.'

Kelly turned to Rabbit. 'You're probably thinking I should have first spoken with you. Made sure it was even possible.'

'No.' His gesture took in the room, the faces on the screens. Her team. 'They need to be involved from the very outset.'

'Can we do this?'

'Maybe. I brought a leaf.' Rabbit smiled. 'Diyani said I would need it. She loves being right.'

'Where did it come from?'

'Austin. Same as mine. The local cops found six. They were going to burn them. But Agnes was on site.'

'And so she went looking for you.'

'Something like that.'

Darren turned away, then came back and said, 'Agnes and Grey are ready.'

The conversation with Agnes Pendalon and Grey Mathers went more smoothly and quickly than Kelly had expected.

She started by having Pamela summarize the events that took place at the private air terminal. While Garten talked, Kelly had Darren run the security tapes.

Kelly listened and watched with a sense of inevitability. She had the very strong sense that this was the moment and deed she had been aiming for since she had sprawled in the dirt above the Texan arroyo. She recalled studying the slow-moving Rio Grande, guided by the man who could define the unseen.

Pamela did a professional job of describing the moment when the impossible became a memory she would never forget. The security footage provided punctuation to their words. The images would have made no sense without Pamela's commentary. Her shaky voice, the effort required to maintain stable control, only heightened the strangeness.

Pamela described exactly what the security footage showed. A motley collection of families entered the highly exclusive enclave of private jets and serious money. They could not have stood out more if they had carried signs declaring themselves to be part of the alien invasion.

Pamela confronted them, and they meekly shifted from the main lounge to a windowless security room. The families moved without protest, almost as if they expected nothing less. As if that was why they had come in the first place.

Pamela locked the door and had a brief word with the lone airport security guard on duty in the private air terminal. The overhead

cameras showed her directing the other agents into position outside
the locked door. She lifted her phone.

When it happened.

Denton Hayes stepped through the main doors. He was accompanied by Greg Alderton, the pale young man who served as the
group's spokesperson.

Kelly spoke for the first time, identifying the two men.

The security camera showed Pamela's evident shock at the pair's
appearance. Denton walked over, while Greg held back, not nervous,
not afraid. Watchful. Intent.

Then Pamela and the agents, along with everyone else in the
terminal, simply collapsed.

To Kelly and the observers, it looked just like what the airport
security chief had feared: a fast-acting nerve agent struck the entire
terminal at once. Staff, TSA, passengers, all of them. Just folded
over and passed out.

Except for one thing.

Denton and Greg remained standing.

Denton was clearly shocked. And frightened. He backed away
from the prone agents and kept moving until he collided with the
side wall.

Then the locked security door clicked open.

A narrow older woman rushed forward and embraced Greg
Alderton. Or rather, she tried to. Greg pried her arms off as he spoke
with others emerging from the security room. He pointed them
toward the bus and Denton's vehicle parked out front.

One of the younger people seemed to have difficulty walking,
but she shuffled forward on her own steam. Two others were in
wheelchairs. They carefully threaded their way around the prone
bodies.

When the others had exited, Greg spoke to Denton, who then
pushed himself off the wall and left the terminal. Cameras covering
the main entrance showed them loading into the bus and a Toyota
minivan. They drove away.

A few moments later, everyone woke up.

Agnes Pendalon needed a moment to say, 'Kaiser?'

'We're behind the curve, ma'am. There's only one way I can see
for us to catch up.'

'And that is?'

'An experienced agent needs to join in. Ingest or absorb this alien technology. See if it's possible to utilize these new abilities to our benefit.' Kelly gave that a beat. When the room and screens all remained silent, she added, 'Rabbit is an excellent analyst, and his work has been first-rate. But for us to succeed on this mission—'.

Agnes broke in with, 'Hold where you are, Kaiser.'

Her screen went blank. Three seconds later, so did the one showing Grey Mathers.

The minutes stretched out, but Kelly didn't mind. She stared at her reflection in the empty monitor and wondered if this was why Agnes had selected her as mission chief. If Kelly might be willing to take this step, see the need and go for it. Then she decided it didn't change anything one way or the other.

Her mind switched back to the memory of a discussion she'd overheard between Nathan and his father, when they had talked about mission blindness, the moment when emotions took over and the clarity a good leader required was lost. But she didn't feel much of anything just then. She was not just committed. She was at peace.

Agnes and Grey appeared together. Their chief said, 'There's someone who wants to have a word.'

But two people joined on separate screens. Avri Rowe, the President's Chief of Staff, was the one who spoke. 'General, can you hear me?'

General Skarren, head of DOD Intelligence, replied, 'You're coming through loud and clear, sir.'

'I thought it was time you and I met, Agent Kaiser.'

'It's an honor, sir.'

'Who is there with you?'

She took her time and introduced her entire team, including Darren's group in DC. Finally, 'And this is Jon Alvero, AIC of Homeland's LA office. His assistance has proven to be of vital importance.'

'Vital,' Rowe said. 'That's the best word to define what you are all involved in. Vital we maintain our nation. Vital we forge a cohesive strategy for moving forward. Vital we have a core team as solid, as prepared and as successful as your group.'

'There's a lot still to be done, sir.'

'You took the words right out of my mouth, Agent Kaiser. Great start, everyone. Kelly, may I call you that? I'm here if you need me. Same goes for General Skarren. We clear on that, Agnes?'

'Most certainly, sir.'

'An honor and a pleasure to meet you, Kelly.'

'Thank you for taking the time, sir.'

When the screens showing Rowe and Skarren went blank, Darren Cotton said, 'I just discovered how long I can go without breathing.'

Agnes said, 'Agent Kaiser.'

'Ma'am.'

'You have the green light. You may proceed when ready.'

THIRTY-FIVE

Denton left the private air terminal in a crowd of brand-new friends.

The traffic heading east was snarled to the point where, time after time, the freeway came to a complete halt. Now that they were underway, however, Denton no longer felt the crushing weight of a hundred silent voices shouting at him to hurry.

He had been repeatedly warned to remain as close as possible to the bus. Under no circumstances was he to allow another vehicle to slip in between them. Which meant he became the target of numerous angry drivers who leaned on their horns and shouted through open windows when he refused to let them merge.

The Mercedes bus was a lumbering beast with tinted windows. It carried well over the maximum load stated on the accordion doors. Baggage filled the holds to bursting. The rear window was completely blocked by backpacks, carry-alls, food hampers and a wheelchair. The driver, Greg's father Terrance, was unaccustomed to handling such a load, which resulted in over-braking and lurching accelerations.

The Toyota minivan Denton had rented was equally burdened. Seats intended for a maximum of seven held nine, plus more baggage and a fretting infant.

Just the same, Denton shared the group's cheerful frame of mind. Every time the baby went quiet, a little girl of four or five began singing. Despite everything, Denton was tempted to join in.

Maintain a distance under ten feet. Those were his instructions. It meant his vision was effectively limited to the bus's rear end. The silver Mercedes logo remained his target. He felt as though it was imprinted on his brain.

Denton shared the Toyota's front row with the lone crew member assigned to his ride. Astrid was a young woman in her late twenties; her wheelchair was packed in his rear hold. Denton thought of her as a fractured porcelain doll, painted in the most delicate of shades. Her crystal green eyes were far too large for her fragile features. Denton liked her immensely.

Astrid rode perched between Denton and a grim-faced older version of herself. Astrid was as pale and cheerful as her mother was leathery and strong and full of bile.

Astrid sat half on her mother's lap and half on the central console. Her limbs were pale and flaccid. Denton suspected she lived with a lot of pain. But Astrid refused to let it dominate. She was fascinated with everything. And wanted nothing more than to talk. 'My condition, and we're not talking about the legs that still don't work. My other condition. That one rendered me nearly speechless for twenty-eight years. Right, Mom?'

'It could have been longer.' Her mother had not introduced herself to Denton. Nor did she glance his way. 'I wouldn't mind.'

Astrid ignored her. 'Give me half a chance, I'll talk your ear off. You listening is optional.'

From her other side, her mother declared, 'No good will come of this. You mark my words.'

'In case you haven't noticed, Mom can find bones in a bowl of custard.'

'That is no way to talk about your elders, young lady.'

'I wouldn't know. Not having had much practice.' She pointed out the windscreen. 'You're getting too far away.'

Denton nudged the Toyota a fraction closer. 'What's with keeping this distance?'

'I could tell you, but then I'd have to kill you.' Astrid grinned. 'I've always wanted to say that.'

'Seriously.'

'Seriously, Denton. I can't tell you. But it's important. Right, Mom?'

'The way these two are driving, we're bound to wind up in a terrible accident.'

They stopped in Anaheim at a filling station complex, almost a mini mall, with multiple eateries and a small supermarket. Even here, the group's tight cohesion was maintained. Denton was directed to use the pump next to the bus, then afterwards they parked side by side. Everyone who used the facilities or bought food was accompanied by one or more of the crew. Which meant reducing their speed even further. Just the same, Denton saw no need to either complain or question. He was too busy coming to terms with exactly what he had gotten himself into.

The straight answer was, he had no clear idea.

Beyond the crew traveling with Denton, there were many others connected to them and their journey. Denton definitely picked up on their presence, as well as a sense of communal gratitude. They all seemed glad he had signed on. But there was no sense of intrusion. He realized early into the journey that this group was not into reading minds. Whatever he had entered into, this new ability he now shared, it wasn't about listening in on private thoughts.

The concept of communication was being taken to a totally different level. One that did not invade his space. If he wanted to reach out, he could, and they responded with a warm and silent hello. Otherwise, he was left alone.

And yet, even in his solitary state, things were different. How precisely, he could not say. Yet.

Connor called Denton's satphone while they were parked at the first rest stop. Denton studied the screen for a long moment before deciding their conversation had to wait. There were several items he still needed to work through before they spoke. The drive's slow pace actually served him well.

She phoned another three times as they took the 5 to the 210, up through Pasadena, then the 14 north of the Angeles National Forest and the San Gabriel range. When they stopped a second time in Palmdale, Denton was ready to call the attorney back. She answered with, 'I've been worried.'

'No need.'

'How are you?'

'I'm good.'

'Really?'

'Yes. You need to know, I've taken the next step.'

Connor did not ask for clarification. Which pleased him in ways he could not actually put into words. She asked, 'Are you glad you did?'

'I am. Yes. But I'm not ready to discuss this . . .'

'Whatever it is.'

'Transition works. I heard one of the crew use that word. It fits.'

'Crew?'

'Let's leave that for later. Right now, I need you to try to get Byron on the line.'

'He said I could interrupt him whenever you called. Stay right there.'

The line went silent, then a few moments later the NovaCorp CEO came on with, 'Is it as I feared?'

'That and more.'

Byron gave that a long beat, then said, 'Let's have it.'

Denton did his best to be succinct. But he also wanted to offer them an orderly, step-by-step procession of events. Otherwise, the entire situation would be, well, impossible to accept. Thankfully, their halt at this second rest stop went as slowly as the previous one. Astrid was seated in her wheelchair, lounging in the minivan's shadow, seemingly immune to the desert heat. Not watching him, but listening closely. And apparently enjoying his tale.

When Denton finished, Byron said, 'I need to think this over.'

'That makes two of us.'

'Three,' Connor said.

Byron asked, 'Do you have any immediate suggestions?'

'Given what I'm experiencing, I think we need to assume that, sooner or later, this group will not be bound by temporal awareness. As in, the life-expectancy charts NovaCorp uses to calculate risk will cease to work. At least, with anyone who has made the transition.'

'Or is in contact with someone who has.' Byron sighed. 'What a mess.'

'Not necessarily. Your business model needs to adapt to this new level of available information. But you also have a new source of revenue through Greg Alderton. Assuming he will continue to supply you with trading data.'

'Camila Suarez, his aunt, assures me that is the case.'

'I would start by putting a ceiling on any new policy,' Denton said. 'Maybe base it on income stream, or else raise payments exponentially beyond a certain point.'

'I'll put my actuary team on it today,' Byron said. 'Telling them as little as possible.'

Connor said, 'I've heard back from the CEO of Campion Security. They've confirmed our meeting for early tomorrow morning. Not that we can gain much from it now.'

'You'll need to handle that on your own,' Denton said.

'Should I cancel?'

'After the payout I've agreed to, that would only lead to unwelcome questions,' Byron replied. 'Not to mention the federal agent who has agreed to meet you there.'

'She already has me under surveillance,' Connor pointed out. 'I may leave in handcuffs.'

'Which is why it could be good to make this happen under our rules of engagement,' Denton said.

'Meaning?'

'There's a detective with the LAPD's missing persons division. Celeste Jones.' Denton related their conversations, the detective's offer to help, despite being ordered off a case that no longer existed. Then he waited.

Finally, Connor said, 'That's actually a very good idea. Anything else?'

'Yes,' Denton said. 'It's probably best if you don't go home tonight.'

THIRTY-SIX

Kelly's heart struggled to escape its bodily cage.
Rabbit held out the leaf. His movements were almost formal. His voice sounded softly concerned as he said, 'What I was told, you think of the moment when the need, or urge, was greatest. But you didn't have anything like that, did you?'

'No.'

'Take it.' His hand shook as he passed it over. 'You need to form a connection. But I don't know how you . . .'

Rabbit probably kept talking. But Kelly no longer heard. Her mind was filled to overwhelming with a distinct impression. Or compass heading. The clarity she felt in that moment was unlike anything she had ever known.

Her current mission. Her team. The objectives being missed because they remained constantly half a step behind the curve . . .

Abruptly, she became consumed by a taut force, a single-minded intent.

She felt as though she'd been honing these abilities ever since her first day of training. Gradually taking aim at the here and now.

She did not review the elements required to be a good agent so much as feel it all condense into a single tight unit. Everything meant to lead a team, take them into danger, bring them out. Cutting through all the dross and subterfuge, seeing the goal, the need to protect the innocent, serve her country, direct the men and women who relied on her . . .

She heard Rabbit huff a strong breath. The sound drew her back. She saw . . .

The leaf was gone.

In its place was a shimmering thread, weightless, softly vibrating.

Kelly did not hesitate. She lifted the thread and applied it to the center of her forehead.

And . . .

Nothing.

She breathed in and out. Felt her heart rate gradually retreat from its redline pace. And . . .

Still nothing.

Rabbit asked, 'Kelly?'

She looked at him.

Rabbit jerked back. 'Whoa.'

'What is it?'

'You don't . . .' He forced himself to straighten. 'Nothing.'

Kelly started to press him for clarification, when . . .

That solitary glance at Rabbit *flooded* her with information, emotions, impressions. The trivial and the deeply personal. She stood beneath a torrent of new information.

Then, as abruptly as it arrived, the flood vanished.

'Are you OK?'

Kelly clenched down as hard as she could. Tighter still. And looked over a second time . . .

Rabbit winced, but held her gaze as . . .

She *saw*.

She peered into the deeply secret life of a professional analyst. She *saw* him. The man who took a visceral pride in his new name, the way he had become bound to her team. The lover of this Indigenous-Honduran named Diyani. All of it rushed at her. Rabbit's past was a geek's litany of never belonging, which made her open invitation to join them on this hunt, how they all considered him truly one of them . . .

He was Kelly's man.

Even now, when she had the ability to strip him bare.

She looked away. 'I'm so sorry.'

'Kelly, it's OK. No. More than that.' Rabbit breathed. 'It's *wild*.'

'What should I call it?'

'I have no idea.'

'This is not normal?'

Rabbit laughed out loud. 'Did you actually just use that word?'

Gradually, the torrent receded and then vanished altogether. She found herself able to analyze what this meant, how to keep her team moving forward. 'I want to try something.'

'OK.'

'You and I working together. Take aim at our primary target.'

'The missing crew.'

'Right.'

Rabbit nodded. 'Can I bring in my team?'

'You think I can hook up with them too?'

'Sure. I don't see why not. They're ready and waiting.'

'OK, so what do I do?'

He shrugged. 'No idea. But maybe it would help if we held hands.'

She reached out. 'Ready when you are.'

On the hunt.

THIRTY-SEVEN

D enton continued to follow the bus northeast along the 14, through Palmdale and then Lancaster. The afternoon baked beneath a desert sun. The old state road was a silver-black ribbon, ribbed from frequent repairs. They were passed by numerous trucks and dusty vehicles. But the road was empty enough for Denton to relax, which was good. The strain of maintaining his position, the slow progress and the harsh sunlight caused his eyes to burn and his neck and shoulders to ache. Gradually the minivan went silent, as one after another of the passengers drifted off. When they passed through Rosamond, Denton glanced over and saw Astrid's mother was asleep, mouth ajar, head resting on the side window. Only the young woman leaning against his right shoulder remained wide awake. Denton said, 'It's just us now. Can you tell me why we need to hold this position?'

'Absolutely. Get any farther away and we all die.'

He glanced over. 'Is this an Astrid sort of joke?'

'Hey, I like that. An Astrid joke. A unique sort of humor from a woman who couldn't talk until last week.' She shifted position, settling more tightly against him. 'But the answer to your question is no. The danger is very real.'

Denton pointed to the bus dominating his field of vision. 'Why can't he drive faster? Not to complain—'

'Even if you are.'

'But we could have been there hours ago. Wherever we're going. Which brings me to my next question. Where are we going, Astrid?'

She pointed to a road sign dotted with rusting bullet holes that read, *Mojave, 20 miles*. 'That's our end of the road, Jack.'

'For real?'

'Why would I lie?'

'I could think of a hundred reasons. All of them starting with another not-funny Astrid joke.'

She sighed. 'I like you. You're weird. But nice. In a weird sort of way.'

'We're stopping in twenty miles? Truly?'

'Yes. And to answer your not-question, we have to arrive there at a very specific point in time.'

'Why?'

'Don't know, doesn't matter. Well, it does. Since you probably want to live, right?'

'I'm not comfortable with this do-or-die alternative.'

Astrid settled her head against Denton's seat. 'Then we've both got a very serious problem.'

'What's that supposed to mean?'

But Astrid was already asleep.

Their destination was a brand-new suites hotel half a mile from the main Mojave airport entrance. The airport tower and runway lights gleamed in the gathering dusk as Denton pulled in and parked behind the bus. The parking lot was packed gravel rimmed by new concrete liners. The raw earth to the left of where Denton parked held coils of old hurricane fencing, a portable cement mixer and two construction trucks. Every light inside the new structure was on, making it appear very welcoming to this weary crew. Denton cut the motor and started to open his door. But Astrid shot him a single word. A thought that was also a plea.

Wait.

He and the young lady remained as they were, even when Astrid's mother rattled the wheelchair against the open passenger door and snapped, 'Can you possibly make a little effort of your own?'

'Leave it, Mom. Denton will help me. We need a moment.'

'Well.' The older woman stalked away.

The others from Denton's vehicle walked forward and joined the families climbing from the bus. It was like watching a circus clown act, a never-ending stream of people and luggage gathering under the entrance's overhang.

Then a man stepped through the entry. Denton felt the night freeze. 'What is he doing here?'

Professor Sean Stiles accepted several embraces, shook Terrance Alderton's hand, then leaned over so a young man in a wheelchair could wrap arms around his neck.

All the while, Stiles continued to meet Denton's gaze. Solemn even when he was smiling a hello to the newcomers.

Astrid slipped away from Denton and took her mother's place in the passenger seat. 'I have some things you need to hear. But first you need to be listening.'

'I asked you a question.'

'You'll have all the answers you can handle.' She pointed through the windscreen at Sean. 'From the man there.'

'Astrid . . .'

'I know. Histories are terrible things. I don't have to look any further than dear old Mom to know how they can weigh down a life. She's still angry with a man she hasn't seen in almost twenty years. Not since he decided he didn't want to live with a messed-up daughter, then vanished into a night just like this one.' Astrid reached over and punched his arm. 'But we don't have time for that. I need you to pay attention.'

'No hitting.'

She struck him again. A third time. Her blows carried the force of falling feathers. 'Tell me when you're done sulking and I'll stop.'

'Why are you like this?'

'You mean, so wondrously improved? Such a delightful bundle of joy?' She struck him again. 'Are you listening yet?'

'All right. Yes. Enough with the hitting.'

She dropped her arm, breathing heavily. 'I volunteered for a job tomorrow. I want you to do the same.'

'I asked about Sean.'

'Pay attention. Sean will tell you about Sean, and a lot about tomorrow as well.' She lifted her fist. 'Listening?'

'I told you I would.'

'You look so handsome when you sulk – has anyone ever told you that?' She unfurled her fist, reached over, touched his arm. 'This is really, really important.'

Which was when he was filled with a sense of joining, the first since leaving the airport carpark. Only this time, the urgency carried a deep sense of solemn need. A great vast chorus of mental power. Denton lost his ability to argue. 'OK.'

'I'm dying. I don't have much time. So before you and Sean talk about everything that needs to happen tomorrow, I have a request. A big, huge ask.'

'Wait, you're dying? For real?'

'Do you think I'd joke about that?'

'No, I mean, you look so great.'

'Some things they can correct. At least temporarily. Others, not.' She gave that a beat. 'We all die sometime, remember?'

'How long do you have?'

'I'm checking out tomorrow.'

The calm statement, the flat gleam in her round gaze, the force of unseen multitudes pressing him forward left him wanting to weep. 'I'm so sorry.'

'Thank you, Denton.' Her words almost a song. 'So I want to ask you a favor.'

'Anything.'

'This place has a pool. I checked. You know, on the drive.'

He nodded. 'Through this communion.'

'Wow. Communion. That's new. I like it a lot.' Solemn once more. 'So. My ask. Something I've always wanted to do. Since forever. Will you take me swimming?'

THIRTY-EIGHT

Kelly found the amount of incoming data to be utterly overwhelming.

Only that term, *data*, no longer fit.

She was flooded with a torrent of unnecessary information. Even so, Kelly resisted the urge to pull away. The only way forward was to link with Rabbit and go no further. Let him maintain the bridge to the others. And then . . . What?

She had no idea.

Just as she was about to admit defeat and pull away, she remembered . . .

She was there. On the gun range. Her first day learning how to handle a rifle. Shooting long-range. Her reward for being top of her class with a handgun. They had gradually shifted Kelly to new targets, until she was taking aim at a tiny white speck four hundred and fifty yards away. Then she followed the instructor's directions and resettled behind the scope. Focused down so intently there was no room for anything but the weapon, the target, the conditions.

Ready. Aim . . .

A great deal of Kelly's training had centered upon parsing out all emotions, every possible shred of non-essential information. Focus only on that which was key to her mission's success. The data that was needed to keep her and her team alive.

This has gradually become an unconscious act. Kelly had learned to ignore the clamor of a live-fire situation, the high-stress moments that caused civilians to freeze up solid. And die as a result.

Only now, in this new situation, the hard-earned lessons were under threat. The data-selection process had to be redefined.

She opened her eyes and looked at Rabbit.

Rabbit winced but held her gaze and her hand.

Kelly whispered, 'I don't mean to invade like this.'

'I understand.'

Agnes broke in, her hard-edged face observing from a screen to Kelly's right. 'What is going on here?'

Kelly shifted her chair so that the monitor showing Agnes moved

totally out of her field of vision. There was no way she was going
to insert herself into that woman. Not now, maybe not ever.

Agnes barked, 'Kaiser.'

Kelly took a long, slow breath. Another. While keeping her gaze
on Rabbit, she said, 'Darren?'

'Go.'

'I want to try something. Call it a trial run.'

'What do you need?'

First and foremost, she wanted to ensure these observers could
not impact her focus. 'Barry, clear away all the screens. I don't
mean close the connections. Just get them all behind me and Rabbit.
I need to cut out the visual noise.'

She kept her focus on Rabbit's hand while Riggs and Pamela
moved around the room. Then, 'OK, that should do it. Now I need
a sat photo of the reservation.'

Grey Mathers responded, 'We don't have one. Not from this
summer.'

Agnes said, 'Normally, this time of year there is a temporary
village, mostly of wooden huts. A few more permanent sheds
constructed from sheets of corrugated metal.'

'They fish, they hunt, they plant a couple of small fields,' Grey
said. 'When the first snows arrive, they head south.'

'Winter storms tear the place apart,' Agnes said. 'Come spring,
they return and rebuild. Only not this year.'

Grey asked, 'I can shoot you an image of last year's village.'

'No.' Kelly had a long way to go. But she was coming to understand the task required her to focus. This was her purpose. She
knew that now. Her intent, her training, the abilities that made her
a good agent. This was what Rabbit's team had been missing. She
said, 'Show me a sat image of what is there now.'

'Grey?'

'Give me a minute.'

Kelly did not mind the wait. She used the time to examine this
link with Rabbit. Coming to terms with what it meant. In doing so,
Kelly realized three things.

First, so long as they were open and linked, the language
barrier could be overcome. Of course it still existed. But a
communication *beyond* words was doable. Not by her, of course.
Not yet. Rabbit served as both conduit and interpreter. His link
was Diyani . . .

Which led to the second point.

They trusted her.

The concept took on a whole new meaning. Around all of Rabbit's team, Diyani included, hovered tragic shadows of fear and hardship and loss. And, in the case of Rabbit and Diyani, a brighter halo of love.

These highly personal issues, these private elements of their lives, were fully exposed. It was within her power to examine them more closely. They were trusting her not to take that step. The ability to breach their barriers and know their secrets did not mean she should. Kelly hoped they could sense her turning away.

Agnes broke in then. 'Sorry it's taking so long. Grey has to go through NSA to access the satellite archives.' When Kelly did not respond, she continued, 'Kelly, good tactics require good observations. Anything you can give us in regard to what you're experiencing will help develop future tactics.'

'Soon,' Kelly replied. 'Not yet. I don't have a handle on what's happening.'

'Understood.'

Kelly resumed her internal inspection. She felt as if she was growing a new set of eyes. This time, though, it was formed through sixteen individuals acting as one.

That was the foundation for her third new understanding. This ability did not erase individuality. They remained individuals. And yet they accessed this awareness through a bond unlike anything that had ever come before.

She decided to take this new awareness out for a spin.

She asked Rabbit, 'While we're waiting, can we take a look at when Greg and his team vanished from your sight?'

Rabbit frowned. 'You mean, like a specific point in time?'

Kelly took her time responding. *Point in time.* The issue formed a core component of gathering evidence. Developing a solid timeline was crucial to identifying the perpetrators.

Kelly asked, 'What if we looked at when they exited the airport terminal. Can you do that?'

In response, she felt him link more intensely with Diyani. 'We can try.'

Kelly spoke to the team at large. 'We need to link through the airport security cameras again. Can someone help us with that?'

Darren replied, 'On it.'

Kelly closed her eyes and kept them eyes shut until she heard Rabbit say, 'OK, you need to look.'

Kelly refocused on the outside world. Barry had shifted one laptop back over to where she looked squarely at the screen. She saw, and yet her attention remained mostly focused on what Rabbit and his team were doing.

Then Kelly corrected herself. *Her* team.

Kelly watched the group of newly infested and their families maneuver around the prone bodies.

'Their camouflage starts the instant they leave the terminal,' Rabbit said.

Denton Hayes and the pale young man, Greg Alderton, were the last to exit. Kelly watched as they loaded into the two vehicles, the bus and Denton's SUV, moving at a well-coordinated pace. Adults settled the two individuals in wheelchairs into place. The last baggage was stored, everybody seated and ready. Then . . .

The ability to sense them, feel this intense awareness of who precisely was raised to this new level . . .

Gone.

Kelly said, 'Freeze it right there.'

Rabbit sat there a long moment, holding her hand. Then, 'We can't see them.'

'That's not the point. *Feel* what happened. That transition. One moment there, the next . . .'

Rabbit was quiet so long Kelly feared he was unable to sense what she found so captivating. 'A cloud.'

'Or fog. Something. When we have the satellite feed, we know what to look for. Forget trying to find the group. Same goes for the Hudson Bay community. We want to hunt for the hidden.'

Rabbit's hand tightened on hers. 'Can we do that?'

Kelly had no idea.

Which was when Grey Mathers came back online and announced, 'OK, we have the sat feed up and ready.'

Inspecting the satellite feed took no time at all.

Rabbit and his crew now understood the purpose, why looking for the invisible had been so important. What was more, the exercise using Kelly's guidance had helped forge a stronger bond. They had the confidence to rely on her for their next compass heading.

Taking aim.

Finally Kelly broke the link and reported to Agnes, who then began a lengthy discussion with Grey Mathers, trying to decide how best to work their way through the Washington tangle.

When she could, Kelly excused herself and left the room.

Forging the connection, going on the hunt, had left her oddly drained. She returned to her room and began a long series of stretches, trying to work through the mental weight as well as the stiffness that had settled into her tendons and bones. When she was ready, she texted Darren and Barry that she was going for another run, then she set off.

Just as she reached her turnaround point, Darren Cotton called. 'Looks like they're going to need another couple of hours to set this up, Kelly.'

'Fine by me.' She returned to the apart-hotel, stretched a second time, showered, then made herself a solitary meal. She liked how Rabbit and his crew did not crowd in. Alone still meant just that. She had the sense that she could reach out, but only if she wanted. And they could connect with her again if required. Otherwise, she was free to remain as she had been for the past hundred-plus days. Enduring her solitary existence.

She was cleaning up when Darren texted and said they were almost ready.

Kelly entered the apartment they used as an ops center and discovered everyone was there. All the laptops were open and showed individual faces. It was good to see her Washington-based team included, spread around the room, as though they belonged. As though they were all working toward the exact same goal.

Barry had positioned the laptops holding Agnes and Grey on the long central table. Three more laptops were stationed to either side. These showed Homeland shields. Darren greeted her, then went back to studying something off-screen. Then, 'Heads up, everyone. Thirty seconds. Barry, shift the camera a fraction to your right.' Barry walked over and moved the camera on its black stand, then stepped back. 'Perfect. OK, everyone. Here we go.'

General Skarren, new chief of DOD intel, showed up first. Then the second screen flashed to life, holding the face of Avri Rowe. 'Afternoon, everyone. Good to see you again, Agent Kaiser.'

'Likewise, sir.'

'I understand there've been some changes since you and I last spoke.'

Agnes said, 'Important changes. Vital to our national interests.'

Rowe nodded. 'OK, who is our Canadian contact?'

Agnes replied. 'Gabriel Gagne holds two positions. He is Deputy Minister of the Interior and also assistant head of the department called Crown–Indigenous Relations and Northern Affairs.'

Skarren said, 'That's a mouthful, sure enough.'

Agnes said, 'It was as high as I could get on short notice.'

'So, if necessary, we'll treat this as a trial run. General, you want to handle it?'

'Your team, your show, Avri.'

'Agnes, you start off; I'll jump in if or when it's required. Everybody ready? OK, make the connection.'

The last screen flashed to life, revealing a round-faced man, skin the color of caramel latte. Dark hair streaked with silver. Eyes of onyx, a stone-hard gaze. 'I am officially being required to set aside a very busy afternoon. What's this all about?'

Agnes limited the introductions to herself, Avri Rowe and the general. She then said, 'We need access to your Hudson Bay reservation.'

'First of all . . . Agnes, is it? This is not *my* anything. It belongs to the Northern Cree people. Second, why is your request not going through proper channels?'

'This is a matter of extreme urgency, Minister.'

'Maybe to you.' He took his time, inspecting the faces on his screen. 'Why is the American military involved in this so-called emergency?'

'They are present in an advisory capacity only. Our operation is being handled strictly through Homeland.'

'Out of the question. Your request is denied.' He leaned back and crossed his arms. 'Was there anything else? Or can I get back to my *real* work?'

Kelly broke in with, 'He knows. He knows and he's protecting them.'

Gagne lifted his chin so as to stare down the length of his impressive nose at Kelly. 'Who is this person fashioning insults from smoke?'

Kelly went on, 'We're talking with the Deputy Minister because his former boss has joined them.'

Avri demanded, 'What, at the reservation?'

'Roger that.' Kelly pointed at the increasingly irate Canadian.

'He's planning to join them as well. He's stayed where he is to shield them. But not for much longer.'

'All right, that's enough.' Avri's bark came to the fore. 'Agnes, arrange a call with the Prime Minister. Sir, enjoy your job while you still have it.'

Gagne smirked. 'I was thinking the exact same thing about you.'

When the Canadian's screen went blank, Avri said, 'Everyone stay where you are. We're going to kick this up a level. General?'

'Ready when you are.'

Their screens, and the ones showing Agnes Pendalon and her aide, all went blank. The room and Kelly's team in DC all took a breath, rose from their seats, stretched.

Kelly remained where she was. Still and focused.

Rabbit asked, 'Kelly?'

'Thinking.' Actually, she was captured by the sense of Nathan being in the room.

Three seconds later, he was gone.

In that brief space, Kelly came to a full understanding of Nathan's snowbound message. *Don't.*

He had bridged the impossible divide precisely because of this. Her sudden overwhelming urge to turn away from reality. Use her newfound mental abilities and follow him beyond the veil of life.

But even if she did so, if she gave in to her own demise, there was no certainty she would find him.

Nathan's soft whisper came again, quiet as falling snow, powerful as a thunderbolt.

Hard as it was, she did what he would have wanted.

She took a shuddering breath and drew the room back into focus. She had time to accept a fresh mug, take a sip, then Darren Cotton said, 'Places, everyone.'

THIRTY-NINE

Denton entered the lobby and was handed a key by Terrance Alderton, Greg's father. 'You're on the third floor, midway down on the left. Elevators behind you. But with this crowd, you might prefer the stairs. No luggage?'

'Didn't know I was traveling when I left home this morning.' Home. A faraway word, one that did not fit with his current state.

Unlike his wife, Terrance struck Denton as a man who had met years of hard times with a cheerful nature. 'You're what, a thirty-six waist?'

'On my good days. Otherwise, it's a thirty-eight. And I need a bathing suit.'

'You and I are close enough in size. My trunks are clean but well worn.'

'That will do fine.'

Terrance rounded the lobby desk and opened a door marked *Manager*. A minute later, he returned and handed Denton swim trunks decorated with faded sailboats. 'It's a good thing, what you're doing. Great, in fact.'

Denton nodded and headed for the stairs, glad Sean Stiles had not been present. Avoiding that confrontation was absolutely fine by him.

The suites' interior was much more upscale than Denton had expected – fully equipped kitchen, high-end appliances, marble-topped counter, leather-and-wood furniture, large and beautifully appointed bedroom and bath. Everything was brand new. Two of his dining chairs still wore their plastic shipping wrappers. Despite the a/c blowing on high, the place smelled of paint and cleaner. Denton changed and returned downstairs, hoping against hope he might avoid Sean for the rest of his stay.

What Astrid's mother thought of Denton taking her daughter for a swim, he had no idea. Nor did he have a chance to ask, for Astrid was seated in her wheelchair, towel across her useless legs, wearing a baggy swimsuit of palest pink.

But she was not alone.

Greg Alderton and two more of the crew were with her, along

with a couple of older women. They all greeted Denton's arrival with what could only be described as solemn joy.

Astrid showed him a flame from crystal eyes that burned with the intensity of her anticipation. 'Thanks.'

He wondered why she had asked him. When so many of the others were clearly ready to take his place, be the ones to introduce her to the aquatic world. 'My pleasure.' And in a strange way, it was.

There was a ceremonial quality to the occasion. Denton pushed her wheelchair down the long corridor and out the rear doors, followed by over a dozen silent processionals. He used the pool's electronic winch to settle Astrid into the water, observed by a crowd that grew larger by the moment. 'Are you cold?'

'Too excited.'

He slipped into the water, took hold of her hands, and . . .

Connected.

He had felt a vague link with Astrid several times during the journey. But this was something else entirely. Astrid was part of this new awareness, but mostly she served as the conduit. Because what held him there was the bonding force of *dozens* of others.

They *gave*.

They *supported* her.

They *loved*.

This was how the woman had experienced such a remarkable turnaround, he realized. The potent force, amplified through the joining of multiple lives and hearts. There simply to give. Offer this remarkable woman a taste of what her life had not contained until now.

Just as Denton was doing.

The act of drawing her gently from the chair, pulling her forward, allowing her to come as close to swimming as she could, gliding her through the chilly waters, granted him the opportunity to become part of this unified force. He saw how her spine and muscles could not be repaired. But the power of speech, connecting to the outside world without the lifelong barriers – this they could do. At least for one brief day.

Because what Astrid had said was true. Tomorrow she would leave this earth.

The awareness of her departure, becoming part of this incredible outflowing of energy and love, caused him to shed tears of his own. He knew there was no reason to be ashamed. But he kept ducking his head below the surface, washing away the evidence of how his internal world was being reshaped. All by the act of pulling this woman around the pool. Careful to keep her head above water.

By the time they had made a full circuit of the pool, Denton had mostly regained control. He spotted Astrid's mother in the crew, standing well back, face a stone mask, arms crossed over her chest. He asked softly, 'Why don't others like your mom, you know . . .'

'Join the club?' She nodded, little more than a shiver. 'In time.'

He nodded back, the answer there in the silent communication with the myriad of others. The answer was there between them, not that he had asked. There was a precise timeline for everything that was happening. But those who wanted would join. In time. 'Want to try diving?'

'Oh, yes.'

'Eyes open, deep breath, hold it . . . OK, here we go.'

He squatted and pulled her under, not far, a few inches. Enough so her world became the blue floating void.

Dusk painted the water with copper strokes. He lifted her up, gave her time to breathe, then gently back down again. A third time, then, 'Let's turn you over. Don't worry, I'll keep your head above the surface.'

'I'm not worried, Denton. At all.' She allowed him to swing her around, so she faced the cloudless desert sky. Able to see all the smiling faces that now rimmed the pool, painted by the sunset's gentle wash.

FORTY

When Avri and Skarren's faces returned to the monitors, the President's Chief of Staff launched straight in with his habitual bark. 'OK, Kaiser. Tell me about this place that's not there. And forget about trying to explain what I probably won't ever fully understand. In precisely twelve minutes, Skarren and I are going to brief the President.'

The general added, 'And the SecDef.'

'And others. You may be called upon to join us. But that will probably wait for round two. Right now, I need to know how certain you are this invisible place is actually there.'

'The community is definitely present, sir.'

'On a scale of one to ten.'

'A hundred.'

'You've seen it?'

'I don't need to.'

'Explain.'

'Darren, show them the most recent satellite image, and beside it the one from last year.' When the two images shared the screen, Kelly went on, 'We have focused this new perceptive ability on the entire region. And that section by the lake, where the community existed last year, is most definitely camouflaged.'

'Tell me how you can be so certain.'

'First, there is a definite wrongness to that point on the image. We can't penetrate, but we don't need to. That area by the lake, it holds a total falseness.' Kelly gave him a moment to bark, but when Rowe remained silent, she continued, 'Equally important, we have been tracking a lone individual, one Greg Alderton, who recently joined with the group, and who we believe is now headed in this direction. He too has vanished, and done so using a system that carries the same signature. Darren, show him the airport security footage.'

When the monitor showed Greg and the attorney, Kelly went on, 'This is the last time we actually see him. From this point on, he vanishes. We should be able to track him, but we can't. Instead, we catch these vague whispers of the same camouflage that shields the community.'

'Vague whispers,' Rowe repeated.

'This is one of the issues we currently face, sir. Trying to use words that don't fit.'

He nodded. 'Agnes tells me there is an attorney who has been photographed aiding and abetting.'

'Her name is Connor Breach, a senior attorney with NovaCorp. We're fairly certain she has not joined their ranks. But she is definitely assisting the enemy.'

'Be very careful when going after attorneys with experience in federal courts,' Rowe cautioned. 'I'm not saying don't do it. But take care.'

'Roger that.'

'Back to the town that's not there. Break that down a little for me.'

'When we survey the region,' Kelly replied, 'there is a very distinct flavor. Northern woodlands. A true wilderness.'

'But not at that one point – is that what you're telling me?'

'Precisely. Where the community should be, there is *nothing*. A complete void. We're absolutely certain they are hiding in plain sight.'

'*We* are certain?'

'Myself and Rabbit's team. Sorry, sir, I mean—'

'I know who Rabbit is. And the vital role his team plays. Go on.'

'All of our physical senses, their mode of what we class as a normal biological process, interpret vibratory patterns of specific types of energy. What we see, taste, feel . . . all this is a combination of specific physical contacts to the outside world, interpreted by our brains.' Kelly tapped the side of her head. 'This is a *new* sense. It requires a *new* vocabulary. For the moment, what you need to understand is that we are totally certain, beyond any shred of doubt, that the enemy is building a new semi-permanent community on the shores of Lake Hudson.' Kelly gave that a beat, then continued, 'Then there is the other element. Take it as physical confirmation of what we have sensed.'

'And that is?'

'We've been tracking a missing house, taken from the Beverly Flats area of Los Angeles.'

'Agnes briefed me. So?'

'This is far from an isolated incident.' She glanced to her DC-based team. 'Darren?'

'The count currently stands at one hundred and ninety-three houses, four apartment buildings, two recently completed hotels,' Darren said. 'Plus labs, warehouses – the list is four pages long and growing by the hour.'

'Why are we only hearing about this now?'

'Almost all of it takes place beyond our national borders,' Agnes replied. Kelly thought she sounded tired. Or exasperated. Or both. 'On many of these missing structures, it has proven extremely hard to obtain verifiable intel.'

'Local governments are hiding things,' Darren said. 'No question.'

'This is developing into a list of regions and nations that we class as shadow states. Not with us, not against us. Waiting to see which way the prevailing wind blows.'

'Including Canada,' Darren said. 'Thirty-seven structures vanished. That we've confirmed so far.'

'It's also possible these missing structures represent new enemy settlements we have not yet identified,' Agnes said. 'This new potential camouflage Kelly is describing also means we have no way of confirming where else they are establishing settlements.'

Skarren said, 'Just the same, there's no way we can use this as a lever against the Canucks.'

'We don't need to.' Avri Rowe was oddly cheerful.

'They're harboring the enemy!'

'Yes, they are. And now that we know this, we can take concrete steps to make them pay,' Rowe said. 'By letting them know this threat to our national security won't go unanswered.'

Agnes said, 'Plant a shot across their bows.'

'More than that,' Avri Rowe replied. 'Much more. We want to bloody their nose.'

'I like this,' Skarren said.

'Agnes, we want to startle them out of their complacent Canadian smugness. Wake them up to the fact this is a war, and they risk being planted firmly on the losing side.'

'Take the fight to them,' Skarren said. 'I like this a lot.'

'But cautiously,' Rowe added. 'Whatever we do next, it needs to remain within legal boundaries. We can't go shooting Tomahawks over the Canadian border.'

'Subtle,' Agnes said. 'But clear as day.'

'Precisely. You and your teams are hereby ordered to find us a way to make that happen,' Rowe said. 'Now then. One final issue. I'm looking for something that can bring the rest of the President's team on board. Anything you can give me – a reason for them to go out on the limb. You see what I'm saying? We're talking about confronting one of our closest allies with an act that could change everything.'

It was the most Kelly had ever heard him say. She took that as a sign of how stressed he was. The words also served as a goad. Pushing her to look in a different direction. Use the magnification granted her by the combined force of Rabbit's team. 'Actually, sir, there is one thing. A possibility. Not a certainty.'

'Understood. Let's hear it.'

'Agnes and her team have repeatedly found a group with either physical or mental disabilities at the center of several new outbreaks. We can confirm this trait is repeated within the crew we're tracking. There has to be a single reason, something so intensely vital, they are risking everything. If it wasn't for this group, we wouldn't have any clear lead on where to hunt.'

Agnes said, 'I've wondered about that.'

Cotton said, 'Hive mind? Some trait that makes them more likely to join up?'

'Yes, but to what end? This group we're currently hunting, they've been described as single-minded in their focus. The woman responsible for their day-care center related how they spent hours, days, weeks, breaking down the structure of electronic games.'

'OK, so?'

'So now they *join*. What if their previous disabilities leave them open to erasing individual boundaries altogether? Their focus is magnified, their mental acuity heightened, their so-called disabilities are lessened. Perhaps erased. There's something about their previous existence that makes them extremely vital. This we know. What if it isn't one specific direction? What if *any* direction can be taken?'

It was Skarren who demanded, 'Give us a "for instance."'

Kelly nodded. Thinking it was right for the military mind to jump forward. 'We have a balance of power between nations because the level of armaments is more or less in sync. Say one group manages to take this to an entirely new level. One where the military-industrial complex is turned into a historical relic?'

'It keeps me up nights,' Skarren admitted. 'They can do this?'

'I'm giving you possibilities only, General. But if you want my opinion, I'd say it's already happening.'

'OK,' Rowe said. 'I was worried before. Now I'm frightened.'

'There's more,' Kelly said. 'Right now, the stock and bond and currency markets are dominated by traders who use algorithms to guide their moves. These set up actions in many cases that are independent of direct human involvement. They establish floors and ceilings. They initiate trades.'

'You're suggesting they're working on a next-gen set of market predictors?'

'If you ask me, this is where they might be focused, at least for the immediate future. Our foes are currently establishing multiple new communities. They have needs. Food, equipment, medicines – the list is endless. They are stealing homes, warehouses, hundreds of structures to house their rapidly growing numbers. So they reach out to groups like this one and, say, find a way to make a lot of money, fast . . .'

Kelly stopped talking because Rowe's screen had already gone blank.

FORTY-ONE

Once Astrid was out of the pool and being cared for by others, Denton headed indoors. The lobby and adjoining lounge were filled with families, the children clustered and shouting and laughing. It took him a few moments to understand why. The adults were allowing them to order from Uber Eats. Whatever they wanted. As much of everything. It made for a change from all the unhappy faces he had seen as they left Los Angeles.

When he opened the door to his apartment, Denton found a stack of new clothes and supplies laid out on the kitchen counter – cotton drawstring slacks, sandals, knit shirt, sweater, hairbrush, razor, the works. Denton showered and dressed and returned downstairs to find the dining area off the lobby now holding a veritable smorgasbord. The little town proved to have a vast assortment of restaurants, including an ice-cream parlor that had delivered Styrofoam containers lined with dry ice that smoked. As he loaded a plate, Denton heard several of the adults talking with Sean. For once, the professor's presence did not rattle him. He listened as the adults marveled over how it felt to do something so outrageously expensive. These families were clearly accustomed to guarding every penny. The cost of this spread took their breath away. And something more. Gradually, it was dawning on them all, even the young and sulky, that life might actually be changing for the better.

Denton filled his plate and went in search of solitude and quiet. The day's events pressed in on him now. He returned to the pool area and seated himself at one of the metal tables. The evening remained baking hot, but very different from LA's oppressive conditions. The bone-dry air held a myriad of desert fragrances – creosote and sorrel and scents he could not name. He stared at the empty pool and recalled the moment he had entered LAX's private air terminal.

He had stood by the entrance and watched as a wave of sheer unbridled force swept over the entire building. Every single body within view dropped unconscious to the floor. Everyone but himself and Greg Alderton. For an instant, he had feared this implacable power had stopped everyone's heart. He had stood there beside the proned-out bodies, staring down a stubby side corridor that ended in a locked steel door marked *Security*. Suddenly, the electronic lock had switched from red to green. When the door clicked open, a motley assortment of families had piled out. Greeting him and Greg. Calm and happy and treating Denton like he belonged. Like he was one of them.

They had returned to the bus and Denton's ride, loaded up and headed out. To here. Seated by an empty pool, beneath a silver desert wash of stars. Coming to terms with what it meant to enter this new phase of existence.

Denton finished his meal, pushed the plate aside and knew with utter certainty this very same force had been at work in Astrid. The longer they had remained linked together by hands and water, the more his new awareness took shape. The way these unseen others had joined with Astrid, how they had offered her the temporary gift of everything possible, a final few days of light and clarity and speech, the sheer flood of compassion surrounding it all . . .

The night now served as a mirror, pressing him to view his days from a different perspective. Suffering through a hopeless affair, one that bound him to a woman who would never be his. Twice nearly destroyed by the futile loss. All this formed a well-known path. Only now . . .

Denton faced the alternative. What might have been, how he might have spent his days, if he had rejected the married woman's magnetic draw. Chosen a different course. One that rendered him open to more occasions like this afternoon. Helping others because he could. Grieving without thought of self.

Strangely enough, there was no guilt. No remorse. Instead, the realization opened his mind and heart to a sense of new beginnings. A portal he was being invited to walk through.

It was not just this strange group of families who faced the challenge of monumental change.

It seemed almost appropriate that Sean Stiles chose that moment to walk around the pool, heading towards Denton.

Sean was followed by several adults and a number of excited young children, all of them dressed for a night-time swim. Sean watched the children leap into the water, spoke briefly with the adults, then rounded the pool. 'May I sit down?'

Denton gestured at the empty chair. Viewing his life as a failed
opportunity left him feeling like a shattered gourd. There was no
room for condemning the man he had blamed for causing so much
pain. 'Are you doing this to me?'

Sean did not pretend at ignorance. 'Absolutely not. Just the same,
this mirror you're facing is part of the transition. And since I indi-
rectly supplied you with the leaf, I suppose you could say I have a
hand in it, after all.'

'You always were defined by conflicting aims.' Denton had spent
years wanting to shout at the man. Strip the lofty professor with
his rage. As it was, the words emerged in a toneless drone. 'Wanting
to keep Ryan. Wanting every coed within easy reach.'

'Which is why I volunteered for this duty.' Sean rocked the metal
chair, creasing the night with gentle motions. 'So I could apologize
face to face.'

'Duty?'

But Sean would not be redirected so easily. 'Addicts in recovery
are urged to apologize where possible. Make amends when we can.
Accept the burden of all the pain we've caused others. Making this
transition doesn't change any of that.' He shrugged. 'At times, I
feel like it's made it worse. All the veils I've used to blind myself,
they're gradually being stripped away. The mirror of past deeds . . .'

Denton had no choice but to agree. 'It makes for a dreadful
burden, seeing myself in that mirror.'

'I'm very sorry, Denton. You deserved far better than I ever
allowed.'

'And Ryan.'

Speaking the name silenced them both. Sean nodded. Wiped his
face. Nodded again.

They watched the shouting, laughing children for a time. Long
enough for the night to heal, at least partially. When it was time,
Sean asked, 'Can I tell you what we are hoping will happen
tomorrow? And why we so desperately need your help?'

FORTY-TWO

Early evening found Connor still wading through make-work when Rachel phoned and said Byron wanted her to come up. Connor responded by asking if Jackie Barlow could be included.

When the two women entered together, Byron greeted Connor with, 'I think it would help if you walked us through this latest episode in its entirety. I have the sense Denton only touched the surface.'

'There's certainly a lot to take in,' Connor agreed. She laid it out in detail, starting with the Palisades dinner, viewing the video of a different man from the professor Denton had known. On through Denton's thirty-second meeting in the men's room, the four-car procession back to his home and then the homes themselves. Both of them.

Gradually, her words slowed. Reliving the experiences carried an unexpected impact. As if it was only now, while relating events in this silent conference room, that the true weight of what she had experienced came to life. She related the moment Denton revealed the BMW slumbering beneath the canvas wrap. Which was unimportant in a way. Unnecessary. Except for how it brought the entire episode into crystal clarity. So intense she might as well have been back there again, pulling into the airport parking garage.

Finding Ryan Stiles there waiting for her.

Connor slowed further and related their discussion in almost word-for-word detail. She described Denton's farewell words. *Parti pris*. Explained what they meant. Then on to her entering the airport alone. Meeting the strange young man. Watching Sanjib Gupta be escorted by multiple agents through the terminal. Hearing Greg Alderton's final warning.

When she was done and Byron remained silent, Jackie asked, 'Any chance our guy could have told the lady to meet him at the airport?'

'At that precise location and point in time?'

'I agree, it's a stretch.' She glanced at their boss. When Byron did not speak, Jackie went on, 'Denton owning those two apartments, that surprises me.'

'I was floored. And something else.'

Jackie nodded her understanding. 'It's not often someone fools me like Denton has. Researching what I thought was the real guy, totally missing the deeper truth in the process.'

'Everything you uncovered was real enough,' Byron said. 'Just not the complete picture.'

Jackie asked, 'This agent who confronted Denton – what's her name again?'

'Kelly Kaiser.'

Jackie watched Byron rise and walk to the exterior window. Softly tapped the glass. Same as the first time he had met Denton Hayes. For all intents and purposes lost to them and the room.

Jackie said, 'Sooner or later, Kaiser is going to know you were there. In the terminal. Observing.'

'I agree.'

'That is, assuming she's got one of these . . . What should I call them?'

'I have no idea.'

Byron addressed the window, 'Ask Denton for help with the necessary vocabulary.'

'Will do.' Connor silently added, *Assuming I have contact with him again.*

Which brought to the fore the one little item she had neglected to mention.

How much she found herself missing the man.

Then she saw Jackie's smile. 'What?'

'Oh, nothing.'

Any place else, Connor would have snapped at the woman for her unspoken thoughts. As it was, she found herself struggling not to smile back.

Byron turned back to the table. 'You're going to meet Campion tomorrow?'

'Unless you say otherwise.' Almost hoping he would order her to stay away.

Instead, Byron asked, 'You're meeting the LA detective?'

'Tonight,' Connor confirmed. 'I texted and she's confirmed. It has to be totally off the record, since she's no longer involved in an investigation that doesn't exist.' Connor told Jackie, 'I was hoping you might be willing to come along for the ride.'

'Count on it.'

Byron said, 'I also think some additional security would be in order.'

Jackie said, 'In any other circumstances, I'd say it was overkill. But given what I've just heard, I'll set it up.'

FORTY-THREE

K elly and Rabbit spent the afternoon at a desk by their ops center's front window. Trying to make good on Rowe's challenge.

First, they talked the issue to death. Speaking softly, just the two of them and Riggs. Using her number two as an anchor to the here and now. Trying to define the hunt. Kelly thought it was sort of like identifying the haystack. So they could start searching for the needle.

By late afternoon they were as close to ready as they would probably get. Kelly and Rabbit linked with Diyani's group and searched for a long and futile hour.

When they stopped for dinner, Darren reported that a contact within the Mexican government had come through with another missing structure – this time, it was three and a half acres of green-houses, plus two refrigerated warehouses, a large equipment shed, the works. Kelly suggested he pass the intel to Agnes, then mentally filed it away. There just wasn't room.

She and Rabbit worked another thirty minutes after the break, but Kelly could tell her linked-up team were flagging. 'We'll call it a night.'

'Another few minutes,' Rabbit said.

'No, this is enough.' She thanked Rabbit and through him his group, then turned to where Riggs sat, feet up on the next desk to hers, cradling a mug. 'If you were any more relaxed, you'd be snoring.'

'Too late,' Pamela said. 'He's been lights out for the past twenty minutes.'

'Hey, this is a duty I was born for.' He raised his mug. 'Ricard just made a fresh pot.'

'OK. Good.' Kelly rose and stretched and accepted the mug. Her crew were spread around the room, working phones and computers, helping Darren and the DC team. Together, they monitored air traffic control, checked all the regional airports and private landing strips, kept tabs on reports from military bases and Coast Guard. A state-wide alert had been sent out for the Toyota minivan Denton had rented at LAX. Jon Alvero occupied a station by the rear window.

Making himself part of the team. So far, though, all their efforts had turned up nothing.

Riggs watched Rabbit rise slowly, unkinking his neck and shoulders. 'No dice?'

Riggs had been close enough to follow her and Rabbit's conversation. Kelly replied so all the others, including the faces clustered around Darren back in DC, could hear. 'We haven't found them.'

'Yet,' Rabbit added.

'But we're learning new skills. Pushing the boundaries of what's possible. We're pretty sure now we can focus on an individual even if we don't have a location. And then widen the search.' She pointed to Rabbit. 'Basically, we're expanding on what Rabbit did to find Greg Alderton and the attorney at LAX.'

'That was different. I had a trail. They were close. They weren't masked. That attorney, Connor Breach, stood out like a beacon. We had a lot of things to track.' Rabbit waved his hand at the world beyond the window. 'But the group is masked. The lawyer isn't with them anymore. They're gone.'

'Sounds pretty futile to me,' Riggs said.

'Yes and no.' Kelly gave one brief moment to wondering why Connor Breach had stood out so clearly. Wondering if this was part of their deception. But there was no logical reason she could find for this apparent vulnerability. So she went on, 'You saw that Canadian official. He and all those others, they think they're in control and hold all the power. They've grown used to staying one step ahead. But Rabbit and I are on the verge of defining new methods to track and trace. Soon we're going to show them just how wrong they are.'

A couple of her team applauded. Jon Alvero offered two thumbs up and said, 'Well, all right.'

'We call it scanning,' Rabbit offered. 'We decided to focus on Denton Hayes, both because he's new and because Kelly has met him. We're pretty sure face-to-face contact helps forge a link.'

'We've actually made contact with Denton several times,' Kelly said. 'Which is why we can talk about it with this degree of certainty.'

Ricard asked, 'Why are we only hearing about this now?'

'Because he comes and goes,' Kelly replied. 'We're getting tight little flashes. Long enough to know it's him and ID his general direction.'

Rabbit swung their laptop around, pointed to a spot on the

California road map. 'He's driving northeast. Inland from LA. Staying on what we think are minor highways. Which is probably why the Highway Patrol hasn't been able to help. Where he is exactly, what his final destination might be, we have no idea.'

'We're fairly certain it's just his vehicle and the bus,' Kelly said. 'We have these quick photographic-style images of what he sees. Which is basically the bus's rear bumper. A few tight glimpses of what appears to be two-lane state roads in fairly bad condition.'

'It's like he can't mask himself,' Rabbit said. 'So he drives very close to the others in the bus. Every time he slips back, he becomes visible.'

'So we've been watching,' Kelly said. 'Hoping for a longer break. Enough to alert the Highway Patrol, give them a more precise location. But since we've come back from dinner, there's been a big nada.'

Riggs watched Kelly dry-scrub her face, asked, 'You OK?'

'Tired.' The word didn't go far enough. 'When am I scheduled to go on watch?'

'No watch for either of you tonight.' Riggs was firm on that point.

Kelly was in no state to argue. 'Wake me by six. We're due to meet Denton Hayes at Campion Security.'

'You think he'll show?'

Kelly had been wondering the same thing. 'Probably not. Just the same, we need to be prepped and there on time.'

Jon offered, 'I can handle that.'

Kelly was tempted, but decided, 'Thanks, but no. Whoever shows up needs to be treated as a major suspect. I'm hoping it will be Connor Breach. If that happens, I have a lawyer I want to fry up for breakfast.'

FORTY-FOUR

When Connor and Jackie emerged from the NovaCorp's front entrance, two pale-blue Lexus SUVs and numerous dark-suited security waited out front. Connor thought this was probably overkill but liked it just the same.

They drove to Connor's home, where she showered and packed another overnight bag. When she returned to her living room, she found it oddly comforting to find Jackie seated at her dining table and a security standing by her front door. Jackie rose to her feet and said, 'I'm concerned about Denton's ride still being there at the airport. That is, assuming it's as nice as you describe.'

'Nicer. But I don't have keys.'

Jackie smiled. 'Watch and learn, sister. Watch and learn.'

The evening was faultless. A super-dry desert wind blew strong out of the northeast, offering a temporary gift of mid-summer clarity. No clouds, no smog, not a single fire the length and breadth of southern California.

They drove to LAX, entered the T3 parking deck, climbed the circular route and halted by the BMW. Jackie said, 'This cherry belongs to Denton Hayes?'

Connor nodded. 'Nothing says perfection like German machinery.'

Jackie had the BMW's door popped and engine started in less than two minutes. She returned to Connor's open window and said, 'You should stay with the security and let me drive, you know, in case they have this ride under surveillance.'

'I thought you were a really nice person,' Connor said. 'I was wrong.'

Jackie Barlow lived in a relatively new, very nice highrise in the hills above La Brea. Jackie parked Denton's BMW in the underground garage, then re-emerged and led Connor up to her condo on the seventh floor. While Connor settled into her guestroom, Jackie ordered Mexican – enough to feed them, the security detail and numerous others besides. The lady was nothing if not generous. She and Connor took their meal on a balcony overlooking Hancock Park. They dined in the easy silence of old friends. Afterwards,

Connor stretched out on the sofa while Jackie turned the news on low, thinking she would rest her eyes for just a moment. Ten minutes tops.

The next thing she knew, Jackie was shaking her shoulder and saying, 'It's time.'

Among Los Angeles jazz enthusiasts and musical elite, the Rhythm Room held a legendary status. There were other places with more glitz and bigger names on their stages. The Rhythm Room was essentially a windowless basement, dressed up with brass chandeliers and walls clad in walnut and oak paneling. With the lights on full, it resembled an oversized library. When the bands came on and the glow illuminated crowds determined to ingest every nearly perfect note, the Rhythm Room purely rocked.

A solid caramel-skinned woman was seated at a table one row off the front. 'Detective Jones?'

'I'm off duty, hon. It's Celeste.'

'I'm Connor Breach. This is—'

'I know Jackie. How you doing, girl? Long time.'

'Too long. Good to see you, Celeste.'

She waited until they were seated and refused the waiter's offer of drinks to ask, 'Where is Denton?'

Connor replied, 'I have no idea.'

'Bad?'

'Different question, same answer.' Connor breathed around a sudden ache. 'I hope not.'

Celeste pointed to the stage. 'A guitarist by the name of Jeff Golub starts his first set in ten minutes. He's near the top of my list. Which means once he gets going, you can't interrupt the man. So talk fast.'

Connor knew her rapid-fire account missed more than it explained. Her telling was made harder still by everything she needed to leave out, simply because the explanations she offered would be only partial and merely confuse the core issue. Which was, *I'm so afraid.*

Celeste studied her a long moment. 'Do I have the whole picture?'

Jackie Barlow spoke for the first time since Connor had started. 'Not even close. But everything she's said, I can confirm as the absolute facts. Strange as they may sound.'

Celeste's honeyed gaze remained intent on Connor. 'Will you tell me the rest?'

'If you're sure you want to know.'

'That bad?'

'Worse,' Jackie replied. 'And the problem is, you can't unhear what she'll tell you. If you insist.'

Celeste drained her glass, lifted it and rattled the ice at a passing waiter. 'All you haven't told me. Have you broken any laws in the process of whatever this represents?'

'Definitely not. But the federal agent in charge, Kaiser, would say breaking laws is only part of the picture. Kaiser wants to bundle this up under the Prevention of Terrorism Act. As an attorney in good standing, I respectfully disagree.'

'Feds.' The LA detective shook her head. 'I detest them almost as much as I do attorneys.'

'I actually don't know what to say to that.'

Celeste's smile could have been intended for the waiter who deposited her fresh drink. But she held on to it as she told Connor, 'Present company excepted, I hope.'

Connor breathed more easily. 'So do I, ma'am. Hope and pray both.'

'I assume that means you need my assistance with something.'

'I'm supposed to meet senior executives with Campion Security tomorrow. I suspect Agent Kaiser intends to be present and use this as an opportunity to make me disappear.'

The smile vanished, along with every vestige of softness. 'That is not going to happen.'

'Will you help?'

'Feds involved in a clandestine operation in my town? Count on it.'

Connor rose to her feet. 'Thank you. So much.'

'You're not staying for the main act?'

'That just happened, at least for me.' Connor pointed to the group shifting to the stage. 'The music would be lost on me tonight. I'll see you tomorrow.'

FORTY-FIVE

They left in the calm grey light of an early dawn. Four of them set off in Denton's rental – Astrid, her mother, Denton, and Sean. The young lady's good humor from the previous day was gone, replaced by an apparent desire to fuss with everyone. As he lifted her wheelchair and settled it in the rear hold, Astrid demanded, 'Tell Mom to go back to bed.'

Denton had not slept well and was in no mood to placate her. 'That's not my job. And even if it was, I wouldn't do it.'

'You're a lot of help.'

'That's not my job either.' He shut the rear door, walked around to the open driver's door, slipped inside. 'Anything else? No? Good.'

From her position in the front passenger seat, Astrid crossed her arms and fumed. Sean was seated behind Denton. He glanced at his watch and said, 'We're slipping behind schedule. That can't happen.'

'I'm moving.' But when he started the engine, Astrid wailed softly. The sound was so sad, so filled with genuine anguish, that he cut the motor once more. Not certain what he should do. But definitely not wanting to cause the young woman any sorrow on what she claimed was her last day on earth.

'Now you see why I'm so crabby.' Astrid's mother leaned forward and settled her hand on her daughter's shoulder. 'Astrid has had these awful moments since before she learned to talk.'

'I didn't *learn* anything! And the only reason I'm crabby is because *you're sitting here.*'

'I'm right where I should be, daughter.' She remained utterly unfazed. 'And you would know it, if you'd just hush and think.'

When Astrid's only response was to turn to the side window and burn in silence, Denton started the vehicle and headed for the exit.

'Finally,' Sean said. 'Fast as you can.'

A mile down the highway leading to the airport, Astrid's mother said, 'I apologize for Astrid's outburst. My daughter doesn't like waking up early.'

'That's not it and you know it!'

'It's made her cross since she was in diapers.'

'Not nearly as much as having my *mother* show up where she's *not wanted* and *doesn't belong*!'

Sean said, 'The lady certainly has a way with a point.'

Astrid kept her face turned away from the car's other passengers. 'Are you laughing at me?'

'Not a bit of it.'

'Well, don't you dare start. I've got more than enough bile for you too.'

'Point taken,' Sean said. 'Denton, this is your right coming up.'

There were a hundred different things that could go wrong with their day. So many that Denton felt utterly disconnected from Sean's humor, Astrid's foul mood and the mother's uncommon caring. He started to ask the woman's name. They had traveled together most of the previous day and the point had never come up. Now, though, he decided it didn't matter. Or, rather, in a couple of hours it could hardly have mattered less.

Denton's eyes were grainy, and his neck and shoulders still ached from yesterday's slow drive. He had not slept much, his hours captured by a level of fear he had never before known. He had been shot at a number of times, twice taken part in SWAT-led assaults of heavily fortified gang money drops. Such was the nature of white-collar crime in LA. But nothing had ever infected him with this sort of terror. Denton followed Sean's directions through the strengthening light of a new day and wondered if this was what it meant to grow old.

Their destination was California's largest boneyard. It sprawled over desert plains north and east of the Mojave Air and Space Port. The grandiose name referred more to aspirations than reality. The airport's only significant commercial occupant was Virgin Galactic, and they were rumored to be leaving for their new Texas facility.

The same could not be said about the boneyard.

Boeing, McDonnell Douglas, Lockheed and Airbus all used the vast empty stretches as their airport at the end of the road. Hundreds of partially dismantled aircraft littered the hard-packed vista. The piles of rubble and rusting air frames stretched out as far as Denton could see.

They swung around Virgin Galactic's main buildings and engine-testing facilities. Beyond that stretched a runway long enough to handle the world's largest and weariest jets, even those with burned-out engines and barely functioning brake systems.

Between the space port and the boneyard rose four warehouses, intended to give their occupants a safe place to climb on board without blistering their hands on desert-hot metal surfaces.

Sean said, 'Pull into the second building.'

Everything about the place was oversized. The open doors were tall and wide enough to permit a commercial jet to slip through. Seven forty-five in the morning, the shadows were already blade sharp. When his eyes adjusted, Denton saw the hangar only contained one plane.

Sean said, 'Pull over by the office. Behind the fuel truck.'

'Sean . . .'

'Leave your keys in the ignition.'

'That's a commercial turboprop.'

'An old one,' Astrid said.

'Who's supposed to be our pilot?'

'A joke,' Sean said. 'Hah.' He opened his door, then realized Denton had not moved. The minivan's engine still ran, his hands still gripped the wheel. Sean settled back into his seat, met Denton's gaze in the rearview mirror. 'This is what you signed up for, remember?'

'Sean, there is no way on earth I can fly that thing.'

'Yes, you can.' He gave that a beat, then added, 'It's the end of the line for us, sport. Which means you only need to take off. Landing won't be an issue.'

'I don't have the necessary instrument training to get us out of the hangar.'

'That's taken care of.'

Astrid said, 'It looks ancient.'

'It is. Which is a big reason why our allies within the California air traffic control system will keep quiet for as long as possible when we veer off our official flight plan. Any question about theft will be met with the logical response. Who cares?' Sean rose to his feet and opened Denton's door. Pulled on his arm. 'Let's get a move on here. Timing, remember?'

Reluctantly, Denton allowed Sean to draw him out of the car. He heard Astrid say, 'Mom, *please*. I'm *begging* you.'

'My darling baby bird. What do you think has kept me going all these years?' The car went silent, then Astrid's mother added, 'What kind of life would I have without you?'

Denton opened the rear door and pulled out the wheelchair. He could see that Astrid's mother continued to lean forward, stroking Astrid's neck with one finger. The only sound now was Astrid's soft weeping. He flattened the chair's seat, angry and ashamed and frightened. He turned to where Sean stood smiling at the plane and said, 'I can't fly that.'

'Actually, you can.'

'Sean, that's an Embraer 120. One of the most successful commercial turboprops in history. It is also notoriously difficult to fly. Not to mention it's five times the size of anything I've ever flown.'

'Same basics, though, right? Two wings, engines, tails, all that.'

'No. It's not the same at all.' The man's good humor mocked him. 'And another thing. The Embraer requires two pilots.'

'I'm flying in the second seat.'

'You can pilot a commercial turboprop?'

'Theoretically.'

'Oh. Great.'

'Look. This connection you've been forging. There are two pilots on the other end. Both know this plane inside and out.'

'For real? This can work?'

Sean was already moving for Astrid's door. 'Let's get the ladies settled and find out.'

Sean carried Astrid up the steel stairs, with Denton close behind for support. The cabin's interior smelled of diesel and dust and age. Sean asked the young woman, 'Where do you want to sit?' When Astrid did not immediately respond, he offered, 'There's a fold-down navigator's seat in the cockpit.'

'What about Mom?'

'There's another for the flight engineer.' Sean glanced back. 'Though you might be more comfortable in the main cabin.'

'No,' her mother said. 'I'm flying with my baby bird.'

When Astrid was settled and both women strapped in, Denton moved forward. The pilot's chair was split from collar to knee. Two springs jutted out at the point of Denton's hip and lower back.

Sean slipped into the co-pilot's seat and offered, 'Sit down, push your seat back far as it will go, then check underneath.'

Denton did as instructed and discovered a canvas carry-all. He opened the top and pulled out two heavy-duty saddle blankets and a pair of super-size thermal socks with rubber soles.

Sean was already draping his own blankets over the co-pilot's seat, which was in worse shape than Denton's. 'Fit the socks over your shoes. Old Embraers are notorious for the nose heating ducts freezing up.'

'You know this how?'

Sean tapped the side of his head. 'You need to go ahead and link up yourself. We're falling behind schedule.'

Denton started to point out that he had never experienced anything like a specific message. Much less one containing words so precise he would have known to search beneath his seat.

Not to mention directions for how to fly an antiquated beast of a plane.

But right then he had no choice but to hope for something, anything, that might help make sense of the cockpit's blistering array of instruments.

The Embraer dated from some distant era, long before digital read-outs and automated controls. His seat was surrounded, both above and below the windscreen, by literally hundreds of analogue dials and almost as many toggles and heavy-duty levers.

Denton swallowed hard, then sent out a frantic single-word plea. *Help.*

The response was instantaneous and so clear it might as well have been spoken by a guy perched directly behind his seat.

Don't sweat it, mate. Most of these instruments you don't need. Which is a bloody good thing, since they probably don't work anyway.

Definitely a guy. Definitely British.

I'm Denton.

I know who you are and names don't matter. But timing does.

Sorry. All this is just . . .

Bizarre. Tell me. Right. Now pay attention and let's get this bloody great beast off the ground.

The unseen, unnamed pilot did not take hold of Denton's limbs. Nor did he actually invade Denton's interior world.

But he came mighty close.

The British pilot remained intensely involved. But it was a new sort of connection, one that maintained a certain distance, just like the person was there beside him, rather than *inside* him. Telepathically, of course. But still.

By the time he and Sean finished the pre-flight check and started the engines, Denton was coming to terms with the fact that his privacy was still in place. An internal barrier separated this pilot from who Denton was, what he thought, the memories and past mistakes, everything that he had worked so hard to keep hidden. As they taxied from the hangar, the noise a ferocious bellow, Denton started to ask Sean if he had ever experienced anything like this before. In the end, though, he remained silent. The pilot perched on his mental shoulder kept urging him to focus, to hurry, to get back on a schedule that had never actually been explained.

Denton listened as Sean followed co-pilot's protocol and radioed the tower, identified their plane, requested permission to take off. Their official destination was California's other main boneyard, the Southern California Logistics Airport outside Victorville. Total flight time, thirty-two minutes.

The tower responded with a go. Denton nudged the engines up another notch and they lumbered toward the main runway. Cool, correct, hands steady on the helm, as if he worked with such aircraft every week. Simple.

The unseen pilot continued scanning those still-functioning instruments through Denton's eyes. The plane was a massive lumbering beast, rattling and shaking and groaning in protest over being woken from its desert slumber. The blistering sunlight revealed multiple divots and cracks in the windscreen. Sean reached into the co-pilot's side pocket, came up with two sets of super-dark sunglasses and handed one over.

They lined up with the runway, took a double-hold on the engine's throttle levers, brakes hard locked, engines to full, listened to the bellow grow and the wings shiver, released the brakes, faster and faster down the pitted concrete strip . . .

Take-off.

FORTY-SIX

Campion Security occupied a seven-story glass cube on Wiltshire, just outside the Beverly Hills town limits. At a quarter to seven in the morning, the building shone like a copper monolith. Connor thought the structure was both faceless and forbidding, which suited the descriptions she'd heard of the company itself.

She understood the basic logic behind NovaCorp's desire to acquire this group. Campion was by far their largest competitor in the local and highly lucrative private-security business. But Connor had also considered Campion to be a very poor fit. Their aggressive take-no-prisoners attitude, their armed-response tactics, the cold and somewhat brutal nature of their debt-collection subsidiary, not to mention the mercenary attitude of their senior management – all this was at direct odds with the corporate culture fostered by Byron Hayes.

Connor's first act as the new head of legal had been to urge the NovaCorp board to ax this project. Which had resulted in bitter enemies among the senior executives. The very same executives who had spread rumors of her and Byron's affair.

That time of morning, traffic on Wiltshire was light and streetside parking spaces plentiful. Jackie parked her Acura behind a four-door Chevrolet the color of dried mud and said, 'That has to be an unmarked D-ride.'

Sure enough, Celeste Jones rose from the car and joined them on the sidewalk. She showed no sign of wear from the previous night. Celeste watched three dark-suited security rise from the second Lexus and asked, 'What do we have here?'

'Overkill,' Connor replied.

Jackie shrugged. 'I prefer that to being unprepared.'

'Point taken.' Celeste pointed to the Campion entrance. 'How do you want this to play out?'

'I have no idea.'

'That almost makes sense.' Celeste started for the entrance. 'Well, let's go see what the feds bring to the dance.'

The lobby was a high-ceilinged marble cube, frigid as a mausoleum and not nearly as inviting. Connor gave her name to the guard, who cast her security team a long look before reaching for the phone.

Which was when Agent Kelly Kaiser's two tan SUVs halted directly in front of the building. Thirty seconds later, Kaiser entered the building.

She was accompanied by six others. Two more agents remained standing by their rides. Kaiser fastened on Connor, tight as a gunner taking aim. But the security and Connor's two hard-faced companions gave Kelly a bitter pause.

Kelly's first words were, 'They're with you?'

Celeste demanded, 'This is the fed giving you trouble?'

'Agent Kaiser, Homeland. And you are?'

'An LA detective wondering how you're operating in my district without alerting the local force.'

'We alerted everyone we needed to,' Kaiser replied. 'And your superiors saw no need to interfere.'

'Guess they forgot to pass that memo down the food chain. Can I see your badge?'

'Most certainly.' Kaiser traded her leather portfolio for Celeste's. Gave it a careful inspection, then passed it to a dark-skinned agent with the face of a human blade. She asked Jackie, 'And you are?'

'Jackie Barlow is a director of NovaCorp's investigation and security division,' Connor said.

Kaiser gave the security detail a careful inspection. 'You really think this crew will protect you, Ms Breach?'

'From the bad guys, absolutely. Is that what you are, Agent Kaiser? A bad guy?'

The elevator doors pinged, and Samantha Campion stepped out. The founder's daughter and current deputy CEO was dressed in an aggressively cut grey suit of raw silk that shimmered as she crossed the lobby. 'What on earth is all this?'

Connor replied, 'I'll allow Agent Kaiser to answer that. If she can.'

'Oh, this is rich.' Campion surveyed the room. 'Please tell me you brought a NovaCorp security detail with you.'

'I'm waiting, Agent Kaiser,' Connor said. 'Or would you rather hold your responses for a dark alley, someplace you can grab me when I'm alone? Where your Gestapo-style tactics might go unnoticed.'

Kaiser's phone chose that moment to start ringing. She handed it to the agent standing alongside her and replied, 'I'm operating under the Prevention of Terrorism Act. Pursuing enemies of the state.'

'*Alleged* enemies,' Connor corrected.

Samantha Campion clearly disliked not being the center of attention. 'I would like to know exactly what is going on here!'

'So would I,' Connor replied. 'Very much.'

The male agent handed Kaiser her phone. 'You need to take this.'

'Later.'

'They've located the targets. All of them.'

For the first time since locking gazes, Kaiser's attention went elsewhere. She took the phone, said, 'Go.' Listened intently. Then, 'We're ten minutes out. Start prepping.' She pocketed the phone and said, 'You'll have to excuse me. I'm off to do my job. Arrest perpetrators of criminal offenses. Especially those who threaten our nation's security and our citizens' future. Something you probably wouldn't understand.'

'Oh, I understand, all right. And soon enough I'll be clearly redefining those terms, and your role in all this, where it matters most. In a court of law.'

'Is this before or after I bring you and your boss up on federal charges?'

'That depends how deep you wish to dig your professional grave, Agent Kaiser.'

'We'll see about that.' She motioned to her crew. 'We're out of here.'

As the agents piled into their SUVs, Jackie said, 'Seems to me our lady gave as good as she got.'

Samantha Campion snapped, 'I'm *waiting.*'

'Thank you for your time,' Connor said. 'We were just leaving.'

FORTY-SEVEN

There was a primeval quality to Kelly's rage. She sat in the passenger seat as Riggs drove down relatively empty streets, heading west, maintaining a close proximity to Jon Alvero's ride. Kelly was vaguely ashamed to have been bettered in front of her team. And that was exactly what Connor Breach had done. The attorney had prepared for their confrontation in a manner that left Kelly feeling like an amateur. To have arrested the attorney under those circumstances would have opened their investigation to public and legal scrutiny. Not to mention perhaps involving a dispute with the LAPD. But none of this was what had Kelly fuming.

She had seen in the woman's gaze a bitter contempt. She had heard it in Connor Breach's tone. Her attitude had been one of an attorney with the weight not just of the courts but of absolute right on her side. She considered herself to be untouchable. Inviolate. Kelly was filled with a visceral desire to strip away that woman's confidence. Show her precisely what it meant for Kelly to move forward with true might on her side.

Riggs noticed her state, of course. Very little got past that man. 'Dealing with lawyers is such a pain.'

Kelly forced herself to focus on the most important issue derived from that confrontation. 'She knows.'

Riggs nodded to the street ahead. Grim. 'No question.'

Kelly spelled it out anyway. 'Connor Breach is fully aware of the situation. She has elected to work with the other side.'

Pamela Garten spoke from the rear seat. 'The enemy.'

Riggs nodded once more. 'Which paints the same target on her back.'

'The lady's going down,' Pamela said. 'It's only a matter of time.'

Kelly found a burning comfort in being surrounded by people who shared her focus. 'I hate how she's remaining free to spread the secrets.'

'You want to go back?'

'Can't. Not now.' She shifted in her seat so as to face Pamela.

'Soon as we're upstairs, contact Darren and have him assign a team to work nonstop on Ms Breach. Bring in Jon. Set up a twenty-four-hour net over that woman.'

'It will be a pleasure.'

'Tight as a noose.'

'The lady breathes a word, she's ours,' Pamela assured her.

Kelly asked Riggs, 'How long?'

'Five minutes tops.' He pointed to the empty lanes ahead, then to the heavier traffic filling the inland lanes. 'All the beachfront execs are heading in the opposite direction. We couldn't make better time if Jon lit up the world.'

Kelly settled back. 'Radio ahead. Tell them to alert Agnes. Make sure everyone is ready.'

Because Avri Rowe was correct. It was time to strike.

Kelly rode the elevator in silence, strode down the corridor at one pace off a run, entered their ops center and demanded to her team at large, 'Are we sure we've identified the target?'

'Ninety-nine-point-nine percent,' Ricard replied.

Agnes spoke from the laptop. 'I absolutely agree.'

Rabbit offered his hand. 'I can show you.'

'Not yet. Let's set the stage. Darren?'

'At six eighteen this morning, a vintage Embraer 120 Brazilian-class lifted off from Mojave.'

'This take-off point matches the path we thought Denton Hayes was following,' Rabbit offered.

Darren went on, 'Flight plan listed the Victorville boneyard as their destination.'

'And Victorville is . . .'

Ricard had the California map on the monitor next to Agnes. 'Half an hour flying time. Rifle shot straight south.'

She glanced at her watch. They were a few minutes shy of eight. 'Where is it now?'

'Heading directly north,' Darren replied. 'Maximum speed and altitude for a plane this old.'

'Can an Embraer hold all this group?'

'According to our in-house expert, yes,' Agnes said. 'It would be tight. Minimum luggage. Uncomfortable. But definitely possible.'

The chance to take aim at a verified target helped Kelly push away the morning's frustration. She felt a chilling energy take hold, a fierce hunger to engage and fight and win. 'What is their precise location?'

Ricard said, 'FAA reports they will cross the Canadian border in twenty-one minutes.'

'It's them,' Riggs said. 'We've got them in our sights.'

'Not yet, but soon.' She saw two more faces appear on formerly blank screens, those of the President's Chief of Staff and General Skarrens. Neither man spoke. Kelly took that as permission to move forward. 'OK, Rabbit. Talk to me.'

'We've been working the same pattern we used last night. Only now there's a specific target.'

'Denton Hayes.'

'Right. He is definitely their weak link. Denton flashes into sight. Five seconds tops. Long enough to get a fix that it's him. Twice we've also gotten glimpses of the plane itself, which is loaded to the gills. Denton is piloting this craft. But he's getting help from another pilot further up the food chain.'

She liked the breathless way Rabbit spoke. A young man bonded to her team, sharing their tight and nearly frantic excitement. Hunting beasts waiting to be released. Ready to take down their prey.

Rabbit straightened, a quick lightning reaction to the unseen. 'OK, he's back.'

She reached out her hand. 'Show me.'

FORTY-EIGHT

The flight was awful.

They maintained maximum velocity. Heading straight north.

Mojave tower came on, requesting a status update, noting they were off course. Sean reached over and cut off the radio. 'I guess that means we're committed.'

In response, Denton followed his pilot-instructor's guidance and pushed the throttles to maximum revs.

The plane rattled in a thousand places. The cockpit heating had two settings, sweltering or frigid. Either way, the flooring remained scarcely a degree above icy. Because of the women seated behind them, they went for par-boil.

When they leveled off at eighteen thousand feet, Sean said the same thing Denton had just heard from his pilot-instructor, 'Go check aft.'

Which was beyond strange, since they flew an empty aircraft. But still.

He slipped between the two women, which required Astrid's mother to temporarily release hold of her daughter's hand. Otherwise, they paid Denton no mind. As he left the cockpit, he heard Astrid's mother say, 'You're the only reason I've lasted this long, daughter mine.'

'Mom, don't you dare make me cry. Again.'

'Who's to care? You're my angel. You always have been. And you deserved far better than the crabby old woman I've become.'

Denton shut the door on Astrid's response and passed through what was once the galley. Everything had been stripped out, leaving raw metal siding and rust. Beyond that were the toilets, which he hoped no one would need.

As he entered the rear hold, he sensed a transition.

One moment, he stared at row after row of empty seats, the steel supports rattling and the chairs shivering as if in fear of what was about to happen. The next . . .

All the seats became filled with passengers.

The shift was both swift and gradual. Clouds formed, congealed, solidified . . . and became people. All of them watching Denton. More than that. They were *connected*. To *him*.

He stood there, coming to terms with what he witnessed.

When he returned to the cockpit, he asked Sean, 'You want to go have a look aft?'

'No need.' Sean tapped the side of his head. 'Pretty cool, huh.'

'I guess cool works as well as anything.'

As he settled back into the pilot's seat, it happened.

The only warning Denton had was the sense of a raging lighthouse swinging his way. Searching. Hunting.

That initial contact seared him so deeply his mind felt branded.

Denton experienced a swift transition as the unseen others created a filter or barrier; both words worked and neither was really correct. What was important was how his connection to the woman, their foe, was blocked. He glanced back and found Astrid watching him, face taut and pale both. Her mother had unstrapped and now knelt beside her daughter's seat. Both women ready.

Astrid said, 'Thanks for the swimming lesson.'

'Here they come again,' Sean warned. 'I'm told it's necessary. We can argue about that later.'

Before he could respond, the laser force was back. Gripping him in with volcanic fury.

It was a woman; he knew that instantly. Behind her was a group, the power of their unified focus driving the woman's ability to both search and assault.

Denton's unseen allies remained poised in the background, watching from a distance, themselves hidden from view, yet fueling the vivid sense of the plane carrying a full load of passengers.

Their attacker, he realized, was the agent who had confronted him in the Whole Foods parking lot. Kelly Kaiser. She scathed his brain with two words.

Last chance.

His unseen allies prodded gently, opening a portal, allowing Denton to see how the woman had herself been wounded. The pain she carried was raw and fresh. It fueled her desire to see them destroyed.

The woman realized he was peering into her own private recesses, and as a result she blasted him with a new level of fury.

Then she vanished.

FORTY-NINE

I nstantly upon linking up, Kelly *saw*.

She breathed around the immensity of what they were now capable of. Hunting together, her and Rabbit's team, peering into the decrepit cockpit, viewing the pilot . . .

The connection broke.

Agnes said, 'Tell us what you see, Kelly.'

Kelly now understood what a great hunting beast must feel, tracking spore for days, then finally coming upon—

'Talk to us, Kelly.' Agnes again. Sharp.

'Wait.' She barked the word because just at that moment the link was restored. 'Rabbit, can we look aft?' A few seconds, no more, then they were looking down the main cabin, and, 'OK, the plane is jammed full. But there's a flickering sort of energy to the group. Like a fog or diffuse camouflage. Some are not at all clear. Denton, the professor, one of the LA crew and a woman who isn't linked, they're all crystal . . .'

This was something new, a direct and visceral linkage carrying the force of multiple thunderbolts. She *saw* him. And then, for a single, terrifying instant . . .

He saw *her.*

The connection broke.

Rabbit was the one who said, 'And they've gone again.'

Kelly released Rabbit's hand. Took a long, hard breath.

'Kelly?' Agnes.

'Sorry. The camouflage is back in place.'

Rabbit said, 'It's been like that ever since they took off. Maybe this time lasted slightly longer. But not much.'

'Denton Hayes is tiring,' Kelly guessed. 'He's linked to a more experienced pilot. He's flying an ancient plane. He's working to maintain this masking energy. It's too much for the new guy.'

Rabbit offered, 'I'll keep on him.'

But the links had also brought home just how utterly exhausted Rabbit and his crew had become. 'No. It's time for your team to take a break.'

'Kelly—'

'This is good work. Primo. Make sure everyone knows that. Now I want you all to relax.'

Avri Rowe sounded almost jovial. 'This is precisely what we wanted. Don't you agree, General?'

'I couldn't have detailed it any finer in a war college exercise,' Skarren agreed.

The men's cheerfulness heightened Kelly's own sense of unease. She felt compelled to say, 'I'm concerned about how my view of the plane's passengers was fractured.' She directed her words to Rabbit. Wanting him to say she was worried about nothing. That she was merely having trouble coming to terms with the new possible. 'There was a fog or mist or lack of focus. Something.'

Rabbit wiped his weary face with one hand. 'Yeah, I saw that too.'

'And?'

'All Diyani and I could come up with is, we're seeing what Denton sees. Like we're looking over his shoulder.'

'That doesn't explain it.'

Rabbit nodded. 'Like you said. He's tired. He's trying to juggle too much. It makes for a lack of clarity.'

Skarren broke in, 'Let's focus on what's important. We have a target. And they're going to slip from our grasp if we don't move, and move fast.'

Rowe said, 'We are in complete agreement here, General.'

'Wait one.' The general turned away, spoke off-screen. Then, 'All right. Our fighters are in the air. A formal warning to land has gone out.'

Rowe demanded, 'Is that necessary?'

'Engaging the enemy in a public display of force requires us to maintain strict protocol.' Skarren might as well have been reading the words from a textbook.

Pamela and Darren said it together. 'The plane is accelerating.'

Skarren said, 'There's your official response, Avri. We are now legally free to engage.'

'All right, then.'

Darren said, 'Canadian ATC has cleared them for entering their air space.'

Skarren said, 'Our two F-18s are closing on the target aircraft. Second warning has now been issued. Land or die.'

FIFTY

Denton struggled to refocus on the plane, the flight, the immediate. He told Sean, 'I just bonded with this woman who's been attacking—'

'No time.' Sean switched on the radio, took hold of the mike, and said, 'Canada air traffic control, this is flight 182 requesting permission for an unscheduled border crossing.'

A voice over the radio instantly replied, 'Flight 182, we have you on approach. You are seventeen minutes out. Hold to present course and descend to—'

Whatever else followed was lost to the roar of a fighter jet *slamming* the space directly in front of the cockpit.

Sean shouted into his mike, 'Canadian customs, we hereby request official recognition as applicants for Canadian citizenship.'

'Your request is hereby granted! Provisional citizenship is hereby confirmed—'

A *second* jet roared so close it *slammed* the Embraer with its backwash.

Denton heard the Canadians shout, 'Unidentified aircraft, you are operating in direct contravention of treaty protocol. Flight 182 has Canadian citizens on board and is—'

A first jet made yet another invasive fly-past, while the second jet took up station beside Denton's wing.

He had been warned of this, the takedown described as precisely as Sean was able. The potential outcome had been carefully studied, and their response painstakingly set in place. Denton's role had been just as carefully described, Sean giving it voice while dozens of the unseen allies reached out. Not so much pleading as, well, hoping he would play his role.

Now, in this dread moment, he found himself somewhat amazed that his last thoughts were not of Ryan. She belonged to a past that he had done his best to truly put behind him.

Instead, Denton's final reflections were of Connor. Her brilliance, their few remarkable moments together, a desperate yearning for a shared tomorrow.

If only.

FIFTY-ONE

D arren reported, 'They've requested Canadian citizenship.' A pause, then, 'Provisionally granted.'

'So these Canucks have been forced to show their true colors.' Rowe actually laughed out loud. 'Outstanding.'

The proximity to assault only magnified Kelly's unease. She wanted it to happen. She could almost taste the pleasure of striking their target. But she needed to be absolutely certain. She needed to know.

She stepped away from the others, turned slightly so, physically as well as mentally, she disconnected from the screens and the verbal exchanges. She reached out.

There he was. Denton Hayes. Terrified but calm. But this time the connection remained somewhat vague. She sensed Denton had no idea she was even present. He remained preoccupied, fighting the aircraft's controls, pushing its ancient engines beyond redline. The roar of the wind, the rattling metal frame, the smell of hot oil and age. She detected three others in the cockpit, the professor and a young woman of the LA crew and her mother. All of them filled with various combinations of terror and tension and determination and . . .

Then he was gone.

Skarren asked, 'Do I have permission to engage?'

'Absolutely,' Rowe said. 'Granted.'

Kelly felt the rage solidify into a visceral force. This was her prey. Her kill.

She heard, 'This is General Skarren. Weapons hot. I repeat. Weapons hot. Fire when ready.'

FIFTY-TWO

D enton heard the Canadian tower continue to shout at the two jets, but he could no longer understand the words. The entire process seemed to be splitting his brain in two. One component still operating as the co-pilot's backup.

But by far the major portion of his awareness drew further and further away, drawn by all the unseen minds taking part . . .

The jets backed off. The airspace cleared.

But safety remained a myth. Denton knew that from how the Canadian controller's voice rose to a full-fledged scream, accusing the jets of firing missiles at an unarmed civilian . . .

There was a split second of shrill approach, a single fiery *WHAM*. An instant of feeling the plane blasted apart . . .

Nothing.

FIFTY-THREE

For a single, solitary instant, Kelly reconnected. But not so much to Denton as with the two women seated in the cockpit behind the two pilots. As if unseen minds forced her attention on to the unique intensity of mother and daughter, connected in an incredibly powerful manner. A union so strong . . .

'Missiles away.'

'*Target acquired.*'

SNAP.

Kelly's extended vision was *ripped away*.

The experience carried such force she actually screamed. Fell to the carpet. Spasmed. Then . . .

Nothing. It was gone.

Beside her, Rabbit writhed on the floor. Shouting one word over and over. *Diyani*.

Riggs stood over her. Horrified. 'What just happened?'

She heard her team shouting from a vast distance. Rowe and the general and Agnes and Darren. Faces she could scarcely recognize crowded in. Hands lifted her up, settled her in a chair. Then had to steady her so that she didn't collapse back on to the floor. Kelly opened her mouth, but no words came. All she heard clearly was Rabbit's falsetto shriek. *Diyani*. Weeping and screaming for them both.

Losing something this visceral should have resulted in genuine agony. A pain as vast as the longing she felt for what was now gone. Instead, Kelly felt nothing. A hollow void existed where the ability had formerly resided.

FIFTY-FOUR

For three and a half long days, Denton Hayes lived inside a world of faraway sounds.

He shared a top-floor apartment with Sean Stiles. Together they were housed in the same apart-hotel where he had spent his last night in California. Only now replanted in the northern Canadian community their group called home.

The place even smelled of the same fresh paint.

Directly across from his kitchen window stood the former home of Sean and Ryan Stiles.

Which would have been good for a bitter laugh if Denton could have managed it. But irony and off-center humor were not in his wheelhouse.

Just the same, Denton stood by the window several times every day, watching a new family with three young children play in the unkempt front yard. From time to time, their laughter drifted up, gentle reminders of everything that had changed in his world.

A nurse came four times a day. At least, Denton assumed she was a medical professional. She treated him in that courteous yet off-hand manner of someone who was trained to deal with the afflicted. Which he most certainly was. She checked his vitals and brought him meals and then returned to ensure he ate everything. Evenings, she insisted he take two pills, an antidepressant and another to make him sleep.

He woke occasionally in the night. Recalling the events at twenty thousand feet threatened to tear him apart. Each time, however, the distant whispers became a much stronger chorus. People who mourned with him, and yet who were there to comfort. And show him a healing patience. When he woke each morning, they had again receded to the distance. There if or when he needed. Otherwise, they formed a backdrop of murmured assurance. He was not alone. He never would be again.

They bore the loss together.

The apartment's third bedroom held exercise equipment and a set of free weights. Denton spent hours walking the treadmill, not jogging, using the very lightest barbells, mostly just going through the motions. Trying to anchor himself in the here and now.

Sean suffered far worse after-effects than Denton. The few times the former professor emerged from his bedroom, his features were drawn and so parchment-pale that he looked ready to faint at any moment. Sean seemed incapable of seeing Denton at all. Each time, he staggered into the kitchen, stood looking blindly around himself, then returned to his bedroom. He never spoke.

What little Denton could see of their surroundings held a raw, unfinished look. He thought it resembled a huge residential commercial development that was far from completion. The front windows looked out over forest and several graded lots, ready for the next structures to drop from the sky. Further still were more buildings and a road of rocks and packed earth and distant glimpses of sparkling water. There was very little vehicular traffic, and what there was appeared to be electric. People mostly moved about by bikes, scooters or on foot.

The sky overhead was confusing. Like studying the heavens through tinted, fractured lenses.

On the morning of day four, Denton rose knowing his time of isolation was over.

He was in the kitchen making coffee and inspecting the cabinets, trying to decide if he felt like preparing his own breakfast, when the front door opened and Terrance Alderton called, 'Feel like company?'

Greg's father was a strong version of the man his son would probably never become. Tanned by a life outdoors, full of good humor, his gaze direct and easy both. He spied the coffee maker and asked, 'You made any extra?'

'Help yourself. There's milk, but I can't find sugar.'

'I don't use either.' Terrance took a mug from the cabinet and poured himself half a portion. 'There's a memorial service for the ladies this evening. Thought you should know. No one's expecting you to be there.'

'I want to come.'

'I'll stop by.' Terrance studied Denton's form. 'Your size is . . .'

'Forty-two long.'

'I'll bring some fresh gear.'

'Thanks.' Another sip, then, 'About what happened on the flight.'

'Are you sure you want to discuss this now?'

Denton wasn't. Even asking caused his vision to waver slightly. Just the same, 'I need to know.'

Terrance nodded acceptance. 'We're still defining the possibles – you understand what I mean?'

'Yes.' But what struck Denton the most was that very first word. *We.* He was part of this now. Come what may.

'So two things were at work. First, the how. A system of protection, or shielding, was put in place around you and Sean. It's basically the same form of applied energy that keeps us safe and warm here.' Terrance started to say more, then decided, 'If you're interested in details, you probably need to speak to somebody who actually knows what they're talking about.'

'Portable shield. Got it.'

'As for the other passengers who weren't there, and, well . . .'

Denton liked how Terrance found it difficult to name them. 'Astrid and her mother.'

'You made contact with the connected group assisting our foes.' It was not a question.

'I did. Yes.' The moment came vividly to the fore. 'They were led by the same agent who accosted me in Los Angeles.'

Terrance nodded. 'She and everyone else needed to be warned. And shown the results if they refused to listen. The agent and her team have been stripped of their abilities.'

'I don't understand.'

'You can't harm others and maintain this link. These two options, being linked and willfully targeting the lives of others – they can't coexist.' He swept out the arm not holding his mug. 'All around the world, there are nations and groups seeking to destroy us. Most are considering the same tactics as the organization that assaulted you. They need to be stopped before they begin.'

Abruptly, Denton was aware that Terrance's words were being echoed by many others. This was a very somber group, people assigned an overall . . . well, *authority* was the only word he could think of. It wasn't like a government or a defense force, and yet it was both. What Terrance spoke was reflected in this new connection. People who were grimly intent on maintaining their communities.

And growing new ones.

Terrance went on, 'What you experienced was intended to be the only warning they will receive. From this point on, their motive, a desire to do us harm, will be enough. Either they choose to join in

what we are building or their newfound ability will be stripped
away. Permanently.'

'I miss Astrid.' It was a silly thing to say, in the face of a global
unified presence. But still.

'She was fully aware of what needed doing. She volunteered.'

'She was really going to die?'

Terrance nodded. 'Not that specific day. But in a matter of weeks.
Her body was deteriorating fast. There was nothing anyone could
do about that. Yet. Someday, perhaps. Hopefully. Someday soon.'

Terrance went quiet then. Watching him.

And Denton knew why.

The group, this collection of leaders, they waited with him. The
invitation was there, but only if Denton wanted to accept would they
actually spell out what was involved. Just the same, he knew
they wanted him to continue in something akin to his previous role.

Investigator. Protector of the peace. Cop.

He said, 'I want to help.'

'That's great. Wonderful, in fact.' Terrance possessed perhaps the
widest smile Denton had ever seen. 'Welcome to our tomorrow.'

FIFTY-FIVE

They kept Kelly sedated for five days.

Rabbit was roomed down the hall. He refused to see her. His entire team had lost their ability the same moment as Kelly. That much was clear from her few moments of clarity between doses.

Kelly understood Rabbit's desire to keep her well away. No doubt he and Diyani and all the others blamed her. She ached for them. But mostly for herself.

Agnes Pendalon arrived on day six. 'They tell me you want to be up and moving.'

'There's nothing for me here.'

Agnes studied her for a long moment. 'So it's definitely gone.'

Kelly took a firm grip on the sudden desire to weep. 'Yes. It is.'

'For good? There's no chance of it coming back?'

'Can an amputee grow a new limb?'

Agnes seemed capable of peeling away Kelly's flesh and seeing to the very hollow core of her being. But all she said was, 'I am truly sorry for your loss.'

Kelly clenched her teeth. Nodded. Breathed around the void. Finally managed, 'Moving on.'

'Every moment of this exercise has taught us an immense amount. We need to assume that no future specialist who has become engaged with the tree can participate in an assault. Especially one potentially leading to death.'

For the first time, Kelly felt like she and the woman were in sync. Honed to a razor edge, hardened to where their lives only had room for one purpose. 'What is our next target?'

Agnes was clearly pleased by the question. 'That depends on you. Your team is heading for Canada. A clandestine mission to inspect the region on the Hudson Bay's southern shore. The question is, do you want to lead them?'

'I assume you have an alternative in mind.'

'Only if you want. Avri Rowe needs a new assistant to handle everything regarding this threat. Having our neighbor to the north

declare itself as allied to our enemy will require action. Plus, there
are all the future events necessitating a White House-level response.
We can't keep going back to the President's Chief of Staff every
time there's a bureaucratic snafu, or an official we need to chop off
at the knees.' She paused, then added, 'Or when our teams go
weapons hot.'

Kelly breathed around the offer. Trying to focus on something,
anything, beyond the mammoth void. 'I'd have to give up on field
work.'

'You would.'

'Is there a chance I could return to frontline duty in the future?'

'Theoretically, yes.' Agnes flipped a hand at herself. 'But this
level of access changes everything. If you're not careful, it can
consume you. Of course, some would say that's not altogether a bad
thing.'

There was an intense draw to the offer. A desire to have something, anything, so intense it would fill the void. Or at least grant
her the power to ignore it. Kelly flipped off the covers. Shifted over
so her feet touched the cold linoleum floor.

'When do I start?'

FIFTY-SIX

B y the beginning of week two, Connor was almost ready to accept that Denton Hayes was gone.

The news of a large unidentified plane crashing out of the sky, a brilliant fireball that lit up most of Washington state's interior region, made headlines for two days. Some reports circulated on the web, claiming to have seen a pair of missiles streak overhead just before the plane exploded. The US military and FAA both denied it, of course. But the authorities offered no alternative explanation for how the wreckage had become spread over three counties, a veritable rain of metal debris. Televised news showed investigators pouring over the site. And then . . .

Nothing.

Even the online chatter went quiet.

Connor tried hard to lose herself in work. It was by far the easier way to deal with what was a surprising sense of loss. She missed Denton. She ached for what they might have had.

Telling herself it was ridiculous to mourn a man she scarcely knew helped. A little. Not much.

But it was all she had.

Jackie Barlow insisted on their living together, and Connor did not object. Her movements were still being tracked, only now the teams were professional. These agents were clearly trained at close surveillance. Connor was very grateful for how both Jackie and the LA detective, Celeste Jones, boiled over the feds invading her world. Someone probably should. Just then she couldn't find the energy to be mad about it herself.

Eleven days after the fireball in the sky, Connor was working at her desk, for once lost in the details required for her quarterly report to the board. She was due to meet Camila Suarez in fifteen minutes, as they were making a joint presentation on a string of highly successful short-term investments and how the company needed to prepare for future opportunities. Which almost balanced out a larger-than-expected series of claims and life insurance payouts.

Her assistant, a wonderful genie of a young man named Jamie, knocked on her door. 'You have a visitor.'

She did not look up. 'I also have a standing order not to be disturbed.'

'He says it's crucial.'

'Jamie . . .'

'Connor, really, you need to see him.'

She looked up, only to discover the towering figure of Sanjib Gupta smiling behind the young man. 'Of course.' She sprang from the chair. 'Doctor Gupta, please excuse—'

'No apologies necessary, I assure you.' He didn't actually need to bend over in order to make it through her door. But old habits and all that. The board member and head of UCLA Medical School waited until the door closed to ask, 'How are you faring, Ms Breach?'

The concern in his voice, however professional, brought her close to the tears she was determined not to shed. They didn't help. 'Coping. Barely.'

'Yes. Which is why I am here, actually.' He motioned to the chair by her desk. 'May I?'

'Sorry, sorry, can I offer . . .' When Gupta silenced her with the grand motion of a prince, Connor drew over a second chair. 'What can I do for you?'

'A very fine sentiment, but the wrong question. I am here at the behest of a dear friend. A gentleman who wants you to know he is doing fine.'

This time, the tears would not be held back. 'Really?'

'Most certainly. He was wondering if you might like to join him.'

'More than just about anything in the world.'

'In that case, my dear' – Gupta reached into his jacket's side pocket and extracted a carefully folded silk handkerchief – 'he has asked me to give you this.'